# KATIE KINCAID COMMODORE

## Andrew van Aardvark

# Katie Kincaid: Commodore

## Author: Andrew van Aardvark

## Editor: Margaret Ball

Copyright © 2023 NapoleonSims Publishing

www.NapoleonSims.com/publishing

Cover image copyrights:

Spaceship one - Illustration 227705779 / © Codawaldem | Dreamstime.com

Spaceship two - Illustration 176589242 / © 3000ad | Dreamstime.com

Spaceship three - Illustration 63786679 © Algol | Dreamstime.com

Space station - Illustration 8814949 / Alien Space Station © Luca Oleastri | Dreamstime.com

Figure created From LaFemme model in Poser | www.posersoftware.com

Space ship interior: 127380755 @ SDecoret | Dreamstime.com

Galaxy - Illustration 210228619 / Space © Ievgenii Tryfonov | Dreamstime.com

Paperback ISBN: 979-8-38768-452-4

Hardcover ISBN: 979-8-38768-771-6

# Table of Contents

## Prologue:

*So, dear, deeply encrypted diary, they say pride goes before a fall.*

*They rarely had the guts to say it to my face.*

*The heavens know I understand people often thought I was arrogant, over-confident, and rash, but I don't think that was fair.*

*I know for a fact, I tried not to be. I was, and always have been, more interested in results than anything else, and that includes stroking my ego.*

*And, therefore, I tried to be realistic.*

*I can't say I always succeeded.*

*A case in point being our debut on the galactic stage.*

*I was already famous at the time of first contact. Only Admiral Tretyak may have been more famous, and I was younger, more photogenic, and more exciting. My relative lack of any interesting personal life only gave the journalists more to speculate about.*

*So when I turned down command of the First Contact Expedition, I thought I was showing a commendable lack of ego and demonstrating an awareness of the fact that I was not cut out to be a diplomat.*

*And when I accepted command of our first anti-pirate patrol instead of diving deeper into Earth politics, I once again thought I was being realistic. I'd long realized I couldn't ignore politics. It gets into everything, but I believed I was playing to my strength as a military leader.*

*Be assured, any future historian, this is not false modesty. I'm claiming I tried to be realistic, not that I was modest.*

*So believe me, when I write that I had no idea that galactic politics was going to turn out far more complex, subtle, and murky than anything Humans back on Earth had managed.*

*And that I'd plunged myself right into the middle of it.*

*This is the story of how that worked out.*

*You'll probably find it amusing. You know we survived my blundering about.*

*At the time, I was far from sure that'd be the case.*

## 1: Sitting Ducks

*"The human race is like a growing child who discovers with amazement that the world consists of not just of his bedroom and playground, but that it is vast, and that there are a thousand things to discover, and innumerable ideas quite different from those with which he began."*

Page 5 of "Reality is Not What it Seems" by Carlo Rovelli


Katie was in class when the sirens sounded.

Susan next to her grunted in exasperation. "Not this again. They already had a drill this morning."

The bone thrumming whoop of the sirens subsided slightly, as if in answer to her complaint, and words rang out. *"This is no drill. This is no drill. Alien attack imminent. Battle stations. Battle stations. Alien attack imminent. This is no drill. This is no drill."*

Katie, Commodore Katherine Anne Kincaid of the Space Force to be formal, exchanged glances with Commander Susan Fritzsen, an old friend from the Academy. They'd already begun moving out of sheer habit. All those drills. But now they and all their classmates snapped to and quickened their pace. They had mere minutes to make it to the shelter of their bunker before the blast doors came slamming down. Slamming down and isolating any laggards from safety.

They briskly exited their classroom and started a steady jog down the corridor outside. Their haste didn't stop the usually phlegmatic Susan from continuing to comment. "Damn, and that class was actually an interesting one."

They'd been taking logistics. They were attending the Space Force's new Command College preparing for promotion to flag rank and logistics are a key part of professional high command. Unfortunately, unless you're really into shipping and accounting, they tend to be a bit boring. Today's lesson, on van Creveld's classic book, "*Supplying War*," had actually been interesting. That book had revolutionized the understanding of logistics both prior to and after the industrial revolution.

So, Katie understood the reason for Susan's chagrin. She also understood it was partly a cover for just how dire and frightening the current situation was. "And so inconvenient that alien pirates chose to attack just now."

"Yes," Susan replied as they found seats in their assigned bomb shelter. "Surely, it's bad enough they might kill most of us off and bring about the end of the world as we know it. Did they really have to time it so badly?"

"Enemies tend to be like that. Inconvenient," Katie said.

"Be nice if we were on board ship where we could help do something about it."

"At least you're likely to get another ship."

"Ouch, sorry, Katie. I forgot."

"Yep, doesn't look like I'll ever get to sit on the bridge of my own ship again and play god in command of all she surveys. Instead, I'm going to get to try herding a lot of people like you. Prima donnas with delusions of grandeur."

"Ah, poor Katie got promoted too fast. Shouldn't have played war-winning hero if you didn't want that."

"It seemed necessary at the time."

Susan nodded. "I think we're all glad you did, but you know the reward for a job well done."

"Too well. Just seems the problems get bigger and bigger and more complex, doesn't it?"

"It does. Mainly because they do. And we both know you don't think there's anyone better qualified to command a fleet in the Space Force than you. I love you, Katie, but modest you're not."

Katie sighed. She looked at the ceiling and then around at their classmates, who were carefully pretending that they weren't listening to Katie and Susan's conversation. "No, and that's a good thing," she said.

"Another Katie philosophy lesson?"

Katie grinned. "It's not like you can go anywhere. And, frankly, this is important. When things are uncertain and the stakes are high, when your life and all you hold dear are in play, it's natural to worry. In fact, it's perfectly normal to feel fear."

Susan pursed her lips, an unusual degree of emotional display for her. Usually Susan was blandly upbeat. "Worrying about things doesn't help."

"Most of us aren't reincarnated Nordic warriors who calmly accept life is the pits and then you die and that all you can do is face the fact with stoic flare."

Susan smiled. "Nice to be recognized for the outstanding individual I am."

"You're weird, so blandly weird that people hardly notice. Only most of us aren't like that."

This assertion was punctuated by the sound of the blast doors crashing closed. A sound that didn't just assault their ears but also rumbled through their seats and into their bodies. Most of the people in the crowded shelter flinched, and looked around startled, despite having known what was coming.

Susan just looked amused.

Katie shook her head. At least, it looked like everyone had made it to the shelter in time. And finally, the sirens had stopped. "You're incorrigible. Anyhow, my point was that in times like these people aren't calculating machines or even cold-hearted warriors. They're human. They need the people making the life and death decisions for them to seem confident. Confident, not modestly unsure."

Some nods of agreements from the colleagues around them greeted that statement. Their classmates and the college staff weren't even pretending not to be listening now.

Susan's eyes crinkled mischievously. "So, what would normally be a character flaw in someone else is actually a virtue for you?"

"Exactly," Katie said. She looked around at their captive
audience and grinned. "We all know this attack isn't likely to
reach us here at Goddard Station. Even if it does, it's not likely
to hurt us here in our little, well-armored hidey-hole, is it?"

Sporadic nods of agreement answered her question.

"But, all the same, I'm sure it's hard not to be a little
*concerned,* maybe? Never fear, however, it's not my fate to die
before triumphing in battle over these buggers, whoever they
are." She grinned.

That got laughs.

Susan looked determined. She nodded. "I can't wait to be
back on a ship showing these bastards what a mistake they've
made."

"Amen," Katie agreed.

\* \* \*

The Grotto of Decision was dark and damp. Only a single beam
of light conveyed by an ancient series of crystals and a few
candles lit it. The cool walls sweated moisture.

A tiny pond in the center with a few bits of moss around its
edges added to that moistness. In times past, it had doubtless
seemed an oasis and a place of respite from the searing
dryness of the surface above.

A place where considered cool decisions could be made
away from the heat and urgency of the hunt.

The Huntmaster fervently hoped it would be so today. It
seemed to him that his fellow members on the ruling
Triumvirate of the Great People were determined to rush
headlong into a dangerous hunt without learning the nature of
their prey first.

The Great People had long ago expunged all competing
predators from their home planet. They had long ago learned
how to take down their home system's prey without exposing
themselves to real danger. Even having moved out to the stars,
they had failed to encounter real competition. That despite the
technological advantages many of the races already there had.
The Great Chief-King and the Great Broodmother were chafing
at the lack of challenge. Between them, they outvoted the
Huntmaster.

The Great People were aggressive predators, but they were not foolish or arrogant ones. They were not so lacking in foresight as to trust their fate to a single individual; hence the fact that they were ruled by a Triumvirate, a council of three. Unfortunately, as the member of the Triumvirate tasked with gathering intelligence, as well as making detailed plans, the Huntmaster was the only council member who had some true understanding of the nature of the other space faring races.

He was outvoted by the Great Chief-King, who worried most about his restless sub-Chiefs and warriors, and the Great Broodmother, who was most concerned about finding resources to support her horde of broodlings whom she'd allowed to outgrow their current resources. Only the Huntmaster understood they were risking the existence of their species in this hunt.

The Huntmaster had to somehow convince at least one of his colleagues on the council of the danger.

To that end, he'd arrived first in the Grotto. This amounted to spending what the species he was currently studying called "*political capital*" in order to underline how seriously he took the question.

Of course, being the first member of the Triumvirate to arrive didn't mean he was the first individual to do so. Two individuals of lesser importance would be present for the meeting even if they'd have no vote.

One, the Princess, greeted him with a slight snout dip of respect. "How goes the hunt?" she said.

"The hunt begins. The prey is unaware, but an unfamiliar one," the Huntmaster answered. A fuller answer than strictly necessary, but although supposedly the Princess was only present as her father's apprentice, she was already a force that needed to be respected. As her presence because of her male siblings all having had unfortunate accidents indicated. She was worth cultivating as an ally.

The other, second individual, was less a possible ally and more a snake in the grass that needed watching. That individual, the recording Scribe, was acknowledging the Huntmaster with a sustained deep bow and by carefully looking past him and not right in the eyes. The Huntmaster didn't believe the surface deference extended to the Scribe's heart for a moment. Not even for the time of a lunge. Not even for the small unit of time the Galactics called a Tok.

The Huntmaster depended on the work of scribes, both past and present, but did not trust them just because of that. They didn't risk themselves in the hunt, but ate of what others had killed. They thought of themselves as smarter and more knowledgeable than others and dared to believe those qualities more important than courage, prowess in stalking, and the strength needed to bring prey down. They needed to be culled at regular intervals and it'd been too long since the last such culling.

The Huntmaster looked away from the Scribe and gave a slight tongue flick to politely acknowledge his subservience. The Scribe assumed a neutral stance, and they all waited.

They didn't have long.

A "*Tok or two*" or "*less than a Katok*" as the Galactics would say. A "*few seconds*" as the Humans would. The Huntmaster had diligently immersed himself in the subjects of his study and sought to look at everything as they might to better understand them. One ancient and respected Human huntmaster had taught that "*to know your enemy and to know yourself is to win a hundred battles*". It was fortunate that Humans did not appear to heed this wisdom for the most part. That their culture contained it at all was justification for considerable wariness.

Having strode in with his head high, the Great Chief-King looked squarely at all those that had preceded him and spoke to the Huntmaster. "Lost in thought, old huntmate?" He clicked his teeth in amusement.

The Huntmaster clicked his teeth and gave a tongue flick of pleased amusement in return. He'd always worked well with the chief, who was a great leader. "It is a complicated hunt with multiple sorts of prey on unfamiliar ground. It means much to learn and contemplate."

"Indeed, and which way does the wind blow?"

"Some of our prey may be very dangerous indeed and even the weakest are jackals that will swarm us if we allow ourselves to be wounded by the stronger among them. We must stalk carefully and sniff every breeze. Attend every little noise."

The chief replied with a slow-blink of his eyes. A galactic would have shuffled their feet. A Human would have "*shrugged,*" which was a gesture where they raised then lowered their shoulders. "The Broodmother grows impatient. It will take sharp arguments to convince her to wait longer."

Only long practice kept the Huntmaster from staring at the chief in dismayed challenge. The Great Chief-King was saying in effect that he would side with the Broodmother in whatever she decided and that the Huntmaster needed to convince her of the need to proceed cautiously on this hunt.

They all had to wait patiently for the Broodmother's arrival. She didn't arrive until a little after the appointed time for their meeting. A bad sign. It was a disrespectful and haughty gesture that strongly suggested that she was in no mood to compromise.

She sauntered in. She completely ignored the Princess and Scribe. She deigned to give the Great Chief-King a nostril flare and slight snout dip of respectful greeting. The Huntmaster got a haughty snout lift. "You have a report, Huntmaster?"

The Huntmaster did not appreciate being treated like a minion reporting rather than a co-equal on the council, but chose not to make an issue of it. He gave an open mouth huff of thoughtful contemplation before answering. "Indeed, Broodmother, a very important report. There are strange scents on the wind."

The Broodmother slow-blinked at him. "Proceed."

"We are apex predators and have not had any true competition for many generations. Indeed, since the triumph of the Great Clan, we have not even had much competition among ourselves," the Huntmaster began.

"Indeed, our hunters grow impatient for challenge," the Great Chief-King said.

"And it is past time we exploited our success," the Broodmother added.

It went downhill from there.

The Huntmaster did his best. He detailed all they knew that suggested a need for caution. The fact that the Galactics' technology was generally superior to that of the People, and that there were more of them. That it was a fact that too many of the People still lived on the surface of their home hunting ground. He reminded his colleagues that the Galactics they knew of all feared other races further away who were supposed to be inclined to intervening whenever they thought local races were becoming too powerful.

He reminded them that there was much they didn't know that was cause for caution. Not least the appearance of a new, young race, the Humans, who were reputed to be much more numerous and aggressive than the older, more sedate Galactics they'd already encountered.

It was all for naught.

When the Huntmaster was done, the Broodmother lifted her snout and said, "It is the role of the hunters to risk themselves to feed the broodlings."

The chief slow-blinked at the Huntmaster. "The Broodmother is not wrong," he said. "You may start the hunt by scouting carefully. You may have our hunters stalk sneakily hidden in the grass, but hunt we must. And we must not delay the kill so long that our broodlings go hungry."

The Huntmaster dipped his snout. "So be it."

\* \* \*

As Katie entered one of the Command College's small conference rooms, Admiral Tretyak stood to greet her. "I imagine you're wondering what all this is about?" he said.

Katie wasn't completely in the dark on the point. She was due to graduate the Senior Command Course in a few weeks. Also, it'd only been a little more than a week since the Space Force had beaten off that alien raid. That raid had represented only the second contact the Human race had had with any aliens besides the Star Rats, who had taken residence out around Saturn. Well, out around Saturn until recently. Recently it'd been announced that vast areas around both Hudson's Bay and in Siberia had been turned over to them in exchange for significant transfers of technology and other information.

So the whole future of humanity was in play. It wasn't hard to guess that Katie, as one of the Space Forces' more senior officers, and certainly its most famous, was going to be part of the Space Force's response to the crisis. She could easily guess that her exact role was going to be the topic of this meeting. A rather irregular meeting, but it was a crisis. That still left a lot of not insignificant detail for her to guess at.

"Well, it's not hard to guess it's something to do with the current crisis, but beyond that, I've got no idea," Katie said. She looked around the room. In addition to the Admiral, five other individuals were present. She knew them all. Three were old friends.

In addition to Susan Fritzsen, Colleen McGinnis, who'd been her roommate at the Academy, and, Amy Sarkis, her cabin mate on her first ship, were present. Colleen was a commander in the intelligence branch now. Amy was a lieutenant commander in charge of a scout group.

Also present was Commodore Pierre "Pete" Radison, who headed the Space Force's research division. It was so Top Secret that until just a couple of years ago the public hadn't even known it existed. Radison had been an old friend of Katie's grandmother.

"Commodore Radison, I hope you're not here to try to convince me to go into research again," Katie said.

The commodore shrugged and smiled thinly. He seemed amused. "No, that ship's sailed. I'm here to help the admiral brief you."

Katie inspected the last individual in the room. A mere senior lieutenant, also with intelligence insignia. "Lieutenant Robert Hood," she said, "you were an enlisted electrician the last time we met. Told you you'd end up getting drafted and given a commission."

The man in question nodded ruefully. "And you were right. Been a lot of surprises the last few years."

Katie nodded back. "Seeing you, I know there's skulduggery afoot, but it's good all the same." She'd not known Hood long enough to become friends with him, but he had come through for her in a pinch. Katie had him pegged as the sort of person who could be counted on to do so again come the need.

Katie looked at the admiral as she seated herself. "So, what's up?"

"Well, you know how the media and public are celebrating

our victory against the alien incursion?"

"Yes, you think it's premature?"

"Exactly. Using the information the Star Rats provided us, we knew where the attackers were likely to appear and precisely how to handle them."

"So far, so good."

"So far. There were two ships. We destroyed one and managed to capture the second one mostly intact."

"And?"

"Well, too bad we're already calling the Kannawik 'Star Rats'. It'd be a better label for this new race. They're called the 'Zneet' or informally 'Snouts' by the galactic community, it seems. Small-time traders and thieves when they can get away with it according to what the Kannawik and others tell us. It wasn't a serious attack by a genuine alien force, it wasn't even a pirate attack really, it was bandits at most, but more like an attempted mugging by some small-time thugs."

"And the only reason we managed to handle them is because they came in fat, dumb, and happy, and we knew they were coming. Other aliens? Other actors?"

"Your assessment is correct. Small time thugs with the most basic star drives and weaponry. We figure that they were probably the dupes of other actors who wanted to probe our defenses. And, yes, Star Rats and others. It hasn't been announced yet, but we cut deals with two other starfaring races for information and technology. We're just completing a set of ships in secret that incorporate what we've been given. You'll be getting command of them. We're here today to discuss how you're going to use them."

"Forgive my idle curiosity, but what did it cost us?"

"Most of the interior of Australia and the better part of the Sahara, and most of the deepest parts of our oceans. Two different species with two different environmental needs."

"Ouch. Good to have allies, I guess. But did we really need to sign away large parts of Earth?"

"I think so. I advised the government to pay whatever we had to. Look, Katie, we're at a huge disadvantage here. We don't have a technological edge even with what we've bought. We don't have more than a handful of up-to-date ships and they're only just now reaching completion. Most of all, we don't have enough people qualified to command them."

"So you want me and the rest of the folks here to work up some sort of plan for a miracle?"

"No. I've got a plan. I think you'll like it. So much so that your first knee-jerk reaction to it is going to be to say 'yes'. Only I want you to listen me out and then think it over. Think it over for several weeks while checking out the assumptions it's based on. This is too important of a junction in our species' history for us to blindly act without the most careful consideration."

Katie frowned. Herself, she was a fan of getting stuck straight in and seeing what happened. But if humanity's fate depended on what she did with a handful of ships, she could understand Tretyak's caution. "Okay. So what's this plan?"

"First, you've probably heard our first contact expedition didn't go that well."

Katie sucked her teeth. A bad habit, but although the official news was upbeat, it was also curiously lacking in detail. Reading between the lines, humanity's first attempt to contact wider galactic civilization had flopped. She'd actually heard rumors that crew had had to sell wedding rings and coin collections to pay for a day's docking fees at the local trade hub. And then been treated with scant courtesy by a low-level functionary. "Only some rather sensational rumors," she said. She detailed what she'd heard.

Admiral Tretyak sighed. "I'm afraid those rumors were accurate. It was worse than that, really. That low-level flunky was blunt. The elder races up the arm from us have a few rules. Races confined to their planet are to be left alone. Their planets are off limits. Races with space travel but not FTL are to be left alone. Their systems are entirely off limits. The Star Rats arriving here was a mistake because of our having developed so quickly and just bad luck on their part."

"So far, so good," Katie said, deliberately playing the straight man. She wasn't the only one at this briefing.

Admiral Tretyak grinned in a decidedly unamused way. "Exactly. They made it abundantly clear once you had interstellar travel you were fair game. That if we or any other such race can't defend ourselves, it was just '*so sad, too bad*'. They opined that we badly needed help. They then made it clear that help wouldn't be free."

"Encouraging that they apparently bothered to research us and our culture."

Somehow Tretyak managed to look even grimmer and more exasperated. "Indeed. The furry asshole in question was one of a species called 'Limers'. They're even more like monkeys than Humans, but with worse attitude. He was the local representative of something called the 'Trade Union'. He trotted out the whole no-free-lunch lecture."

"You're kidding?"

"No, I'm not. Wish I was. He used those exact words 'no free lunch'. Also the acronym TANSTAAFL; '*There Ain't No Such Thing As A Free Lunch*'."

Katie just blinked. She was at a loss for words.

The Admiral surveyed the disbelieving faces around him. The only exception being Lieutenant Hood. Katie had to suspect he'd been briefed on the incident earlier for some reason. Tretyak continued, "So, yes, ladies and gentlemen, we've met aliens who are apparently fond of our classic science fiction. Representative Grok, we suspect it's not really his birth name, explicitly confessed to being a fan and went on to say there's a common galactic saying to the same effect. One that translates as roughly: '*Nothing for nothing*'."

Katie snorted. "And what was it that he wanted?"

Admiral Tretyak smiled. "If we send a squadron to do an anti-pirate patrol around their trade hub and they judge it effective, they'll kindly open relations with us. Allow us a trading post on the hub and even defray necessary expenses. They want our answer in less than a month and to see the ships in not much more than two."

"And if we don't, we're on our own."

"Precisely."

"Well, it's ugly. It's pretty clear they've got us over a barrel and intend to take full advantage, but I think it's equally clear we don't have much choice."

"I agree. So does my staff," and with this the admiral nodded at Colleen and Hood, "and so do our intelligence people."

Katie thought that was an interesting hint as to what Colleen and Hood had been up to. A bit beside the main point right now, though. "You want me to command that patrol, right?"

"Right."

"I'd be honored," Katie answered.

"Good, but I want to delay making it formal. In fact, I want you to seriously consider whether it's a good idea. Both whether you're the best one to command it, because, Katie, we could use you here both to help in our system defense and politically. Also consider whether we should even send the squadron. They're not asking us to do this out of the goodness of their hearts. It could be they know we're likely to get chewed up. It could even be that they're in cahoots with the pirates and are trying to weaken our defense of the Solar System."

"Or both," Katie said. "You know, we both know that I'm not really fond of waiting around for someone else to take the initiative. Also, I'm not sure what good I'd be politically."

Radison spoke up at this point. "You haven't used it, but you still have a high profile and most of the people who took their lead from your grandmother now look to you."

"You've stayed in touch?" Katie asked. She wasn't sure how she felt about spooks dabbling in politics.

"Yes, just informally," Radison answered.

Katie paused before answering. "Right now there seems to be a broad consensus on what needs to be done. Everybody realizes what's at stake and is doing whatever is necessary. I'm not a personal fan of Andrew Cunningham's, but he and his Realistic Conservatives are pushing the government to do even more than they are."

"He's on board with more government power because he figures he'll get his turn at wielding it," Radison replied.

Admiral Tretyak grunted. "We've got enough problems without second guessing the politicians, but Pete's not wrong. Your opinion carries weight with the public. You say something is needed, and no matter how unpalatable it is or how much sacrifice it'll mean, people will listen."

"Okay."

"Also, let's be clear: putting together an anti-pirate patrol will strip our defenses here at home. It's an awful risk."

Katie nodded. "So, you want me to think it over?"

"Yes, you and the rest of the people in this room. We intend Commander Fritzsen to be your flag captain. McGinnis and Hood will be key members of your intelligence team. We need to know more about what we're facing."

"A good reason for taking on the patrol."

"Indeed. And to see that you don't walk into any ambushes, you'll have Lieutenant Commander Sarkis as the head of your scout group. All subject to your approval, of course."

"Yes, sir. We've all worked together well in the past. I consider most of your suggestions good friends as well as superb officers."

"Great, then we can get on with the main briefing then. Commodore Radison will start by bringing us all up-to-date on the new technologies your ships will be employing.

The briefing took hours with minimal breaks. Food and coffee were provided during one. At the end of it all, Katie was tired and her head bursting with new information.

The basic choice remained the same, however. They needed allies and information, and taking their best ships and people out on the requested anti-pirate patrol would give them both.

Only at the cost of leaving humanity's home almost defenseless.

And Tretyak was giving Katie, as the one who'd have to make it all work, the final say.

No pressure.

* * *

Rob Hood, now Lieutenant (senior grade) Robert Hood and with a degree in exo-anthropology to accompany his shiny new commission, swatted a mosquito. Apparently, neither his commission nor his degree entitled him to a job in a nice, comfortable office. One free of stinging insects.

Here in the muskeg of what had been northern Canada, he'd have been happy just to be able to unclench his teeth. He dared not. The damned bugs were so thick that he couldn't fully open his mouth without swallowing a bunch of them.

And although this part of the world might be well below

zero in the winter, it was currently summer and hot and very muggy. Rob itched all over and the exact reasons were multiple and unclear. Having to slog his way through a swamp cluttered with stunted but nevertheless often thick little trees with many scratchy branches didn't help. At least modern technology ensured they couldn't actually get lost.

That their guide was proficient at spotting what bits of ambiguous surface were safe to stand on, and which weren't, was another good point. At least they weren't likely to get stuck or drowned here.

Small favor, but welcome.

Their guide, strangely enough, wasn't from the area. He wasn't even from Earth. He was a Star Rat. This was one of his first visits to the terrain humanity had ceded to his people in exchange for their help. His name was Water-sniffer. He'd assured Rob and Tanya that they had no hope of actually being able to produce the native sounds of his name and that the translation was fine.

Water-sniffer was delighted to be here. Apparently, he'd waited his whole life for this opportunity. Which was the whole point of the exercise. It was Rob's and Tanya's job to wheedle as much free information out of him as possible. Having him happy and loosened up was theoretically conducive to that.

"You're pleased with your new home, Engineer-Scout Water-sniffer?" Tanya asked the Star Rat. Ensign Tanya Wootton was fresh out of grad school and a complete and utterly single-minded geek. Rob suspected she'd have happily fed a finger or two to a rat for the chance to be here interacting with a real live alien.

Between that and her youth, she didn't seem in the least bothered by the bugs, the heat, or the exertion of their long hike. So she might be an arrogant academic and a geek, as well as a mere slip of a girl, but she was one tough and incredibly focused geek girl.

Given that, Rob didn't dare complain. His ego wouldn't allow it.

"Ecstatic," Water-sniffer replied. "This is both a dream come true and a profoundly religious experience for me."

"How exciting. Please, tell me all about it."

Not the most subtle of interrogation techniques, but Water-sniffer didn't appear to notice. "We Kannawik are a people profoundly attached to our land. Others might see us as dedicated to shaping it to our own needs, but in truth, we first and most of all seek to understand it and to bring out its full potential. Acquiring that understanding and fulfilling that mission is the primary drive of all of us. Without a land to call our own and to sympathize with, we are partly dead inside. We live in a constant state of grief."

"How sad," Tanya responded, "and yet the people of your pond have lived in space for many generations, I understand."

"Yes, sad. So true and so sad," Water-sniffer said, turning and putting a paw to his breast. Rob wondered if that gesture was genuinely native to his species or something he'd learned to help in dealing with Humans. "Still, it is the way of the universe. A species is lucky to survive reaching the stars. No species can afford to have most of its individual members live as their lucky ancestors did on a planet's surface. Planets are the wombs of species. But one must leave the womb and one's mother, eventually."

Tanya looked stunned at that, but recovered quickly. "Surely it's possible to protect a planet?"

Water-sniffer looked at Rob and paw to his muzzle coughed. He turned back to Tanya. "It is good to be young and innocent, but surely not. Planetary surfaces are indefensible. If any significant portion of a species' industry or population is present on a planet, they will be targeted and destroyed. Worse, there's always the chance this will hurt the precious ecology of the planet."

Rob sighed and nodded. "That's exactly right. That's exactly what our general staff has concluded. They're drawing up plans to evacuate as much of our population and industry to space as possible." He looked right at Water-sniffer who'd turned to inspect his Human followers. "Never fear. Our leadership understands this, even if they've yet to figure out how to break the news to our population."

Water-sniffer shuffled from one foot to the other. And nodded his head back and forth, too. Rob had been trained to recognize these motions. They were both the alien equivalent of shrugs. The first motion was part of the lingua franca employed by Galactics of the many species that traded with each other. The second motion was that native to the Star Rats themselves. "Yes, doom stalks many of your species' individuals, but some of you, maybe many of you, will survive and find your places. You are doing much better than most newly arrived among the stars."

Tanya's mouth dropped open, and she stopped dead. They ceased making even the slow progress that they had been. Of course, she swallowed a fly.

Rob and Water-sniffer waited patiently for her to stop coughing.

"That's horrible. I can't believe it," she finally choked out.

It was Rob's turn to shrug. He'd long understood that life could be cruel. He still didn't know how to explain the fact to people who had no personal experience of it. "I'm skating to say even this much because SFHQ has declared it all Top Secret, but they've studied the hell out of the issue. Nobody likes the conclusion. But it's what every starfarer we've talked to has said, and it's what our analysis always ends up concluding. It looks like it's just a fact of life in a rather unfriendly galaxy."

Water-sniffer clicked his teeth in affirmation. He then remembered to nod Human style. "It is sad, but it is so."

"I need to think," Tanya said.

"Let's keep going while you do that," Rob said. "I want to get out of these trees. It's stifling in here, and I'm sick of eating bugs."

It was almost another hour's trudge before they cleared the tree line and made it out into the open. Rob thought maybe he could see the ocean in the distance. He wasn't sure. What he was sure about was that there was a breeze now. A cool breeze that blew most of the bugs away. A great relief. They all stopped to look around and enjoy it.

Tanya seemed to have recovered from her disbelieving shock. At least some. "Water-sniffer, if planetary surfaces are so vulnerable, why did you want this area so badly?"

"Even if the vast majority of us can never live on a planet's surface and enjoy the luxury of real air and water and genuine nature, we can hope to visit it at times."

"So, basically, planets are just big theme parks?"

Water-sniffer stroked his whiskers. "And places of religious pilgrimage, too. I understand your people once had several large entertainment parks where you went to worship a mouse with large ears."

Tanya blinked. Surprised wordless again.

Rob struggled manfully to swallow a laugh.

Tanya recovered first. "It's going to be years, more like decades, to move everyone into space. Even if they stopped prioritizing the building of warships. We don't have that long, do we?"

Water-sniffer clicked his teeth.

"You'll help us, won't you?"

Water-sniffer turned away and stroked his whiskers a few times before turning back to the young woman. "We've already risked a great deal to help you as much as we have. You must help yourselves now. For more help you must give help to us too. Nothing for nothing."

Rob nodded. That was the way the world worked.

## 2: New Toys

*"In his vision, shared by nobody else at the time, the universe was crisscrossed by lines of force - electric, magnetic, and possibly other kinds. The points where these lines met were the points at which we perceive matter to exist."*

Page 102 of "Faraday, Maxwell, and the Electromagnetic Field: How Two Men Revolutionized Physics" by Basil Mahon and Nancy Forbes.

It'd been a long day. It'd started with Susan and Amy showing Katie around her new flagship. The darned thing actually smelled new. It looked new. It was absolutely raw with newness. Almost every surface glowed with new paint. The few that didn't hadn't been quite finished. The distracted, busy crew rushing about, half of them at least looking a little lost, were another sign of its newness.

Katie hadn't mentioned these observations to Susan. The *Bonaventure,* the first star carrier ever built by humanity and Susan's new command, was obviously her pride and joy. It was something that might not be apparent to anyone who hadn't known Commander Susan Fritzsen as long and as well as Katie had, but to Katie, it was obvious. She didn't think she'd ever seen Susan so excited or so happy about anything.

Grimly, Katie couldn't help thinking it was almost a pity she was going to have to order her friend to take her new baby in harm's way. They'd ended up their extended tour of the ship with a quick supper in Susan's cabin and had then retired to the flag command center to start thinking about how they might use her.

In a way, the *Bonaventure* was more a mobile base than the offensive platform wet navy carriers of the twentieth century had been. But although they had yet to figure out exactly how they were going to use her, or even where, it was clear they were going to need to take the battle to their enemy and that that would entail real risk.

If Katie had been prone to worrying herself sick, it would have given her a bellyache. Once again, she felt she'd been thrown into the deep end. Only this time, not just her own fate, but that of the entire Human species rested upon her ability to learn how to swim well enough to make it to the pool's other end. Yeah, situation normal; all fouled up, and absolutely no pressure.

"Well, Amy, it looks like you've got the most critical job," Katie said. "It's going to be vital that you find the enemy before they find us."

"That's right, Amy," Susan said. "You let those alien pirate bastards scratch the paint on my baby and I'll track you down in Hell and somehow make your existence worse."

Amy grinned. "Didn't know you had that much imagination, Fritzsen. You do know warships are supposed to fight, don't you?"

Katie shook her head. "Down, girls. I think it's pretty obvious that we're going to have to fight. Otherwise, we're ceding the initiative to our enemies, whoever the hell they may be, and we can't afford that. So, Amy's scouts are going to have to screen and scout ahead. Then we'll commit the squadron's main strength with the *Bonnie* at its core to a decisive battle. Only we're going to need good intelligence, so Amy knows where to look. And so I know how to win the main battle."

Susan's happy glow dimmed a fraction. "Maybe Colleen and that lieutenant you obviously have a thing for should have been here."

Katie grimaced. She didn't like being reminded of her lack of a personal life. It was a fact, too, that she felt oddly comfortable with Rob Hood. It was also a fact he was in her chain of command. He reported to Colleen, who was head of her intelligence group. He was, therefore, thoroughly off limits. "We're all very short on time," she said aloud. "We're responsible for operations. We need to get to know the *Bonnie* and our other ships and the people manning them. Colleen and the other spooks, they're tasked with learning about our opposition and also any possible allies. Not a small task."

Amy looked uncharacteristically grim. "We know it's going to be tough, don't we? There are a lot of different actors out there, aren't there? And they're all looking to see what we're made of, right?"

Katie smiled. Amy's normal happy optimism made her a comforting friend, but Katie wanted her scout group commander to be at maximum alertness. Looking for monsters in every possible corner. Being the opposite of complacent and happy. "That's right. Which is why it's so important our scouts keep us from being surprised."

Amy managed a small, twisted smile. She heard the subtext. "Yes, ma'am. Once again, the scouts get all the hard work and not the glory."

Susan grinned. "You get to scuttle away when the going gets tough. Some folks seem to think that if we do this anti-pirate patrol, it's going to be mostly just a show-the-flag thing with a few skirmishes. But you know, I don't think this is just a trial task the Galactics are giving us. I think it's a serious test and I'm not getting the feeling they expect us to pass it."

Katie nodded calmly. She'd thought this through and had come to much the same conclusions herself. It was reassuring that her friends, who were also key parts of her command team, saw things the same way. "I agree," she said. "Tretyak wants us to be sure it's a good idea before we commit to this anti-pirate patrol. But I don't think we have a choice. I agree it's a test. A tough one probably, but one we have to take if we hope to survive on the galactic stage."

"Survive at all," Susan amplified blandly.

"Survive at all," Katie agreed. "Welcome to the big leagues, guys."

\* \* \*

The *Bonaventure* was a big ship. It not only had room for a whole scout group of Town class FTL capable scouts, each of them a small interstellar warcraft in their own right, but for a scout group command center, right next to the Scout Group's own dedicated briefing and conference room.

It almost made Amy feel important.

It didn't because Amy already felt important. She'd understood full well how important her role was even before Katie had made it clear to her. Amy would have happily traded that importance away if she'd believed there was anyone else capable of doing her job better. Only she didn't. The Space Force had been small and hidebound before the Smuggler War and then First Contact. Many of the few hundred people in existence with experience of warship command had acquired most of that experience in scouts. Mostly on routine tasks and without acquiring the background in engineering and logistics that Amy had.

They might know how to command a scout, but they knew less about how to keep a group of them properly supplied and working well.

Also, crucially, they didn't know Katie Kincaid well. They didn't know her mind and how to work effectively with her. And Katie wouldn't know them the way she knew Amy, either. It was almost embarrassing how much their command group was dominated by friends of Katie, people she knew and trusted. Only Amy strongly suspected they weren't going to get much time for that command group to jell as an effective team.

Katie or Tretyak, Amy suspected the two of them working together, had stacked the deck with people that already knew each other. It might not be fair to many outstanding officers who didn't happen to have the luck to know Commodore Kincaid, but it made perfect sense.

With the fate of all of humanity in the balance, fairness to individuals took second place.

"Why so grim, Lieutenant Commander Sarkis? It's going well, isn't it?" Bobby Maddox asked.

Bobby was the *Bonaventure*'s CAG, Commander Air Group. They held the same rank. Bobby was a lieutenant commander, too. And the org chart showed them both as direct reports to CMDR Fritzsen as the *Bonaventure*'s captain. Administratively, that was accurate, but operationally, Amy reported directly to Katie. Amy's Scout Group was the Flotilla's eyes and ears. Amy had no doubt Katie would want to speak directly to the scout captains and their sensor operators at times. So, in one sense, Amy was responsible to a higher power than Bobby.

Only, practically, and again operationally, Bobby was responsible for both the *Bonaventure*'s defense and the running of its flight deck and operations. Amy and her scouts were his guests, and it behooved her to remember that and work closely with him. Also, in a pinch, his fighters had priority over her scouts.

Fortunately, Bobby was both easy to get along with and amazingly efficient at his job. He was right. The flight drills they were currently engaged in were going well. Smoothly and without any glitches, if a bit more slowly and tentatively maybe than was ideal. Considering they were all very new to this, and it was something nobody had ever done before, that was better than they had any right to expect.

"Yep," Amy replied, "it's going great. I have to say I'm impressed. I would have expected a bit more confusion, but you must have figured it all out in detail and briefed everyone very carefully."

The ship shuddered as suddenly a full set of fighter drones were fired off immediately on the heels of the recovery of their full squadron of "Wasp" class torpedo bombers. A little mistake in timing and it could have meant not only the loss of expensive equipment, but of lives. The equipment was nearly irreplaceable in the little time they had before deploying. The lives, and the experience they embodied, were absolutely irreplaceable. Not only did it take a good twenty years to grow a competent and well educated human, but never again would the Space Force have the time to train people the way they had their existing cadre. Only they had to train realistically for it to be worth much, and that meant taking some risk. Yes, it was a minor miracle it was going as well as it was. Something they both ought to be intensely grateful for.

Bobby grinned. He knew all that as well as Amy did. He half turned to her and held a hand over his heart. "I'm hurt," he said. "You didn't think I had it in me, did you? You thought just because I'm a laid-back, informally friendly sort of fella, that I didn't take this seriously enough." He shook his head in mock woe. "I'm disappointed, Amy. Just saddened."

Amy stared at the command display table in front of them with its schematic depiction of local space and tried manfully not to smile. She failed. Looking around, she noticed she wasn't the only one. Her entire command staff was charmed and amused by Bobby Maddox. Much better than back bitting resentment, she supposed. "Bobby, Bobby, Lieutenant Commander Maddox, I mean, you're incorrigible."

"Incorrigibly adorable, yet effective, you mean. And you haven't answered my question, have you? You're usually pretty upbeat and can-do yourself."

Amy nodded and bought a little time by pretending to inspect the plot before them. It showed one of her scouts coming in hot. It was going to have to decelerate brutally to have any chance of landing on the *Bonnie* without overshooting and coming around for a second try. But in the scenario being modeled, it had little choice. Red symbols representing enemy pursuit craft, actually local system defense craft simulating them, were hard on its tail. Bobby's fighters were racing out to meet them, but a scout ship in a dogfight between fighters was a fat target. That scout had to reach the protection of the *Bonnie*'s hangar as quickly as possible. "I guess I'm the one guilty of not being completely serious this time. Before now and seeing this, it didn't seem completely real. It seemed more like some staff exercise or a science fiction story than something actually happening. You'd have thought after Ganymede I'd have known better, but it's just coming home to me how serious this is. How much depends on us."

"Yippers," Bobby said, "you've got that right. It's serious and there's a lot more at stake than just our careers or even our lives. All the more reason to stay positive and enjoy the blessings we have while we can."

Amy smiled. "Thanks, Bobby. I know you're right. We're going to beat this thing. And we're going to be happy doing it."

"Happy warriors is us!"

\* \* \*

Katie was getting top priority on everything. It worried her. It was very convenient and arguably necessary, but it worried her.

"This is highly irregular, isn't it?" Lieutenant Rob Hood asked as they came to a section of access corridor that was temporarily empty except for themselves.

And there it was. Normally, Katie would have expected some pushback on the shortcuts and departures from normal routines she was taking. She was used to that. And as much as it had irked and frustrated her at times, she now recognized it'd kept her honest. Occasionally prevented her from making serious mistakes even. Now she was the only one second-guessing herself. "Well, yes," she answered, trying to buy time to formulate a proper answer. "I guess the question is whether that's a good thing or a bad thing." She sighed. "And whether we have much choice, really." She stopped and turned to face her head of galactic social, political, and economic intelligence. "Short on time, but you're right. I need to think about this. You're likely one of the few people I can honestly discuss it with."

Lieutenant Hood gave her a crooked smile in response. "Because I'm one of the few people in your command group not working flat out on something critical that needs to get done by yesterday."

Katie gave Hood a quelling look. "Partly, but let's be clear. Your work is vital. I've got two questions critical to the future of our species I have to answer and you, and your geek girl PhD Ensign from academic hell, are the ones I'm depending on to give me the information I need to do so. Capeesh, Lieutenant?"

Hood gave a sharp, chastened nod. "Capeesh. So, in the interest of clarity, let me spell it out. Those two questions are: one, are we really going to send our only effective warships on what might be a wild goose chase and leave the Solar System undefended, and, two, if we do opt for the possible wild goose chase, what does that goose look like and how do we catch it."

Katie snorted. "Usually, I rather like colorful language, but let's rephrase that. I need to know what the success criteria for the mission are, and, of course, I'd like some idea of how I might achieve them."

"Right, just like what I said." Hood showed no sign of repentance. "Let's cut to the chase. For the first time in your life, you're scared shitless by something."

Katie grunted. "You know better than most that I don't scare easily."

"True, and I've studied up on you, Commodore. Not just news reports, I've got to know some of your friends and colleagues recently. It's pretty clear you've seen this crisis coming a long time and you've shaped your whole life to being the one who can solve it. Right?"

Katie nodded slowly. It was true and something she rarely admitted to, even to her closest friends. "True. I'm afraid you're working for a paranoid megalomaniac with delusions of grandeur."

"Heroic delusions of grandeur," Hood corrected with a faint smile.

"Sometimes, Hood, heroes are needed."

"When I was younger, I didn't believe in them, but you've convinced me. Me and plenty of others."

Katie was surprised to find herself blushing. She managed a nod.

"Umm, excuse me? Commodore, ma'am?" an uncertain voice said, breaking into their conversation.

Katie and Rob turned to see a young, rather flustered, leading spacer engineer rating who had the name "W. A. Jackson" emblazoned on the left breast of his uniform ship suit. Between them, they were blocking the young man's access to the Engine Room. He might have squeezed past a pair of other ratings, but not a couple of officers and not when one was the commodore.

Katie smiled. "No problem, Jackson. Sorry for blocking your way."

Jackson turned pinkish, then rallied. "Is it a surprise

inspection, ma'am?"

"No, no," Katie replied, "I'm just looking around informally to see how things are going and taking the chance to get briefed by Lieutenant Hood here while I'm at it."

Hood seemed to be having trouble keeping a look of amusement off of his face.

"Yes, ma'am. Well, it's going pretty well. Everything seems to be working according to the book we got, but, ma'am, I'm damned if I understand the innards of this new tech. Anyhow, the chief is a stickler for double checking everything and he's expecting me back soon."

"Right, I want to see the engines myself. Let's get on with it." With that, Katie turned and led the way to the Engine Room, which lay just the other side of the airlock at the aft end of the access passageway they'd been occupying.

Entering the Engine Room, Katie found herself with quite the view. Normally spaceships are deliberately cramped so that in the event of any unexpected acceleration in any unexpected direction, nobody will have very far to fall. Not so in the Engine Room. It was full of large, heavy, and very complicated machinery. Machinery that its maintainers had to be able to easily access all parts of. Machinery that would periodically need to be removed and then replaced. That all needed room. Plenty of room.

There was a great deal of padding and wide meshed wire netting present to try to mitigate the effects of any falls, but basically the Engine Room was a huge cavernous space full of not just machinery but also pipes, wiring, catwalks, and platforms to work from. It was impressive as well as somewhat intimidating. In the middle of Katie's view, there was a podium festooned with indicator lights and control consoles. In front of it was a grizzled old chief who'd been poring over a thick manual.

Katie recognized him. It was Pavel "Pie-face" Borzakovsky. They'd stood a number of engineering watches together back on the *Resolute*. He'd been a Petty Officer then. She'd been a mere wet-behind-the-ears ensign.

Katie grinned. "Well met, Chief."

"Yes, ma'am. Jackson, you've got work to do on the

Auxiliary Power console, don't you?"

"Yes, Chief," Jackson replied as he hurried away.

Once he was out of easy earshot, Chief Borzakovsky spoke up. "So, ma'am, still nosing around sticking your nose into everything then?"

Katie enjoyed Hood's startled reaction to this. "Stood some long watches with the chief back when he was a mere petty officer and I was just an ensign."

"You seem to get around and make the oddest friends," Hood answered, and then immediately seemed to realize maybe he'd been a bit too forward.

Katie grinned wider. "Met you, didn't I?"

Hood just nodded and sighed. "You got me there, ma'am."

Katie turned to the chief. "So, yeah, I wanted to look around informally and see how things were going myself."

The chief gave Hood a quick glance. "Heard the lieutenant is from Mars and used to be enlisted." He didn't say he'd heard he was a spy and maybe a snitch.

"I trust the lieutenant implicitly," Katie replied gravely. "He does good work, and he's saved my bacon on occasion."

"Yes, ma'am. No hard feelings, Lieutenant Hood?"

"None. I'm fond of being cautious myself," Hood replied.

The chief gave a sharp nod. "Well, ma'am, everything that we can check seems to work as described in the manual here." He thumbed the thick volume he'd been studying.

"But?"

"But it's a complete black box. Engines and gravity generation, at least. I think I've maybe got an inkling of how the anti-matter catalyzed fusion power generators work. Those at least seem like more advanced versions of technology we already had. As for the rest, it's more like it's magic than tech, ma'am."

"The manual doesn't help?"

"No, ma'am. It's so 'do this and this happens' with such a lack of theory that I'm not sure the folks that wrote it really understand the technology themselves. If so, they're not sharing."

Katie looked at Hood. "Thoughts?"

"Sounds right. They're cagey about it, but it's pretty clear most of the Galactics aren't using technology they developed themselves. Not any more. The few that did develop their own technology did it so long ago they've forgotten the original science."

"Forgotten it? These are advanced technological societies. How could they have forgotten the science behind their tech?"

"It seems strange to us, but we're the abnormal ones. This tech is probably at least secondhand, more likely thirdhand or worse. I had this discussion with Ensign Wootton. She's a walking encyclopedia on the Galactics. Her powers of absorption and retention are incredible. Only sometimes she can't believe what the facts she has are telling her. As odd as it seems, we have almost no evidence of any of the galactic races actually inventing the technology they're currently using."

Katie frowned. This was odd, and she wasn't sure how it might be important, but her gut was telling her it likely was. "Is it possible there are only a few sources for most of it and those races are being careful to hide how it actually works?"

Hood shook his head. "I don't think so, ma'am. In every case we've investigated carefully, each group of Galactics was open about having got their technology from some other group. It looks a lot like each species develops its own technology for reaching the stars, but once they get there, they abandon it in favor of some better tech they buy from someone else. Then they stop trying to develop their own."

The chief grunted. "You know, ma'am, that makes sense. Why waste money and time on research to develop your own tech when you can buy better tech off the shelf?"

"And after a while, a single generation even, you'd lose the ability to do your own research even if you wanted to," Katie said.

"That's my tentative theory," Hood said. "It's a big galaxy out there, but it fits what we know of our local section of it. I think even Tanya, Ensign Wootton, I mean, is reluctantly coming around to agreeing with me. She still plays devil's advocate, but she's been pretty half-hearted about it recently."

"Wow, that's amazing," Katie said. "Interesting too, but does it have any operational significance?"

"Again, this is just an impression based on partial evidence, but it looks like the fact that most of the Galactics are using technology they don't really understand makes them very cautious about using it in any but the most conventional and well-tried ways."

The chief chuckled humorlessly. "That makes sense. Just mashing the buttons on powerful gear is likely not to just wreck it, but to get you and a lot of other people killed."

Both Hood and Katie nodded at that. They both had the background to understand what the chief was saying.

"And, as an interesting example of that, ma'am, that might have practical operational importance, I've found a rather interesting entry in this big book here."

Suddenly, Katie was glad she'd made this trip. "Go on, Chief."

"There's apparently something called a 'A *Dire Emergency Jump from an Arbitrary Start State*' for our jump drives."

"And that means precisely what?" Hood asked.

"Well, normally you have to be on a precise vector, at the right location in a system, within a limited range of velocities, and with no acceleration when you trigger the jump to reach a specified location in another system, right?"

"The Squids were pretty damned emphatic about that," Hood replied. "Otherwise, they said you were lucky if you only missed where you were going and ended up hopelessly lost. Most likely, they said, you ended up smeared over some random portion of creation. Exactly what they meant wasn't clear. It was apparently couched in very poetic and 'emphatic' language. Tanya thinks there may have been Squid swear words embedded in their description. She was rather excited by that. Anyhow, aren't the jump drives locked against being triggered if the parameters aren't correct?"

"Apparently, those lockouts can be overruled in the event of an emergency. Faced with certain destruction of some sort, you can make a random jump from almost anywhere it seems. But it's just that, random, though apparently the odds are you'll end up somewhere between one quarter to a couple of light years away. Usually in the other direction from the closest source of major energy."

Katie chewed a lip. "That could be handy."

"Well, maybe, ma'am, but the manual makes a couple of other things clear. For one, there's no certainty you'll come out someplace where there isn't already matter which will result in a very big explosion. Also, it makes it clear that it's random on a ship by ship basis. If two or more ships all try this maneuver, they're not likely to come out in the same place."

Hood sucked in a breath. "Willing to bet getting back from someplace that's a light year or more from any other place might be a little difficult navigationally, too. Can't safely use the jump drive from an arbitrary location and using the interplanetary drive would probably mean a trip back of months or even years."

Katie snorted. "I can see where the '*dire emergency*' label came from. Also, I wonder how many other little surprises like this there are. Things that some species are aware of, but others aren't."

"Don't know, ma'am. Helluva of a thing, ma'am. Don't really like how much I don't know. Don't like going by guess and by golly when so much is riding on it."

Katie sighed. "Welcome to the club, Chief. It is a helluva thing, but we've got to do our best."

"Yes, ma'am."

\* \* \*

He was what the newly pertinent Humans would call a spy and a fixer.

Unlike them, he considered it a high calling. One both honorable and conducive to ethical outcomes.

Currently he was slinking about on a Fringe Trade Hub formally called "Far Seat of Trade to the Trailing Edge Gamma". "Far Seat" if you wanted to be politely informal. Most of the denizens of and visitors to the station weren't so polite. They called the place "The Butt End of Nowhere." "Butt End Station" or "Butt End" more often.

The being, who generally asked his acquaintances to call him "*Shadowguide*" in whatever their native language was, didn't think this harsh judgment was entirely fair. True, the place was beyond the edge of what could be considered the civilized galaxy, but it was prosperous, clean, and safe. The various individuals of various species using the broad corridor that Shadowguide was lurking in all seemed to be doing well enough, and to be getting along with each other too.

Not something that could be assumed to be true in all Trade Hubs, however hard Shadowguide and his ilk tried to see it was.

So, yes indeed, there were worse places than "Far Seat." Far worse. Shadowguide worked hard to keep things like that in perspective. At all times, he attempted to keep the big picture in mind. That didn't change the fact that a lot of his day-to-day work was distinctly retail.

For instance, right now he was engaged in eavesdropping on a conversation between a dock worker punter and a local small-time entrepreneur.

"Five gold on the Humans passing their trial," the dock worker, a Climber like most of them, said. He scratched the top of his furry head as he did so. It showed he wasn't as confident as he was trying to pretend.

"Gutsy," his bookie, a Snout, said, his whiskers twitching. He obviously felt like he had a live one and was wondering how to best fleece him. "Most of my customers are betting the Scaly Ones will do for them. I'm offering eight to one odds if you want to bet against that."

The dock worker shuffled his feet. "I don't know. You're already giving me five to one on their just passing their test."

"Yep, you know something I don't?" the bookie asked, his snout twitching. Good question and one Shadowguide would like the answer to himself.

"Nope, but I don't think anyone else knows much either. I think maybe they're writing off those hairless monkeys a little too quickly. Also, there's that Builder colony in their system. I'm guessing they slipped them a little extra on the sly. Lots of rumors on the docks too that they've been quick to make deals with a couple of other species. Even some of the Tentacles and you know how awkward they are. I figure their odds are at least one in three, maybe even one in two. You're offering one in five. I'm just playing the odds."

The bookie shuffled his own feet. "It's your gold. Only they haven't replied to the request for a patrol yet and it's been a while. Also, the Scaly Ones might be new and kind of aggressive, but we already know they're plenty tough and shrewd to boot."

Shadowguide had to agree with the slippery little Snout on that. The Assheraskillias, or Scaly Ones as they were labeled informally, the Great People as they liked to call themselves, hadn't hesitated to answer the Trade Union's request for an anti-piracy patrol. They'd sent one immediately, and it'd quickly found and rooted out a nest of Snout pirates to everyone's relief. They'd also been cagey enough to not send everything. Someone had tried a sneak attack on their system while their anti-pirate flotilla had been engaged elsewhere. It'd received a hot reception. The consensus was that the only reason a few survivors had been able to limp away was because the Scaly Ones wanted everyone to know what a bad idea it was to mess with them.

Shadowguide also thought the dock worker was mistaken about having Builders in their system being an advantage for the Humans. His sources said they weren't even properly unified as a species yet. The Builders might have slipped them some intelligence and some technology, but Shadowguide didn't believe that made up for their presence, having likely inspired the Humans to develop interstellar travel earlier than was healthy for them. Not that developing FTL was ever too healthy for a species. Just surviving it eluded most of them.

The dock worker made non-committal noises while scratching yet another part of his fur covered anatomy with long fingers at the end of long arms. "Opportunities like this don't come along very often," he finally said. "Not just one species new to space, but two? And one very unusual one at that. I'm willing to bet we're going to see some surprises. Give me eight to one and I'll take your bet about the Scaly Ones and the Humans. If the Scaly Ones and Humans come to blows, I bet the Humans will still survive on their home planet a station orbit from now. I'll bet three additional gold on that."

The bookie couldn't help stroking his whiskers in pleasure at that. He held out a paw. "Done. Two bets. Eight gold in all."

Shadowguide figured the bookie had got the better of the deal. The odds weren't that good for the Humans. The Scaly Ones were aggressive and shrewd, and they weren't going to let a potential rival go unchallenged. They'd try to strangle the newcomers in their crib. They'd likely succeed.

Shadowguide's masters were concerned about the Trade Union's rather excessive local independence and the Scaly Ones were potentially even more of a headache. The Humans seemed likely to be less problematic if they came out ahead. Shadowguide wondered if it was worth putting a thumb on the scales.

## 3: A Grand Tour

*"The disinformation campaign began back in the crib, which first introduced you to three spatial dimensions. Those were the two dimensions in which you crawled, plus the remaining one by which you climbed out. Since that time, physical laws - not to mention common sense - have bolstered the belief in three dimensions, quelling any suspicion that there might be more."*

Page 2 of "Warped Passages" by Lisa Randall

Tretyak's message caught up with Katie and her fleet only hours before they jumped to Alpha Centauri and the new outpost there. The one grandiosely named "Star Station Alpha."

It wasn't real-time. Even if there hadn't been hours of lag between them, the fleet was traveling at a velocity sufficiently close to light speed to create a noticeable degree of time dilation. Einstein, like Newton, had been more extended than refuted. In any case, none of the alien magic they'd been able to buy allowed Faster-Than-Light communication. Travel, yes, but any messages had to go by ship.

Part of the message from Admiral Tretyak was for general consumption. Katie would have it piped out to the crews of her ships shortly before they jumped. It praised them, told them how what they were doing was historic, and how all of humanity was depending on them.

Another part of the message was for Katie personally.

"Katie, it's still up to you. Taking on the anti-pirate patrol is enough of a Hail Mary pass that there's no one else I'm willing to entrust the task to. And if you don't think it's a good idea, I'll work with that. That said, it's looking more and more like just turtling with everything we've got here in the Solar System won't work. Maybe we're not ready for fighting some aliens and making allies of others, but, sadly, the more we learn, the more it seems we don't have a choice. We've been war-gaming it incessantly and every play-through ends the same way. The Earth is indefensible. Planets are just big, fixed, and very vulnerable targets. Looks like it's just a fact. Even with the Galactics as allies, that'll still be true. Only with their help we have a chance of getting most of our industry and people off the mother planet."

Katie snorted at the priorities.

Even though the message was a recording, it was as if Tretyak was there reading her mind. He smiled wanly. "I don't have to guess how you're going to react to my putting industry first." He shrugged. "I'm getting white hair, Katie. I could be sleeping better, too. It's one thing to realize abstractly that your decisions could involve the fate of your species. It's another to actually prioritize saving machinery over evacuating millions of people."

Katie nodded. All of her crew had signed up for the dangers they faced. She still worried every day about her responsibility to each and every one of them. She'd been doing her own share of war gaming with Susan and Amy and others. In almost none of them had she been able to avoid sacrificing some of her people for the greater good. Amy's scout crews invariably had to stick their necks out to get the information Katie needed, and there were always losses as a result. So she certainly felt a great deal of empathy for Tretyak.

"It's been a relief to me that at least some of the Kannawik," Tretyak said, using the polite term for the Star Rats, "are tying their fate to ours. It rather bothers me that as a whole they seem to be hedging their bets. They seem genuinely sympathetic, but skeptical about our chances."

Katie nodded. She hadn't had Tretyak's experience of the Star Rats, but everything Hood and Wootton, her alien experts, had told her seemed to indicate that was the attitude of most of the Galactic aliens. They didn't bear humanity any ill will. Not generally, it varied, not just by species it seemed, by group and even individual. Only they were jaded and mostly interested in their own problems. Continued survival for a species, group, or individual didn't seem to be something the Galactics ever took for granted. They were most concerned with their own survival. They didn't like sticking their necks out for others. It was natural, Katie guessed. She guessed she understood. Couldn't really say she approved. Maybe that proved she was some sort of barbarian.

"In any case, you're going to have a chance to talk to some of our higher ranking Kannawik friends." Tretyak combed his hair with his fingers.

Katie nodded, despite knowing Tretyak would never see the gesture. The trip to Alpha Centauri was partly a fleet exercise, but it was also one step on a trip to visit their Star Rat allies out around Saturn. It was quicker to jump to Alpha Centauri and back to Saturn than to travel directly between Earth and Saturn using their interplanetary drives.

Tretyak continued. "Try to learn what you can. They've been at this game longer than we have. They have a vested interest in our success now. Use that and use what you learn to inform your final decision."

Being in the privacy of her own cabin, Katie allowed herself a deep heart-felt sigh. She wasn't expecting to hear much new from the Star Rat bigwigs. She figured they'd tell her she had to make allies, very politely of course, and that inevitably entailed risking the billions still on Earth. All of which she already knew and which Tretyak had just reiterated. It was to be hoped they might add useful detail and nuance.

Most of all, Katie fervently believed with so much at stake that it was her duty to do her due diligence. She might have to make critical decisions with uncertain outcomes while lacking critical information, but that wasn't any excuse for not crossing all her t's and dotting all her i's.

She might have to gamble, but she was going to be as responsible about it as she could be.

Besides, asking the Kannawik for their input was a good way to butter them up.

It was pretty obvious humanity was going to need all the alien allies and alien goodwill it could get.

* * *

The Huntmaster's entry into the nameless star system had been executed in as stealthy a fashion as the best minds of a naturally stealthy and paranoid species could devise.

The home base for the ships of the Great People's Forward Stalking Ambush group, what the Humans might call a fleet of scouts with significant capacity for reconnaissance by fire, was secret.

The Huntmaster didn't believe any of the Galactics even knew it existed, let alone where it was located. He intended to keep it that way.

But not at the price of leaving his junior hunters unsupervised. They were competent and well-motivated to be sure, but the Huntmaster was convinced in his bones that part of the reason for that was that they knew he was watching them. Always watching, even if he only intervened when it was clearly necessary.

And so he was here at a base buried under the surface of a barren moon that orbited around a nondescript gas giant. That gas giant's orbit precluded the chance of any habitable planet in the system. The nameless system also lacked a decent asteroid belt to provide minerals. It lacked everything but location.

An ideal location for the Huntmaster's purposes.

There was no reason for anyone to come to this system or to transit it, but it was close to the Far Seat Trading Hub. The station that was the center of Galactic activity for the local area. The nameless system was an ideal vantage point for surreptitiously watching the Galactics. Watching and, when the time came, striking to pick off any stragglers. Perhaps with some luck, they might someday be able to spook the whole herd and stampede them over a cliff. A grand day of feasting, that would be.

But for now, they were watching. Watching for easy prey that had wandered off from the main herd. The Humans looked like they might be such.

The Huntmaster greeted the Stalking Ambush leader with a polite tongue flick. The leader was his subordinate, but also his hunt mate. The Huntmaster had no need to prove his dominance. "The hunt gathers," he said.

"It does," the Stalking Ambush Leader, Foremost Stalker, agreed. "Only too slowly for my taste. These cattle can't do anything in a hurry. The Humans haven't even responded to the Galactics' request for a patrol for pirates yet. The Galactics, for their part, don't push them and tolerate their hesitance. Our offer to perform the duty instead has met only delay too. It is all infuriating delay."

The Huntmaster clattered his teeth in amusement. "Daring is a good quality in a scout leader. Strategists must have more patience. It would be strategically beneficial if the Humans made the mistake of refusing the offer and allowed us the honor of the duty."

Foremost Stalker's nostrils flared.

"Yes, yes," Huntmaster answered the unspoken comment. "It would be more satisfying to hunt worthwhile prey and have the wind in our faces and blood in our mouths, but it is our duty to act in the best interests of the entire Great Pack and not to just enjoy the hunt. I doubt if the Humans will make the mistake of turning down the Trade Union request, however slow and clumsy their decision-making apparatus might be."

A slow-blink showed Foremost Stalker considering this. "Their tendency to dither will make our hunt easier in the end, but I almost regret it."

"Do not underestimate them, Ambush Leader," the Huntmaster replied.

Foremost Stalker snorted. "I have studied the terrain and this prey. They are more prey than predator, and this terrain does not favor them. Even without our direct involvement, the piratical vermin of this region may prove too much for them. Our patience in this hunt may leave our bellies empty."

"A competitor strangled while it's still a weak youth is still a threat removed," the Huntmaster said. "We're not used to competitors or non-traditional prey. It behooves us to step quietly."

"It's hard to think of this prey as a threat, let alone competition."

"I have studied these creatures you call prey. Like ourselves, they have been the most successful predators on their planet. Our home was always demanding. Their planet was sometimes too easy for them, but also often very cruel. They eat grass sometimes, but at other times they fight for meat. Also, unlike most species that make it into space, they are not far from their predatory roots. They have not yet had the time to tame themselves and become dumb and herd-like."

Foremost Stalker dipped his snout in understanding. "Yes, but although they may have been top predators on their home planet among the stars, they are prey. They don't have the knowledge of the terrain, the refined senses, or the teeth and claws to be otherwise."

"Perhaps," the Huntmaster replied, "it may be so, but it is not good huntcraft to assume it all the same. In any case, we will know soon."

"I eagerly await it," Foremost Stalker replied, "all is in place. My hunters wait patiently, but eagerly."

"As it should be."

\* \* \*

The rings of Saturn were magnificent. Too bad Katie wasn't here to play tourist.

"It was generous of your people to cede this planetary system," commented the Star Rat she was meeting. His name in the, for Humans, unpronounceable Kannawik language translated into English as something like "Follower-of-currents". Katie decided to call him "Follower" in the privacy of her own mind.

"Realistic," Katie replied. "You know very well we'd never managed to send more than a scientific expedition out this far and had no permanent presence here in the Saturn system."

"True, but most sentients only learn such realism as the result of hard experience." Follower stroked his whiskers. "Most species have an exceedingly strong emotional attachment to what they consider their home system. All of it, even the parts they may have known only as wandering points of light in the sky. But maybe our experience of this is based on those, who having just discovered star travel, are possessed of a spirit of optimistic triumphalism."

Katie sighed. She was making a point of being open and frank with Follower. It was going to be important that the Star Rats and Humans co-operated closely. That co-operation had to start with individuals. "Our people aren't immune to that. Only, though it was before my time, I think your arrival was a shock to us. It shook a lot of us out of our complacency, and developments since have only emphasized the lesson. We're not alone, and we're not even that important. We really can't hope to continue as before. We're not even guaranteed being allowed continued existence."

"A hard lesson for the young to swallow."

"A real splash of cold water."

"An interesting expression, but yes, if the shock is sufficient, a lesson, however unwelcome, may be learned. Pleasantries aside, let us get to the point. You, Commodore Kincaid, have a critical decision to make. We have heard yours is the deciding voice in whether the Humans will answer the local Trade Union's request for an anti-piracy patrol. How say you?"

Katie grimaced. She suppressed an urge to ask just how the Star Rats were so well informed on the supposedly internal decision making of the Space Force. Follower had asked a good question. He deserved an answer. "It's a risky proposition. I don't see much choice about it though. We have to do it. We're going to have to send the bulk of our up-to-date fleet, too. We're going to be leaving the Solar System without much in the way of modern defense."

"Yes, it is a risk. One we will share with you. Only, as you've said, it is one you must take. It pleases me and those I represent that you see this."

"Thank you, Follower-of-currents."

Follower folded his paws and bowed. A gesture of respect. Katie responded in kind. "Can we continue to expect help?"

Follower stoked his whiskers. "From some, of the sort

already provided, but not much more. Some of us have thrown our lot in with you Humans, but many will leave the ship if they see it sinking, as you say."

Katie kept her feelings to herself. "Is there any way I can convince your leaders to do more?" she asked.

Follower flicked his tail. A sign of negation, according to Katie's studies. "Very little," he replied. "You must understand it is the fate of most species, those that survive at all, to wander as lost tribes among the stars doing what they need to pay their way. Most lose their home world and are unable to find new planets to establish roots on. It is good to aspire to more. It is not reasonable to expect it as a matter of course. You must understand humanity holding onto the Solar System is not a good bet. Our leaders must respect that. They play the cards they have, not the ones they wish they had. You have my sincere regrets."

"I understand," Katie answered. She did. Intellectually.

The rest of the meeting was just polite chit-chat.

* * *

Katie's fleet was on course for what would be only its third interstellar jump as a group. This one would be historic. It was no local hop that was more a test than for real. This one was the start of a deployment that would likely determine humanity's future.

If they managed to impress their prospective allies among the Galactics, the so-called "Trade Union," and to survive the effort intact, humanity would no longer be alone.

And, ideally, when they returned victorious, the Solar System would still be intact, too. Katie and her fleet not only had to be victorious, they had to manage to be so quickly and decisively before any potential competitor sniffed out the home system's weakness and took advantage.

Yeah, no pressure.

"It's awesome, isn't it?" Amy, who was standing right next to her, quietly commented. They were both overlooking the very impressive holographic operational display that formed the centerpiece of Katie's flag command center. They were waiting for one of the pair of Amy's scouts they'd sent ahead to return with the news that the coast was clear.

Katie grunted. "A lot of new ships with the best crews we could muster and technology beyond anything we could have imagined just a few years ago."

Amy nodded and smiled. Not her usual warm, genuine smile. Katie knew Amy knew Katie well enough to hear the reservations she hadn't expressed. Reservations it wouldn't do to explicitly state. Their ostensibly private conversation could be overheard by the command center's staff. The Space Force's command centers were, after all, explicitly designed to allow easy full bandwidth communication between the members of close knit teams.

Katie herself had argued for this sort of design. She'd strongly averred that neither an AI alone, a single commander supported by software, nor a team linked only electronically could achieve the effectiveness of a good team physically sharing the same space.

Katie knew Amy mostly agreed with her about that.

Only it was also obvious that Amy was finding it a little inconvenient just now. She took a moment figuring out how to address the issue indirectly. "It's a lot of ships, all with their different strengths."

"Yep," Katie answered, knowing full well that Amy wouldn't let that short non-committal statement stand. Amy was nothing if not relentlessly upbeat and determined to make sure everyone else was cheerful and optimistic, too.

Amy surveyed the crescent shaped formation of their flotilla in the display before them before replying. "Let me see what we have here. Us in the middle on the *Bonaventure*, along with Bobby's fighters and my scouts."

"All ready to quickly deploy at the end of each jump according to a preset plan, which is why you can afford to be keeping me company here in my command center," Katie answered, going along with the game. She knew this conversation was for the benefit of their eavesdroppers and the messmates they'd share their gossip with.

"I'm your eyes."

"Which I guess makes Hood my ears and Colleen what? My sense of smell?"

That got a small genuine smile out of Amy. Katie could see

she was working hard not to chuckle or, heavens forbid, even giggle. Amy cleared her throat. "And right next to us is the *Freedom*, a powerful cruiser, the first of her class. Able to defend the *Bonaventure* or provide the knock-out blow of an attack as needs be."

"The *Freedom* is pretty capable, I have to admit," Katie replied. "Strong missile defense, a large number of long-range missiles for offense, some torpedoes for those hard to blast to oblivion targets, and chaser and rear beam weapons for closer in ship to ship combat. Yep, the *Freedom* has it all. Too bad she was so damned expensive and we only have one of her."

Amy wasn't having that. "There's more like her in the pipeline. And look, we've got a lot of smaller but still capable ships. They're going to allow you a lot of flexibility and we're going after pirates, not into some sort of fleet action."

Katie nodded solemnly. "True." She really hoped that it was true. She really wasn't sure what they'd be facing. This expedition was as much a reconnaissance of their local galactic neighborhood as it was a patrol at the behest of potential allies. None of which she wanted to discuss in public.

Amy nodded, a glint of understanding in her eyes. Katie had grown up an only child. Sometimes it weirded her out how her friends could seemingly read her mind. Amy continued their little charade. "Four destroyers in two squadrons of two each. Six frigates in two squadrons of three each. And, finally, nine corvettes, each more powerful than anything we had a couple of years ago, even forgetting the artificial gravity and FTL drives, in three squadrons of three. Like I said, it's awesome."

"Okay, it's awesome. Powerful, flexible, well-structured and it should be up for anything we encounter. It's the best all of humanity could provide. It's the most powerful military force the Human race has ever deployed. And it's mine to command. Talk about awesome, it's an awesome responsibility. It's my duty to be as prudent and responsible in doing so as I can be."

"Sure, but it's still awesome."

Katie couldn't help a small laugh. "I surrender. It's awesome."

"Can't win all your battles, Commodore Kincaid."

Katie nodded. All too true. Only Katie wasn't sure she could afford to lose any of them. Humanity had put all its eggs in one basket and handed it to her. Sure, her fleet was powerful and flexible, and the best humanity could manage. But did that mean it was enough?

She wasn't sure.

## 4: Meeting New People

*"To trust immediate intuitions rather than collective examination that is rational, careful, and intelligent is not wisdom: it is the presumption of an old man who refuses to believe that the great world outside his village is any different from the one he has always known."*
Page 60 of "Seven Brief Lessons on Physics" by Carlo Rovelli

Half a dozen plus jumps later and they still weren't routine. Katie had made a point of being in her flag command center for each of them. She'd also made a point of having one of her senior officers or staff present each time so she could temper the waiting with some informal briefing. She never had enough time for everything she wanted to do, so she did as much multi-tasking as possible.

"It's been uneventful so far, hasn't it?" Rob Hood said. He was her current guest. He and his young sidekick Ensign Wootton were her experts on the Galactics and the wider geopolitical situation. Colleen was generally responsible for providing the information needed to make plans. Amy was going to be her eyes during the actual execution of operations. Hood and Wootton were responsible for briefing her on local galactic politics. They were responsible for identifying prospective allies and possible enemies. Strictly speaking, perhaps their advice should be filtered through their boss Colleen, a.k.a. Commander McGinnis, head of Katie's intelligence branch. Only neither Katie nor Colleen saw the need for an additional layer between Katie and the experts. She might as well get her news from them directly, with all the nuance intact.

Although Wootton was arguably the more educated of the two, she was not only the junior officer, but also someone Katie found mildly but distinctly irritating. Hood, on the other hand, was someone she was willing to trust implicitly. An outsider focused on getting things done rather than spinning complicated theories and proving how smart he was.

"So far," Katie said in response to his question. "I'm happy with how smoothly the flotilla is handling routine operations. Given how new to this we all are some awkwardness wouldn't have been a surprise."

Hood nodded. An ex-NCO in the Space Force and then a small businessman after his supposed retirement, he had some experience of running things in the real world. Usually glitches and surprises came up at the best of times, especially when trying something new. "Very good people, hand-picked for this and highly motivated. It can make a real difference. Also, I think you already knowing most of your senior commanders and staff has helped."

"I was worried that excluding people I didn't already know was a mistake, but there were already too many unknowns in all of this. I wanted to minimize the chances of unpleasant surprises in staffing."

Rob Hood smiled. "I appreciate the vote of confidence, but this isn't why I'm here, is it? We're getting close to Far Seat Station and you want to go over what you're going to find there one more time, right?"

Katie smiled. "It's important enough and I'm new enough to diplomacy that getting my lines down pat is worth the trouble."

Faint lines of amusement joined his smile on Hood's face. They both knew Katie was also nervous and wanted some reassurance, even if neither of them was going to say it out loud. "Tanya has done excellent research on this. New species entering space happens periodically, but it's not frequent. She had to dig through the archives the Star Rats and others gave us. This anti-piracy patrol request is basically a very standard test by the local Trade Union representatives. They want to know what to expect from species new to interstellar travel."

"So it should be pretty pro forma?"

"Usually there would be some fighting, but only with small numbers of weak pirates who are too incompetent to get out of the way."

"Because the competent ones will all retreat temporarily, because stand-up fights aren't good business."

"Precisely, makes you wonder about the point of it all, but it seems the Trade Union figures pirates aren't a problem that can be solved. Only one that can be managed."

Katie sighed. "Well, I'll admit that's rather unsatisfying, but practically speaking a few skirmishes one-sided in our favor aren't anything to complain about."

"Be efficient and direct about it, but humble and respectful of the already established races and interests, and we should be fine."

"There will be wrinkles, though, right?"

Hood frowned. "Always some. Biggest unknown is that as it happens, we're not currently the only newcomers to the stars. There's a race that looks like a cross between lizards and velociraptors that are new too. This is very unusual. It shouldn't be a problem, but it's unprecedented. It's a wrinkle we can't be certain about."

Katie took a small breath in lieu of a deep sigh. Part of the job was maintaining a confident demeanor at all times. "So what do we know?"

"The Trade Union says, however scary they look, that they're rational and even polite. They passed their patrol test with flying colors. They were prompter than us in replying to the request and conducted their patrol very efficiently. They were very formal and correct with all the Trade Union officials and even humane and considerate in how they treated the pirates they captured. There's some evidence the Trade Union was pleasantly surprised by their restraint. Apparently, they consider most of us 'new races' as basically bloodthirsty barbarians."

"Ouch. So, a hard act to follow?"

"That's right. Also, though I've got no solid justification for it, these lizard people make me kind of nervous. I think they'll bear keeping an eye on."

"That's not very reassuring."

* * *

Some people said jump didn't bother them. That wasn't true for Amy. It felt like someone twisting her stomach around a stick and pulling it out every time.

This time was no different.

The cockpit of a Town class scout might be kindly described as cozy. Practically speaking, they were crammed in like sardines. There was no way Amy could hide how sick jump emergence made her when the SFS *Lockhaven* popped out into the nondescript system of an unnamed red dwarf.

Unfortunate, as her mission here was as much to boost morale as it was to monitor her crews' performance, also maybe to find ways to help them to do their jobs better.

Those jobs were among the most crucial of a whole slew of very crucial jobs. It was Amy's scouts that had the job of keeping the fleet that was humanity's last, best hope from blindly wandering into trouble.

LTJG Windsor, the *Lockhaven*'s engineering officer, spared her some sympathy. He was less busy than the others. "Can't help how we're made," he said. "A lot of us have issues with jump. I'm glad it just makes me want to puke for a few seconds."

"Still a problem, I think maybe," Amy answered, trying to sound calm, rational, and able to cope, even if she was feeling a little off. "Do you think it might be a tactical problem because of crews being not at their best right after jump? Does anyone know how jump affects aliens?"

Even as she spoke, and despite inertial compensators based on their newly acquired gravity manipulation tech, acceleration rammed her into her combat chair. It'd taken some tens of seconds for that to happen. She'd need to review how long later.

It was LTSG Chanthar, the little scout's captain, who answered for the engineering officer. "Seems if you're alive and sentient, jump is going to disagree with you some. Got drunk with a Star Rat spacer back when we were visiting Saturn. She said the Rats hate it, but Humans seem to be about average in their reaction. That maybe we're more variable in our reaction than some, but not sure because we were so new to it and there was so little data. She muttered something about the other newbies - the Scaly Ones, she called them - being unnaturally resilient to its effects."

"That's valuable information, Adesh," Amy replied. She grinned wickedly at the scout's captain. "I don't suppose you've shared it with the spooks yet?"

Lieutenant Chanthar winced. "No, ma'am. Not yet."

"Well, you're going to have to, but it's worth brownie points in my book. Kudos."

Chanthar relaxed a bit. "Thanks, ma'am."

"Nothing on sensors so far. Looks like it's just us in-system. Place is empty," the co-pilot, LTJG van Tol, who doubled as comms and sensors, broke in to say. This was a real patrol, after all, even if it appeared to be a rather routine and boring one.

Amy nodded acknowledgment.

"Thanks, Sally," Chanthar replied. "Sorry, ma'am. Business first."

"As it should be, Lieutenant. Kudos again," Amy said, grinning encouragement. "So far, I've been pretty impressed by you and your crew."

"We try, ma'am. But you know, ma'am, even a dinky little system with only a half dozen planets all pretty close together and you could probably hide the entire Space Force in it and we'd never know. Just so you and the commodore know an all clear is just a best guess, not something we can ever be sure of."

"The commodore is downright paranoid, though she tries not to show it," Amy answered. "We brainstormed and gamed this every which way we could and I'm afraid the best we can hope from you is a bit of warning. If you can keep us from being surprised, you've done your job. Any more is welcome, but we don't expect it. Particularly in the couple of hours we give you to look around."

"I know if we took any longer, it'd not only hold up the whole fleet, but we'd be out of communications for an uncomfortably long time."

"True, we worry when we don't hear from you folks regularly."

"Good to hear that, ma'am. I think."

Amy chuckled. "Good news, bad news for sure. Yes, I know you're doing your best. And, yes, I know it mightn't be good enough."

"Yes, ma'am."

\* \* \*

Rob Hood hadn't had time for a personal life, let alone any romance, since he was a kid. After his parents had died, just surviving had been a full-time job. Then the Space Force proved to be his big break, but it'd kept him very busy. Even after his supposed retirement, it'd kept him busy, and that was not allowing for the demands of building a business from the ground up.

And then back to school, post-secondary school he'd never been properly prepared for and was out of practice for. That before allowing for the fact he'd effectively done four to six years' work in just over two. Yep, Rob had been one busy beaver.

It'd left him totally unprepared to deal with someone like Ensign Tanya Wootton. At least on a personal level. On a work level, they were both fanatics totally dedicated to developing an understanding of the alien species who populated the local part of the galaxy. The aliens humanity had to learn to get along with.

But inevitably, all the close contact this involved meant work was leaking over into the personal. Totally inappropriate, and Rob was very uncomfortable with it.

Tanya was starting to notice. "You seem very distracted. You know this is very important. You have to get your head in the game, as the saying goes."

"Right, sorry," Rob replied. Why was he apologizing to his

supposed subordinate? "There are a lot of moving parts here and it's not completely clear to me which parts are significant and which aren't. I was trying to contemplate the overall situation and get a fix on where everything fits in." Technically correct in a vague sort of way. Rob was damned if he was going to be specific about what was bothering him.

"Oh, I think I can help with that."

"Fill your boots, girl."

Tanya tried to frown at him, but her happiness at having a captive, almost willing audience for expounding on what she'd learned apparently overrode any inclination to be annoyed at what might be considered disrespect. "Well, if we're going to be informal, we're living in the hinterlands."

Rob gestured at the holographic display between them. It showed a flattened pancake of a myriad colored dots. A map of the local part of the galaxy color coded by political status.

Tanya smiled. Rob knew she'd worked damned hard on the display and was happy someone had taken notice. The young ensign took a deep breath and launched into a spiel worded to sound informal, even folksy, but which she'd obviously pre-scripted and memorized. "For those of you with a North American background." She smiled, showing cute dimples at Rob. She knew that although he was Martian, his parents had been Americans originally, and that was where he'd established the home base for his business. "You could say we're in Indian country and we're the Indians."

Rob gave her a thumbs up. Given what had happened to America's original inhabitants, that should serve as a wake-up call to her audience.

"We don't suffer the epidemiological problems they had, but in every other respect we're worse off. The technological gap was worse and it still might be. That depends on our ability to make modern weapons as opposed to having to trade for them and always being at a disadvantage."

"Not much the fleet can do about that," Rob observed.

"I'm getting to that."

"Sorry."

"This means it's imperative the fleet protect our fledgling production facilities even though many of them still have a critical dependence on parts produced in surface-based factories."

Rob nodded, but also gave his young subordinate a hand wiggle.

"What?" she asked.

"A good point and a good lead-in, but if you find a pithier way of putting it, that'd be great."

"I'll think about it. Anyhow, right now, we're still too dependent on the good graces of the Trade Union." She pointed to a string of bright blue stars scattered throughout the display before them. "And a number of alien groups we've been able to make deals with. The Trade Union can be thought of as the analog of the various European fur traders and the other aliens as other Indian tribes." She paused and looked at Rob. She was obviously wondering if he thought this oversimplified analogy was acceptable.

Rob nodded. "We don't want to get into the theory of conflict and competition between large scale civilizational structures with a multi-species heterogeneous composition. Putting people to sleep while discussing matters of life and death importance is not an achievement we want to aim at. It's an analogy. Having set a baseline, you can then describe how it doesn't work as well as how it does."

Tanya beamed at him. Nice to know she cared what he thought. She continued, "The so-called Mid and Elder Races located up arm from us can be considered to be the analogs of early modern Europe. We don't know much about them beyond the fact that they're far away, and far more advanced and powerful than we are. Also, they're not all that preoccupied with us right now. But they do keep their fingers in the pie because they realize that we're likely to develop in the future. There are clear reasons to suspect they're determined not to let what happened in Earth history happen to them. The older, more powerful Galactics aren't going to want to let the New World dominate the Old World they're part of. Our contacts with local races all report rumors that the Older Galactics will intervene to prevent any of us barbarians from getting too big for our britches."

Rob smiled. "Nicely put."

Tanya dimpled back at him. "For better or worse, it is unlikely humanity is on the radar of the Elder Races, or even of the Middle Powers. However, the local area is an unstable mess of squabbling factions, likely a situation to their satisfaction, and we do need to deal with that."

"Very good. That it for the intro?"

"Thank you. I have one more point to make."

"Okay."

"The two most important local powers we need to deal with are the Trade Union and the Great People who are lizard analogs. Think of the smart, fast dinosaurs in the classic movie and that's what they'll remind you of. From a historical point of view, they're reminiscent of Germany just prior to the Great World Wars of the twentieth century."

"That it?"

"Yes, then I'll ask for questions and use those to give more actual detail. Do you think we should plant some questions to help guide the conversation?"

"Informally, I can talk to some colleagues about topics we'd like to cover. I've got one obvious question: what are the chances of our taking on the Trade Union or these lizard people and winning?"

"Oh, that's easy. Non-existent. The Trade Union could crush us without half trying, if they got halfway organized and wanted to. That's unlikely. Despite being large and having a distinct advantage in tech, they're not really a military power. It's not their thing. Probably, unless we really annoy them, they won't bother us either. No profit in that. They could doom us with benign neglect. They basically control the access to really advanced tech from up arm. We're more on a par with the Great People theoretically, but they've got a decades long head start on us, and they're fully unified. Frankly, I think they're just more organized and efficient. Their whole society is set up for conflict in a way ours just isn't."

"That's disturbing."

"It is what it is."

"We live in interesting times."

"We sure do. Isn't it great?"

* * *

Apparently, the Far Seat Station Trade Hub was either lacking VIP facilities or Katie didn't qualify.

But she had been met politely at the shuttle docks by a friendly, garrulous even, mid-level official with an escort of a half dozen station police. That was something.

Better than the greeting the first contact expedition had received. Of course, they hadn't brought a whole fleet of warships along with them.

Her greeter was one "Far-farer-for-profit". He resembled nothing so much as a rather weird, erect, highly animated orangutan. Orange, furry, and long-limbed, he belonged to a species informally known as "Climbers" according to the briefings she'd received. "Limers" to be formal. Apparently they were a mainly space-based race who specialized in building and then operating stations.

"Far," as Katie resolved to call him in the privacy of her own mind, wore a purple-tinted, gold-chased harness with multiple pouches attached, and a short kilt. Thought of like that, it seemed faintly ridiculous, but actually it somehow came off as elegant and dignified.

Their police escort was also composed of Climbers, similarly dressed, but their harnesses were simpler and colored green and orange with basic black trimmings. Tags festooned with trade language symbols announced who they were and established their ranks. Katie could piece out the trade language if she concentrated, but it was still work. Work that tended to give her a bit of a headache.

"So, what do you think of our humble trading post, so far?" Far asked her.

Katie looked around and took a deep breath. The place was a crowded, cacophonous bazaar. Katie felt morally certain Far could have managed to take her to the higher-level Trade Union officials she was meeting by a quieter route. This was another test of some sort. "It's very noisy and crowded. There're all sorts of different people."

Far bobbed his head. Vigorously. Katie had been told that this was the Trade Talk gesture that denoted a smile. In which case Far's gesture amounted to the slick, too frequent, too wide smile of a used car salesman. His English, quick, colloquial, and perfectly accented, gave the same impression. "Yes, yes," he said. "What is a trade hub but a place for many to get together, get to know each other, and make deals?"

"Get to know each other?"

"Yes, indeed! How can you make good deals with those you don't know? Know what they want? Know what they are willing to pay? Know what they can afford to offer?" Far paused and stood looking around them. "Know how much you can trust them?" he finally continued.

Katie blinked. This was a little out of her wheelhouse. In the Space Force and even in Earth politics, you dealt with people you had to according to more or less established rules. Some of those rules might be unwritten, but they were nevertheless pretty well understood. Katie realized she didn't have much experience picking who she'd work with or with deciding on what basis. She'd never done much buying and selling in an open market. Managing business contacts was something she had absolutely no experience with. "Can't rational intelligent beings make mutually beneficial trades without it being a big fuss?" she asked.

Far stopped again, scratching his head with a long arm as he did so. That done, he made a deeper, more decisive head bob than had been his wont. Was this his equivalent of a genuine smile? "I can see you will be much more easy to work with than some of the cheapskates around here."

Katie fought to keep a surprised frown off of her face. Had this creature just suggested she was a naïve fool, ripe for the fleecing? Or was the compliment genuine and Katie was simply being too paranoid? "We're here to help the Trade Union make this region safe for honest merchants," she said. That seemed an innocent enough thing to say.

Far dipped his head in what Katie understood was the Galactic equivalent of a Human nod yes. He waved at their escort to start moving again. The concourse they were in was crowded enough that Katie appreciated that escort. She wasn't sure she could have elbowed her way through the press of haggling, selling, and shopping beings without causing an intergalactic incident.

Their police escort and the crowd seemed to understand

each other well enough. The crowd parted way for the police readily enough, but calmly without any apparent fear or resentment. In turn, the police didn't seem inclined to resort to overt intimidation and were patient with the odd individual that might be slow to move out of their way through inattention. Katie figured there was a positive message there. The Galactics, as heterogeneous and self-interested as they might be, seemed good-natured and willing to get along.

Katie decided to share that thought. "A lot of very different and busy people, but everyone seems to get along."

That elicited a sharp head bob from Far. "We work hard to create a venue for profitable commerce. I'm pleased you recognize this. It bodes well for a future in which your species finds a constructive economic niche."

"Not too distant of a future, I hope," Katie replied.

Far continued walking but spared Katie a short half nod, half bow. A sign of respectful acknowledgment, maybe? "We all hope so. In the meantime, you have the means to help us discourage those who attempt to profit in non-constructive and unfriendly ways."

Was Far just an escort or had the negotiations already started, Katie wondered. "A certain level of support, supplies of food and fuel as well as information and somewhere for my crews to get rest and recreation would help," she ventured.

Far responded with a head dip, a motion that was slower and more prolonged than his habitual bobs. A gesture of affirmation. "Assuming all goes well with my superiors, you will be provided with adequate quantities of fuel, food, and life support consumables. Mooring slots and the use of several shuttle docks as well. Finally, minimal but comfortable barracks will also be supplied at no cost to you. As long as they behave in a civilized way, your crew members are free to make full use of the station's facilities and trade for entertainment, superior meals, or accommodations at the usual market rates. I've arranged for money exchangers to set up tables at the docks where your crew can exchange your Earth currencies, gold, and other valuables for the gold tokens we use. I trust this meets with your approval?"

"Sounds good," Katie answered. "Your superiors will

provide intelligence and suggest objectives, then?"

"Yes, I've only a little over a GaTok's worth of experience," Far said. "What you Humans might call a few years, a decade and a bit. I'm still too inexperienced to be a principal in serious negotiations."

Which meant by Far's standards Katie was completely inexperienced and unqualified to be performing the role she was. Maybe that explained the faint air of condescension the furry alien seemed to give off. "So, experience is critical for success in Galactic society?"

"Yes, of course, and when it is lacking surviving that lack requires great luck and even then tends to be very costly for all involved."

Katie wasn't reassured in the least by that. If that was how Far saw her and humanity, it was surprising he wasn't actively hostile. "Maybe that's the price required."

The alien official shuffled his feet in what Katie knew to be the equivalent of a shrug. "Maybe. Sometimes considerable investment is required before any profit is realized. Risk is unavoidable if undesirable, and always there are investments that need to be written off. The ones that succeed must pay enough to compensate for that and still leave enough for a reasonable profit."

"I have specialized in military operations," Katie answered, "but even I understand those basic truths. Sadly, I imagine we Humans can expect to pay a considerable risk premium in our initial dealings."

An emphatic head bob. "Indeed. It's good you see that. There may be hope for your species after all."

Great. Katie had no good reply for that. "Thank you," she said insincerely before deliberately turning the conversation to small talk about the Trade Hub and its inhabitants.

For all the surface tolerance and affable demeanor of the Galactics, it was clear that the galaxy was a harsh and unforgiving place.

It was what it was.

## 5: On the Edge

*"A remarkable feature of Lagrange's method was that it treated the system as a 'black box'. Knowledge of the inputs and the system's general characteristics was enough to be able [to] calculate the output; you didn't need to know the details of the internal mechanism."*

Page 205 of "Faraday, Maxwell, and the Electromagnetic Field: How Two Men Revolutionized Physics" by Basil Mahon and Nancy Forbes.

The Huntmaster was letting Foremost Stalker do most of the talking. That had been his policy for all the several hands of sleeps he'd been present for on their secret forward base.

It wasn't that Foremost Stalker couldn't use some instruction in taking a wider, more strategic view of their great hunt, but rather that the Huntmaster believed it was important that he not undermine the independence of thought and aggressiveness of his subordinate. The very fact of the Huntmaster's continued presence could easily be interpreted as showing some lack of confidence. That was unfortunate, but with the very fate of their species perhaps in the balance, the Huntmaster's priority was keeping a close eye on their prey.

"It may be true that it'd have been better if the Human prey had shown their true stomach and failed to arrive on the field as the Trade Union grass eaters asked," Foremost Stalker was saying, "but I'm pleased. Even if it's only the scent of blood on the wind from the harassment of the scavengers we've driven before us, it's better than a hunt with no sighting of any prey."

The Huntmaster understood that his subordinate was attempting to be diplomatic in expressing his feelings. He didn't want to discourage this laudable attempt. Still, he saw an opportunity to provide some mild correction. He resolved to take it. "It is not the sort of course any truly strong-blooded member of the People has any taste for, but one Human sage has the right of it," he said.

"Truly?" Foremost Stalker replied. He dipped his snout quickly as he did so. He seemed more surprised and puzzled than resentful. Good.

"Truly," the Huntmaster answered, "a battle avoided but won, unnoticed even by the unwise, is the best battle of all. Notice I say battle not hunt, for although we speak constantly of the hunt because it is our nature to do so, struggles between large groups of technologically advanced sentients are not truly hunts. They are something else we do not have good words for. Something those with our high ranks and great responsibility must strive to understand."

"So not '*battle*' in the sense of the contests between different groups of hunters among the People in the days of division, but not purely a '*hunt*' either. It is not the same as the finding and taking down of prey that at best can defend itself if fleeing fails," Foremost Stalker said. "Something else."

"Just so," the Huntmaster answered. "How do you think you would characterize it?"

"I can see, Huntmaster, that I have much study to do in addition to the many responsibilities you've given me here. A first, faint smell of the trail is that these star faring aliens have all been hunters at some point, but also often prey. More have ended up the meals of others in the end than have survived. Those that remain desperately seek to be accepted as fellow hunters rather than prey. But, I'm puzzled. They seem to wish to be hunters that don't hunt. How can that be?"

"It is a faint and complicated trail," the Huntmaster

answered. "Surely you know the aliens have different methods of finding food than we do?"

"Indeed, Huntmaster," Foremost Stalker responded with a respectful snout dip, "very different and, to me, at least, rather revolting. They garden much more than our Broodmothers do, do they not? I hear too, that their kills are not always clean, that they act as blood suckers and milk stealers. The stomach turns at the thought."

"Many of the aliens have ways that are different and strange in truth," the Huntmaster said, "nevertheless, it is our responsibility to keep our feelings in check and seek to understand them. The Humans, in particular, have a set of practices they call '*domestication*'."

"An odd word. Have we none that is similar in meaning?"

"No. The Humans picked plants and animals to make into permanent wards. They care for them after a fashion, permitting them food and shelter and freedom from immediate death in exchange for being useful. They have predator animals they used to assist in hunts. They also have herd animals that they are parasitic upon for milk in particular, but which they kill for meat only when those animals are at their fattest."

Foremost Stalker stared directly at the Huntmaster, eyes wide, nostrils flared, and maw wide. He was surprised and revolted. The Huntmaster forgave him his impropriety because of that. "Calm yourself, my best stalker," the Huntmaster said, "it gets worse. Deep in their history, various sub-groups on their very varied home planet did the same to other sub-groups of their species."

"What?" Foremost Stalker responded. "They made some of their own people into herd creatures despite their being naturally predators?"

"Yes," the Huntmaster replied. "Revolting as that might be, they did. And I suspect not only they, but some among the Galactics, are trying to do the same to competing species."

Foremost Stalker went very still and blinked slowly. "I do not envy you your work, Huntmaster. It seems very unpleasant. Truly, this seems like so much Rat Cat Scat."

The Huntmaster gave a snout dip of agreement. The Rat

Cats were small, warm blooded, scurrying vermin that followed the herds of prey about, mostly scavenging what they could from the kills of others, although it seemed they'd eat anything given the need. The People eliminated them whenever possible, but it was no more possible to annihilate them all than it was to eliminate all the tiny little flying bloodsuckers that also followed the herds, preying upon all. Kill one, and there always seemed to be a dozen more. The Rat Cats were no threat most of the time, but on occasion when they found a weak animal that had become separated from the main herd, they'd swarm it and bring it down. It was not a pretty thing. Even more ugly was that their droppings spread a disease that weakened those that caught it. Worse even than that was that its effect was not merely physical, it was also mental. The Rat Cat Scat disease made its victims docile, lethargic and inattentive to their surroundings. For the People, who valued their mental acuity, it was most horrifying. Although the disease mostly affected the already weak, the very young but most of all the very old, it was feared by all of the Great People. Foremost Stalker's short comment was multi-leveled and wide ranging in its implications. It was clever and annoying to the Huntmaster in equal measure.

The Huntmaster chose not to take offense. "And yet now that we're among the stars, which are mostly dominated by others, we have no choice but to stalk down such paths," he said. "Stalk with care and patience."

Foremost Stalker slow-blinked. "There comes a time in the hunt when you must commit to your final lunge and pounce upon the prey."

"Truly, and that time must be selected carefully," the Huntmaster answered, "and I will choose it."

"Truly," Foremost Stalker agreed with a differential snout dip.

The Huntmaster gave a tongue flick to indicate he was pleased with this. Still, it was clear to the Huntmaster that he dared not wait too long to bring this hunt to its conclusion.

Sooner rather than later, it'd be time to see what sort of prey the Humans were.

\* \* \*

Katie hadn't known what to expect, but it hadn't been something like a tea party. A tea party with a flavor half way between feudal Japanese and Victorian Alice in Wonderland.

It was a dim and decidedly low-tech environment. One distinctly lacking in displays, communication devices, and anyone other than the principals she was here to meet. There were no aides, interns, or secretaries present. No servers to set out plates or serve tea.

The imposing views the room provided appeared via full walls of transparent metal. Not via the high-quality flat screens that would have been used by Humans. The view on the side she was facing, behind the Trade Union Bosses she was here to meet, was of a vast expanse of bright stars. One was somewhat brighter than the rest. Far Seat Station Trade Hub was far out from the primary of the system.

Behind her, providing most of the light in the room, was a view of a serene park-like concourse. It had trees in big tubs. Real trees. They'd been shedding leaves. Katie and her escort had passed through it to get to this conference room.

That concourse had been in dramatic contrast to the busy, very packed bazaar of most of their route. Before leaving Far and her police escort outside, Katie had had a chance to ask him about that.

"This is a residential section for successful business people," he'd replied.

Since she was attending an important business meeting in this 'residential' section Katie took that to mean the station's bigwigs mixed their places of business and residence. Looked like the Galactics didn't distinguish between work and play the way humanity's dominant culture did. She had a vague memory of Hood or Wootton saying as much in passing. They'd tried to keep to the high points, but the info dumps they'd stuffed her with had still been immense.

"Your tea is satisfactory?" asked "Sharp-eye-for-profit," a Climber, and apparent head of the Trade Union council. Katie resolved to think of him as "Sharp" and wondered if he was related to Far.

"Excellent," Katie answered. She'd been wondering if this was real Earth tea or simply a very similar hot beverage. She was now leaning towards real Earth tea, but of a quality she'd never been able to afford.

"We enjoy it also," Sharp said. "In fact, as a product that appeals to multiple species, it has considerable potential. We'd take it as a personal favor if you could expedite the export of it in quantity upon your return to your home planet."

This wasn't exactly in accordance with the ethics the Space Force had pounded into Katie, but Hood and Wootton had warned her about this, too. "Of course," she replied, nodding before remembering to dip her head in the gesture commonly used by the Galactics.

One of Sharp's compatriots shifted slightly on their low seat. Katie hoped this wasn't a comment on her faux pas. In addition to Sharp, there were four other Trade Union Bosses present, though so far beyond the initial introductions, none of them other than Sharp had spoken.

The individual that had squirmed was a Varkoid, a "Big" in Galactic slang, by the name of Larkov. Larkov of Far Seat apparently. He resembled nothing so much as a super-sized anteater. Apparently he headed the local branch of the Merchant's Guild.

Next to Larkov sat the "Head Organizer of the Crafter's Benevolent Society," who resembled an extremely cute sea otter. Large for an Earth otter, he was only half the height of the "Big" next to him. His people were called the "Swish" formally and "Swimmers" informally. He seemed fond of stroking his whiskers and watched Katie with bright, intelligent eyes. He'd been introduced as "Faint Ripples".

The pair to the other side of Sharp were similar in appearance to "Faint Ripples", but Katie had been well briefed and recognized them as members of two entirely different species.

One resembled nothing so much as a giant meerkat or prairie dog with odd face fur. Katie had been briefed on this species and that was exactly what Hood had described them as; intelligent, very social prairie dogs that had developed an advanced civilization complete with advanced technology. They were the closest thing to industrialists that the highly merchantile Galactics had. The species was known as the "Ras-

Kas," "Grass Lovers" in Galactic slang. The Galactics seemed to be inordinately fond both of formal terms and making fun of them with slang.

The grass loving individual in question was apparently named "Kweet'Sweet'Aaah," the third syllable being a sign of high rank. She'd also been told he'd be handling the logistical support for Katie's fleet.

The final Trade Union Boss belonged to a species Katie found all too easy to recognize. He was a "Zneet" or "Snout," one of the rat-like creatures that had attacked the Solar System not too long before. Apparently, his race had a reputation for being opportunistic. Some were honest traders, but many were con artists, thieves, or outright pirates.

This particular Snout, "Kaa-Ree" by name, was an honest arranger of entertainment, it seemed. He'd bobbed his head sharply when Sharp had said he'd be responsible for ensuring Katie's crews enjoyed their time at Far Seat Station.

Both "Kweet'Sweet'Aaah" and "Kaa-Ree" viewed Katie with a bland interest she found unnerving. She felt like she was on trial. Not like she was meeting with new allies.

"Very good," Sharp said, ending the long pause that had followed Katie's agreement. Had that been a deliberate tactic designed to unnerve her? "We've made all the necessary arrangements to support your fleet for one of your weeks. That should be long enough for you to prepare. We've determined a patrol route for you to follow at that point. We'll send the necessary information electronically to your staff after this meeting."

That was it? They weren't even going to tell her the details, let alone discuss them? Unfortunately, despite her feelings, Katie had to be diplomatic. "Are there any points of special importance you'd like to emphasize?" she asked.

"No," Sharp replied. "You should find all the arrangements more than adequate and our best minds have planned the patrol route with information you don't have and we're not free to share. That's good tea. You should finish it before leaving."

Katie felt her face go stiff with outrage. She'd been dismissed with only the thinnest attempt at politeness. Had humiliating her been the whole point of this meeting? Was this all about putting the newcomers in their place? She didn't know, and the stakes were too high to wing it. She needed to swallow her anger. She hoped they had missed her change of expression and put a purse-lipped smile on. "Of course, I want to return to my ship so that I and my staff can review the information you've provided us with as quickly as possible. But not at the price of wasting this delicious beverage."

She finished her tea with as much haste as was consistent with decorum and left.

They didn't talk much as Far-farer-for-profit and his policemen escorted her back to the docks.

Katie had a lot to think about already.

* * *

Shadowguide had spent much time, many a long BaTok, studying Human body language. They'd been careless about keeping information about themselves secret. They acted as if they believed they were the only intelligent beings in existence.

A disconcerting trait, but as he watched the Human leader traverse the bazaar back to the docks, he couldn't help thinking a very convenient one. Anything less than intense study from plentiful sources and he'd not have recognized the tight shoulders and slightly stiff walk of "Commodore Kincaid" as signals of displeasure.

His follow denizens of the trading floor were pretending to ignore the little parade, but actually watching it closely. They were all trying to get a fix on the nature of these newcomers.

One of them, a Snout that sold tiny souvenir trinkets he bought cheap and marked up as much as the market allowed, went so far as to comment on it. "Well, I'd be willing to bet our esteemed and wise local leadership, being the big fish in a small pond, managed to insult the Human."

A nearby Varkoid dipped its head at that. "Truly, they worry more about establishing their own importance than making the sale."

A fellow Swimmer who'd been inspecting re-furbished data chips at the stall next to the Snout's small stand chipped in. "The Humans are a captive market now. They have to buy what the Trade Union is offering, but it's never wise to send a customer away unhappy. Repeat business is good business."

Many slight head dips among the local part of the throng greeted that.

Shadowguide added his own to them. He was being careful to fit in.

But he also agreed wholeheartedly. This situation bore watching.

* * *

Lieutenant Robert Hood could feel a headache beginning. It was desperately important to properly brief Commodore Kincaid on the threat they were facing. Soon, like a week ago, shortly after they'd arrived at Far Seat, wouldn't have been too soon. Only there was only one of Rob and he'd mostly concentrated on figuring out the internal structure of their nominal Trade Union allies. They had the formal story from the Star Rats and other species they'd flogged parts of Earth to for intelligence and technology. Unfortunately, their information was mostly a little outdated. And, worse, it was "official" information that reflected what the Trade Union wanted to present to outsiders. The up-to-date information on the Trade Union's internal politics that the commodore needed was lacking.

It'd been Rob's job to make up that lack as best he could. His best hadn't been very good. Gathering that sort of information took time. And he hadn't had much time.

He'd had to delegate the task of gathering information on the pirates to Ensign Tanya Wootton. As trying and arrogant as he found her at times, there was no doubt of either her capability or her willingness to work hard. She'd done her job well and was now briefing Rob on what she'd learned.

It wasn't her fault the news wasn't good.

"So, the Trade Union just accepts endemic piracy as a fact of life?" he asked her.

"Yes," Tanya answered, "in fact, some of my sources suggested they wouldn't wipe it out if they could."

Rob rubbed his temples, trying to relieve the ache there. "Why?"

"The Trade Union offers both insurance and *free* help to members in trouble. It protects members on important routes. If the threat gets too large or too close to vital places, it goes so far as to organize expeditions to cut the pirates back down to size. Only it exacts a price for all of that."

"So, if the pirates were to go away tomorrow, the Trade Union would lose both income and influence?"

"Exactly."

Rob sighed. "So, to be clear, they're not really interested in getting rid of the pirates at all?"

Tanya frowned. Rob, the heavens help him, couldn't help thinking she looked cute when she pouted. "First of all," she huffed, "the pirates are not a single organized entity."

"Right, they're a whole collection of various opportunistic small groups and individuals who're rather indifferent to the law and the rights of others. Got that."

Tanya looked frustrated. Again cute. Again, neither appropriate nor useful. They had a job to do. "What law?" she asked dramatically. "And, repugnant as it might seem to us, they seem to find our concept of 'rights' rather amusing once you get finished explaining it to them."

Rob blinked. This was something of a role reversal for him. He was used to being the outsider who couldn't bring people to realize that their assumptions based on their own narrow cultural bubbles weren't universally applicable. "I'm sorry. It is very hard to overcome your basic assumptions, isn't it? So, I guess the local galactic scene is much more Hobbesian than anything we Humans have seen for centuries."

Tanya grinned. It looked good on her. It completely wiped away the pinch-faced look she sometimes had when she was feeling disrespected or was otherwise frustrated. "That's right. But it's even worse than that. Out here, not only is your ethnicity not guaranteed survival, even your species isn't. Also, not only is there no Leviathan to guarantee security, there's no real hope of one developing. There are rumors of some whales further up the arm, but the rumors also say their only interest out here is to keep any competition from developing."

Rob couldn't help smiling at how happy the young woman seemed about delivering such bad news. "Okay," he said, "that jibes with what I've been able to learn. Let's get back to the pirates. Does this mean we can expect them to be pretty disorganized and piecemeal in their resistance?"

Tanya gave a contemplative nod. "Probably."

"But?"

"But sometimes a greater degree of organization arises internally."

"A strong leader or better organized sub-group?"

"Yeah, or also sometimes one better organized group of non-pirates decides to co-opt them to use in a deniable fashion against their competition."

"The Lizards."

"No real evidence, but I don't think it's something we can rule out."

"Great. Any other good news?"

"Well, yes, one thing, I don't think we can necessarily count on them to just fade out before us if we put on a show of force. They may fight back desperately, even against bad odds."

"Why? If they're in this for the profit, why fight?"

"Because they're not so much businessmen as very aggressive beggars with nowhere to go. Basically they're marginal fringe groups who can't make a living by co-operating with the Trade Union and other groups. They have families and stations and are living on a knife edge. No matter how bad the odds, some of them likely have their backs against the wall and will fight to the bitter end."

"Ouch."

"Yeah, I don't imagine the commodore is going to like this news."

"I suspect not."

## 6: Making Contact

*"A system in equilibrium, very near its state of maximum entropy, has no thermodynamic arrow of time. The fact that our world does have such an arrow means that it is very far from equilibrium. Its initial conditions at very large negative time were such that its entropy was very low, and, as mandated by the second law, began to increase with time—an increase that is still, on the average, going on. Thus, we can say that the time asymmetry arises not from the laws of physics themselves but from the initial conditions of our universe."*
Page 82 of "Time Travel and Warp Drives: A Scientific Guide to Shortcuts through Time and Space" by Allen Everett and Thomas Roman

Katie had a bad feeling.

Objectively, maybe her bad feeling wasn't justified.

Her fleet was forming up precisely despite however hungover she knew many of her crew members were. And, despite how hectic it had been for her and her command staff, the last week had gone smoothly. Give the Galactics one thing: they knew how to entertain. Kaa-Ree, the Trade Union boss, had come through in spades. He'd done everything but lay on dancing girls from Earth. Food, drink, and "cultural exchange events" featuring a lot of music and dancing had been incessant and varied. Even more startling, Katie didn't think her people had been overcharged much.

"You don't like how they're greasing the wheels for us either, do you?" Susan, standing beside her on the *Bonaventure's* bridge, asked.

"Nope, I feel like one of those cows being herded down the slaughterhouse chute."

Susan chuckled. Katie loved steak and had insisted on seeing where it came from back when they were both still cadets. "I told you, you wouldn't enjoy learning that your favorite food was dead animal bits. Let alone seeing the poor burgers on the hoof being led to the slaughter."

Katie nodded. "I think it's important to understand how things work, even if some parts make you uncomfortable. You can't really do anything without its having consequences and it's important to face up to those."

"Yep, us animals eat other living things, even if some people argue plants, fungi, yeast, or insects don't count."

Katie looked around at Susan's bridge. Its crew were all busy with their tasks. A jump was coming up, and the *Bonaventure* was the center of the fleet. Also, they were used to Katie's presence. One benefit of making frequent, unannounced, informal tours of the ship. Nobody was paying much attention to Katie and Susan's conversation. "Trust you to be cheerfully grim. Important point here is I don't think anyone is going to grant humanity a place among the stars without exacting a cost."

"And you don't like the fact you haven't been told how much yet."

"Exactly. I don't think one uneventful patrol, even with a lot of ships and clearing out those few pirates who somehow haven't noticed we're coming, is all they're going to ask. I expect a lot of extra charges on the bill."

"Yep, they've laid out our exact route and given everybody who might care a week to get ready for us."

"Could be just a routine show-the-flag kind of thing and sloppy security on the part of folks who are basically just civilian traders," Katie said.

"On the other hand, maybe they just handed anyone who figures we need cutting down to size a chance to set up a trap."

"Or both. Could be the Trade Union figures it's a chance to take care of two different problems at once by setting us and the pirates against each other."

"What about those lizard people?"

"I wish I knew. Everything we know about them suggests they're naturally very aggressive, but they're being very careful and correct. It gives me the willies, but we have absolutely no evidence of their planning anything hostile. Maybe they're waiting and watching to see if there'll be a chance to play us, the Trade Union, and the pirates all off against each other. Or maybe they have problems at home they're not telling anyone about. Hood and Wootton couldn't tell me much. Nobody has had any success gathering information about them. They're tight lipped and very good at taking care of spies."

"They just disappear and are never heard of again."

"Yep, officially the Trade Union doesn't admit to having spies. They've formally restricted all trade with the Lizards to Far Seat and nobody is supposed to enter Lizard claimed space."

"Only the Galactics are rather entrepreneurial sorts and shady small time traders and outright smugglers abound."

"That's right, and rumor has it that anyone who goes anyone near Lizard space tends to disappear."

"Ouch. So you've got to wonder what they're hiding."

"That's my job."

"And Amy's and Colleen's, and your favorite Martian lieutenant's too. Glad it's not mine."

"No, you just have to be ready for anything. The *Bonaventure* is the core of our fleet."

"She's a good ship with a good crew. We'll do our job."

"Good. It's good to be able to count on something."

\* \* \*

Rob wondered if anyone else saw what he did.

"Ma'am," the flag command center's sensor officer announced to the center's staff and Commodore Kincaid in particular, "drive flare towards zenith. Looks like they're on a jump approach to the jump point for system 0132574. That's a small uninhabited M3 system roughly perpendicular to our planned patrol route. Nothing there really, ma'am."

"Thank you, Sensors," Kincaid replied calmly. A fraction too calmly for it to be genuine in Rob's estimation.

Kincaid was not happy. Not happy and being very careful to not show that fact.

It was the third such flare and departure for a nowhere system by a still distant and unidentified ship within the last few hours. And this was in the first system out of Far Seat on their mandated patrol route. There'd been scouts out, redundant scouts out, waiting for their arrival, ready to report on it to someone somewhere.

Somewhere out there was a mind guiding their supposedly unorganized pirate opponents.

Rob could see that and he had no doubt Kincaid could, too. Hence her unhappiness.

It being his turn to serve as her foil during the long watches in the command center, Rob manned up and spoke. "So they're organized? I guess the question is what are they planning."

Kincaid inclined her head to him and smiled thinly. "No, the question is what I plan to do."

"Ma'am?"

Another thin smile. "When I act, you'll be among the first to know, Lieutenant Hood."

"Yes, ma'am."

"Patience. It'll take a while for this to play out."

A rather long while, as it turned out. It took a couple of days. All of the remainder of the current watch and all of the remainder of their time in the first system on their patrol route, the first of many nondescript M dwarf systems. Several sleep cycles and multiple meals and a lot of interminable waiting.

They'd jumped to the next system, a K9 one that was just barely larger than another M class one, and were facing yet more pirate scouts, before Kincaid showed her hand. By that point, the pirate plan to continuously harass the Human fleet without allowing themselves to be brought to decisive action had become clear.

Rob knew that Kincaid had been aware this might happen

because, along with Ensign Wootton, he'd briefed her on the possibility. What he didn't know was how she intended to handle the problem. She'd looked thoughtful when briefed, but she'd not shared those thoughts with him or anyone else, to his knowledge. He decided to prime the pump. "They're being more aggressive than in the last system, but they're also being careful not to engage anything more than our lightest units and that only when they have superior numbers," he said.

Kincaid's lips twitched. "Yes, I can see that, Lieutenant."

"They're hoping to slowly wear us down, and then when we finally make a mistake, pounce and exact their pound of flesh."

Kincaid gave a slight nod and looked around at the busy command center. Rob figured she was assessing just how carefully her staff was listening to his conversation with her. She gave an amused and confident smile. "I believe that's part of what they're planning. I would also be very surprised if they don't have a stronger force ready to intervene once they think there's blood in the water."

It was Rob's turn to nod. Not happily. "It's almost like someone shared our exact itinerary with them. Our units are heavier and can win whenever we close with them, but the pirates are faster and more nimble. They think they can control when and how we're going to engage. They think they're controlling the battle."

Kincaid grinned. It was the grin of a predator contemplating a juicy meal. "I think they think that, too. But our itinerary was set by the Trade Union and based on the tech our first contact expedition had. We can do better than that."

"We can move faster than they expect," Rob said.

"Yep. And?"

"We have better star charts than they likely realize."

"Yep, we traded away part of Earth's oceans for those, among other things, but now it's going to pay off. Watch and learn, Lieutenant."

"Yes, ma'am."

"Comms!" Kincaid called out in a carrying voice.

"Yes, ma'am," the communications officer replied.

"Message for Commander Wong commanding the *Freedom* and the commanders of the first destroyer, third frigate, and fifth and sixth corvette squadrons; Commander Wong will be taking command of an independent command consisting of the first, third, fifth, and sixth squadrons as well as the *Freedom*. You are to prepare for detached duty. Detailed orders to follow within the hour. Kincaid out." She looked down at the arm of her battle pod beside her and keyed in some commands on the keypad there, then she continued. "Also, message for Chief of Staff Cartwright; you will find in your in-box detailed orders for battle plan beta. It calls for detaching half our heavy units and sending them on a course parallel to our patrol route before doubling back to catch our opponents in a trap. It will be the anvil to our hammer. Check the orders contained for consistency and completeness and ensure they're distributed to all necessary parties within the hour. Kincaid out."

Rob had many questions he'd have liked to ask. Unfortunately, he couldn't do so publicly without potentially undermining Kincaid. Her staff likely thought she'd based whatever plans she had on detailed intelligence provided by Rob and Wootton. Only Rob knew they didn't have that intelligence. Kincaid was guessing. She was guessing about the opponent they faced, and she was guessing about what they had planned. Educated, best guesses maybe, but guesses for all that. Rob figured Kincaid probably didn't want all and sundry to know she was gambling the fate of the fleet and probably the human race's future on some guesses, no matter how good or necessary those guesses might be. "You don't waste time," he finally chose to say.

"Of course not. There's nothing to be gained by it and potentially a lot to be lost. Whoever is pulling the strings on the other side is doing so remotely from the distant shadows."

"Yes, ma'am, one of the scenarios we anticipated."

"Which was good work. Be sure to pass on my appreciation to Ensign Wootton. I'll make a point of mentioning it to Commander McGinnis. And, as anticipated, it means I'm closer to the action than the guy on the other side. I can see what's actually happening better and faster than they can. And, I can act on that knowledge faster than they can. Not an edge I plan to waste."

"You figure you can get Wong in behind them and crush the pirates before they realize what we're doing and can react?"

"I do."

"Straightforward and effective."

"Indeed."

Rob knew it was anything but. There were a thousand things they could have got wrong or could go wrong, but he could hardly say that.

They all had to trust Kincaid's infamous intuition.

\* \* \*

Katie had sent Wong's detachment off on its end run as soon as the second system on their patrol route had been cleared of spying pirate eyes. The pirates would figure out something had happened eventually, and even more eventually what. She intended to delay those realizations for as long as possible. In an ideal world, they wouldn't have time to figure out what she'd done and react before the jaws of her trap closed on them.

She glanced over at Rob Hood standing beside her in her flag command center. She couldn't help smiling. He was pretending to be calm and happy with the situation, just as she was. They were both faking it.

Katie had studied how the Great Captains of history had achieved their victories in considerable detail. She was a great admirer of Napoleon Bonaparte, at least as a general at the grand tactical or operational level. She was less impressed with some of his strategic and diplomatic decisions, but there was no doubt that when it came to planning campaigns and executing on those plans, he'd been a master.

And he'd always had plans. Multiple plans based on the very best intelligence he could gather. He'd made plans for every possible scenario he could imagine. And he'd had a very active and professionally informed imagination. Sometimes the actual campaigns had even gone according to one of those plans for a while. In the end, however, something unexpected always happened, and he'd had to improvise.

Fortunately, he'd been as much a master of quick improvisation as he'd been of careful planning.

It was an approach that had worked very well up to a point.

It wasn't without its weaknesses.

As Katie was consciously emulating Bonaparte's approach, those weaknesses were of immediate concern to her. It was an approach that made it harder both to communicate what you wanted to your people and to maintain their morale. Intertwined rather than separate problems. The communication problem was that multiple contingent plans you might choose among, abandon, adopt, or discard entirely as events develop, are confusing. Communicating one simple plan that doesn't change is much easier.

The morale problem was partly that people don't like being confused in high-stakes, uncertain circumstances.

Katie suppressed a sigh and looked around her flag command center to see if anybody was picking up on her woolgathering angst. She briefly met Rob Hood's eyes. He knew something was up, but was giving her the time to work it through. Apparently, at least someone understood the problems she faced and was willing to trust her to handle them. Nice. She nodded very slightly in his direction.

So, morale. Truth was that what people liked was the idea that victory was certain as long as they did their own well defined part. Like the lyrics of the old song went they wanted to believe that they'd *fight and always win.* Something only the young and naïve could believe, but everybody wanted to. Somehow, Katie felt much older than her relatively meager years.

Napoleon had addressed the problem by a combination of sheer will, chicanery, and by achieving some spectacular victories early in his career. Katie was pretty sure she didn't want to emulate all of his methods.

Among other things, she didn't have battle-hardened subordinate commanders used to improvising. Larry Wong seemed like a decent fellow and quite competent. But like most of her officers, he wasn't even a member of the "Ganymede mafia". She didn't really know him, and he had no real battle experience at all.

Even Napoleon's subordinates, despite being hand picked from veterans, sometimes failed to march to the sound of the guns when it was needed.

Katie couldn't even expect that level of improvisation in the face of unexpected deviations from plan. As little as she liked it, Katie was being forced to pretend she had a simple, straight forward plan that she just wasn't sharing all the details of.

All the weight of any adaption to unexpected developments was on her shoulders.

And, of course, they could expect the unexpected.

Something of her thoughts must have shown somehow, because Hood chose that moment to speak up. "They seem to have picked up on our being weaker. They're acting more aggressively. As you expected, I imagine."

"As I hoped," Katie replied. "We could have been wrong about their top command being quite a distance to the rear and the forces we're facing following a plan they've not got much discretion to change. If their command had been local, they might have disengaged and devoted more resources to finding out where Wong and the ships with him went."

"So you want them focused on us?"

"Yes, and if they put enough into it, they could penetrate our scout screen and maybe get some idea of what we've done. Wong's got a head start and with our FTL superiority, they probably can't catch up with him in a stern chase, but with enough scouts and some luck, they might figure out what he's doing."

Hood blinked and spoke in a deadpan tone. "That wouldn't do."

Katie almost laughed. She covered it up with a cough. "No, indeed, right now if they follow their plan and we follow ours, we'll destroy them wholesale. If they figure it out, they could escape relatively unscathed. We'd have to either hunt them down in a long drawn out campaign or go home with our job half done." She didn't mention the possibility the pirates might concentrate against one of the two human forces and perhaps overwhelm it. No sense making everybody nervous.

In particular, she didn't mention the fact she was bluffing and that the pirates were probably overestimating the firepower the *Bonaventure* could put out, thinking it was more a large battleship than the mobile base it, in fact, was.

Hood was doubtless smart enough to realize that. He also

had the sense not to bring it up. He just nodded, and they settled into a companionable silence.

A silence that lasted for several hours while they watched the smaller ships on both sides dance and maneuver, expending large numbers of missiles and drones but doing little significant damage to each other. It was a knife dance. Just a technical display of skill until someone made a mistake, but very messy once they did.

It wasn't a completely static picture. Not even a dynamic balance. Slowly but surely, the ships screening the *Bonaventure* as it plowed forward were pushed back closer and closer to it. The tension in the flag command center rose inexorably.

Finally, the sensors officer broke the silence. "Ma'am, the forwardmost pirates are getting close to maximum missile range."

"Confirm that," the weapons officer said.

"Acknowledged," Katie replied with almost indifferent calm.

Not too long afterward, the comms officer spoke up. "Ma'am, Captain Fritzsen wants to know if she should prepare to maintain a constant distance between ourselves and the pirate forces in order to keep the *Bonaventure* out of effective missile range."

Katie grinned. It was rare Susan was nervous about anything. Better yet, Katie was about to turn the screws. "Comms, reply to Captain Fritzsen that she should prepare to go to her maximum safe burst speed and close with the enemy forces."

There was the slightest pause as the comms officer absorbed that. "Yes, ma'am. Replying to *Bonaventure* command that they should prepare to go to burst speed in order to close with the enemy."

"Very good. Thank you, Comms."

It was some minutes before a response came. Katie figured Susan had used them to quickly check with her engineering department. "Ma'am," the comms officer announced, "Captain Fritzsen reports the *Bonaventure* is ready to go to burst speed."

"Good. Comms, message to Captain Fritzsen; the *Bonaventure* is to go to burst speed on its current heading."

"Yes, ma'am," the comms officer replied with exaggerated calm, "message to Captain Fritzsen; the *Bonaventure* is to go to burst speed on its current heading."

"Thank you, Comms," Katie acknowledged and bare seconds later the ship began to vibrate as its engines ramped up to their full power.

Hood beside her watched Katie like a hawk. He knew she was bluffing. Doubtless, he was wondering just how much she was willing to gamble. They were playing a cosmic game of chicken with more than just their own lives at stake.

In the event, after many tense minutes, it became a moot question.

"Ma'am," the sensors officer reported, "the leading pirate forces are maintaining position outside of our missile range. They're backing off, ma'am." He failed to keep a note of relief out of his voice.

"They didn't manage to get up-to-date intelligence on us while we were at the Trade Hub," Hood commented.

"No, I didn't think they had," Katie said. "Know your enemy. They've failed to, and I'd be remiss in my duty if I didn't take advantage." She smiled at Hood.

Hood snorted. "Yes, ma'am."

\* \* \*

"Ma'am, the *Rossiya* reports its missile magazines are down to half full," the flag command center's comms officer announced.

It was irregular, but Katie had ordered the ships of her task force to report the levels of their munitions stocks to her directly; by-passing the normal chain of command.

As long as her missile stocks held up, the battle was lopsided in the favor of the Human fleet under Katie. Once they ran out, it'd be a different story. Something the pirates knew as well as she did.

Katie's force had heavier units. They carried heavier missiles. Missiles with bigger warheads and greater ranges. It was a huge advantage. So far, the pirates had lost only the occasional ship, but the Humans had lost none at all.

But the pirates had outnumbered the Humans from the very beginning. Now, in this K5 system, that lay half way through their assigned patrol route and the furthest of any from Far Seat Trade Hub - the one she'd always thought the pirates would attempt to spring their trap in, the pirates had thrown their reserves in. They'd almost doubled the number of their ships. They easily outnumbered the Human forces under Katie's immediate command by more than three to one.

It was only one reason they could afford to take losses at a higher rate than Katie's force. Katie's ships, and their crews, were irreplaceable and further from their bases. Defeat would mean a long and ugly retreat.

Katie was betting everything on Wong's force appearing in the pirate rear before the battle turned against her. This system, in addition to the large area between FTL jump points it had, only enjoyed two such jump points. Far fewer than usual. It was a perfect trap. For the pirates if Wong appeared in time. Less perfectly for the Humans if he didn't. Still, with only one, predictable, far-away exit if Katie had to retreat, it was going to cost painfully. She had little doubt some of the more nimble pirates would manage to get between her and the jump point she needed to reach in order to escape. She had to hope that didn't happen.

"Wong's running a little late," Hood, standing beside her as he had been for most of the past few days, opined. "Is it really wise to keep pushing them?"

Katie blessed him with an amused smile. It was a good question. An annoying question exactly because of that. Also, not one she dared answer with a serious risk versus benefit analysis. A confident certitude was what was needed. "We're going to beat these pirates. It's important we beat them not just badly, but destroy their entire force. That means not giving them much time or space to escape once Wong makes his appearance."

Katie, in fact, was considering scenarios beyond even the three Hood had implicitly referenced. Hood had been suggesting that maintaining a separation from the pirate main body that would both minimize losses and make a retreat to their entry point shorter might be a more prudent option.

Katie had countered with it being optimal to push the pirates closer to the jump point they'd entered through. The same jump point they expected Wong's force to appear at. Hood hadn't raised the possibility of going for a full retreat to the entry jump point before their missile stocks fell too much lower. Katie was sure he was as aware of the option as she was.

Katie had considered many more scenarios. Two were particularly promising. One scenario being a full force attack through to the pirate's entry jump point with the aim of joining Wong directly somewhere on his planned route. The second promising idea was deliberately moving off the direct route between the two jump points and engaging the pirates in a prolonged cat-and-mouse game in-system. This was a way of playing for time while waiting for Wong to make his appearance. Both plans would be risky, but more likely to catch the pirates off guard just because of that.

Katie was also keeping her eyes open for the pirates providing her possibilities she'd not anticipated.

She refrained from sharing her thoughts. As much as it galled her, given her preference for being open and honest, she elected to maintain the illusion that she had a fixed plan and all was going according to it. Because, after all, *sure there are lives at stake, but let's just wing it"* isn't an approach people tend to find reassuring. Rather hard on morale in fact.

Hood seemed to understand this. He just nodded and kept his silence.

The silence was broken by the comms officer. "Ma'am, the *Queensland* reports she's down to half full missile magazines."

"Thank you," Katie acknowledged.

Minutes, then hours, passed as the whole command center watched the fatal dance play out on the large multi-colored displays that graced the center's walls where they could all see them.

The tension was occasionally ratcheted up by announcements from the communications officer, first that this or that ship was down to half full missile magazines and then down to quarter full magazines. And still Wong didn't appear.

Katie was beginning to think she was going to have to do

something to buy more time when the excited voice of the sensors officer broke into her thoughts. "Ma'am, large ships exiting the destination jump point. I think they're ours."

"Ma'am," the comms officer announced, "Confirm that. Commander Wong on the *Freedom* sends his greetings. He says he's moving at full speed to engage the enemy."

Katie ignored the sighs of relief that greeted this announcement. "Thank you, Comms. Please, message Commander Wong that we're pleased to see him," she calmly ordered.

The pirates caught between two forces mostly tried to break past Wong's new entries. It wasn't a well co-ordinated or planned maneuver. It was one that quickly proved fatal to them. Even interplanetary distances are astronomical, so it took time, but it became clear most of the pirates were going to be destroyed. None of them surrendered all the same.

Katie turned to Hood. "Lieutenant, you should get some rest. They don't seem to be surrendering their ships, but there are bound to be survivors in some of the wrecks. When we're done reducing their ships to that state, I'll need you to find and interrogate those survivors. Understood?"

"Yes, ma'am, with a little luck maybe we can find out who's in command on the other side and where their base or bases are located."

"I trust you're relying on skill, not luck, Lieutenant."

"Yes, ma'am, but it never hurts to be lucky, does it?"

Katie's lips quirked at the dig. "No, it doesn't."

* * *

With the exception of the on-duty watch, Katie was alone in her flag command center. Given its large high-quality wall screens, she was coming to think of it as her "Flag Bridge". It was the place from which she commanded her fleet. Usually there would have been a guest, one of her subordinates or a member of her staff present, and she'd be getting or giving an informal briefing in between absorbing information and making decisions. Not right now. They were all busy right now. The last couple of weeks since their departure from Far Seat Station had been hectic. Katie was glad of the time to herself. She needed to reflect on events to date. Reflect and maybe adjust her plans.

So far, things seemed to be going well. They'd received a pleasant surprise when they'd reviewed the patrol itinerary the Trade Union Bosses had worked out for them. Its very existence, requiring them to arrive in certain systems at specified times, was an insult and a dangerous restriction on their operational flexibility. Katie had only accepted it because she'd felt she had no choice. But when Katie and her staff had looked at it they'd realized that it had been tightly coupled to the FTL drive performance of the first generation exploration ship Earth had sent on its "First Contact" expedition.

The wholly human-developed technology of that ship had been crude and its crew had been very careful in how they'd used it. Katie's ships all had jump drives based on technology the alien Squids had transferred to humanity. In principle, it was similar, only it was much more refined, and Katie's crews had a much better idea of how to safely use it. The star charts the Squids and others had also provided helped a lot, too. Katie's fleet was capable of traveling a multiple system route through the stars at a rate two or three times faster than the Trade Union bosses had assumed.

Faster than the pirates they'd faced had assumed as well.

And Katie had taken full advantage of that fact. The pirates had apparently intended to conduct a fighting retreat, culminating in an ambush in the current K5 system.

Instead Katie had sprung an ambush of her own. The pirate fleet had disintegrated. Katie's people were now busy mopping up.

Katie didn't think this was the end of it, but she was having to wait on intelligence gathered from interrogating prisoners. Mostly Snout prisoners, which was a bit of a problem, as even with translator devices, only Hood and Wootton understood even a little of their language.

But Katie was convinced that so many ships had to have a base or bases somewhere and she wanted to know where.

"Ma'am, Lieutenant Hood on the line for you," her comms officer announced.

"Put him through on speaker."

"Yes, ma'am."

"Commodore, I have a prisoner I think you should see. Probably in your day cabin," Hood said without preamble.

"Very well, I'll see you there ASAP," Katie replied.

A short while later Katie found herself, Hood, the Marine commander von Luck, two of his marines, and a very nervous Snout all crammed into her day cabin.

Hood looked around and took a breath. "Tee-Nah, here speaks English."

"A lucky break," Katie said. "Is he willing to co-operate and does he know anything useful?"

The Snout, Tee-Nah, bobbed his head vigorously. "Yes, indeed, fearsome and exalted Human leader Commodore Kincaid. I'm eager to help. I'm not a navigator, but I have observed carefully and can put you on track to find the base you seek."

"A single base?"

Another head bob. "We were gathered together and brought here and those that did so wished to keep us and our families close to hand."

"You weren't all here willingly?"

"Who seeks a fight not knowing their opponent and, therefore, its outcome?"

A good question, Katie had to think. A lot of Human leaders throughout history, but she wasn't going to say that. "So will they surrender? Do you hope to save your family?" she asked instead.

The Snout covered its eyes with a paw. Not a gesture Katie was familiar with. She looked at Hood. He shrugged. Finally, the Snout spoke without his usual head bobs. "No. No, they will fight, and it is unlikely anyone's family will survive." The Snout heaved a heavy and all too Human sigh. "But if this one survives, perhaps he can start another."

Katie was at a loss for words.

Hood filled the gap. "Why are you fighting us?"

"The Trade Union," the Snout hissed, "will not trade with us on fair terms and when we take what we need, it sends those like you to hunt us down."

Katie grimaced. "So, do you and your people hate us because of that?"

The Snout chittered.

Katie looked at Hood.

"Laughter," he said.

"Yes, yes," Tee-Nah agreed. "It is funny in an unpleasant way. Don't think the Traders care for you. Don't think they care who wins in our struggle."

Katie didn't like that. "Surely, the Trade Union wants to keep the trade routes safe?"

"They want to keep possible competition weak and needy. They and the other powers don't care who supposedly wins as long as we both lose."

"Cynical."

"Realistic."

* * *

Amy was on the SFS *Lockhaven* again. Patrolling ahead of the main body. Their mission was critical. Or really, their *missions* were critical. And that wasn't the only complication. As little as she liked it, Amy was putting short-term success above people's feelings or even the long-term good of her scouting group. As much as she wanted it to be a happy and effective team in the long run, right now, she needed short-term results.

"Why so grim, boss?" Lieutenant Chanthar, captain of the *Lockhaven*, asked. The little scout was crowded, its cockpit more so, and you really couldn't hide your feelings from your crewmates for long.

"So many trade-offs," Amy answered, trying to put her feelings into words.

Chanthar gave a humorless chuckle. "True that." He grimaced. "We're on schedule, but it doesn't really give us enough time to even superficially scan even a small system like this before having to tell the main fleet if it's safe."

"That's one of them," Amy agreed. "It took us decades to explore our Solar System and now I want you to do the equivalent in a few hours. It's a hard task, but I know you and the crew of the *Lockhaven* are up to it."

All of them laughed at that. They didn't lack confidence, but they knew they weren't miracle workers either. "Yes, ma'am!" Chanthar declaimed cheerily.

Amy grinned. "Seriously, I know you'll do your best, but the best I really hope for is that the *Bonaventure* and her escorts don't walk right into an ambush on the emergence point."

"Be kind of nice to find the base these bastards are working out of, though," Lieutenant Windsor, the engineering officer, commented.

"Working on that," LTJG Sally van Tol, the co-pilot, comms, and sensors officer, replied.

Amy nodded. "Don't get too frustrated, Sally. Finding them might require a bit of luck, but given that they're not regular military and don't have military levels of discipline, it's not too much to hope for."

"As long as we're on our toes and listening carefully," van Tol answered. "Got that."

Amy patted the co-pilot on the back. "Now, now," she said in a mock motherly tone. "I know you're trying."

Ignoring the chuckles of her crewmates, Sally twisted around to look at Amy. She was visibly struggling to keep a straight face. "It's that there's just so much noise and so little signal."

"I understand," Amy said. "Do your best. We are trying to build up libraries of both what standard systems look like and what sort of emissions the pirates give off. Good part of the reason I'm here is to see what else I might be able to do to help. Spot little things you guys mightn't think are worth complaining about."

Sally nodded as she turned back to her console. "Appreciate that, ma'am."

The chatter died off after that as everyone concentrated on doing their jobs. There wasn't really much useful to say.

Sally broke the silence. "Well, I'll be damned. I've got a flare. Up towards the zenith. Looks like a high-powered reaction drive pointed almost straight away from us. Make that multiple flares. I think we've got multiple boogies on the run-up to jump, ma'am. And, with just a little luck, we're going to be able to pinpoint exactly where they're going."

Chanthar looked over at his co-pilot. "Good work, Sally."

"I'll second that," Amy chipped in.

"I wonder if they're going to be waiting for us on the other side?" Lieutenant Windsor asked.

"I wonder who I'll send to find out, Jim," Amy said.
Grim chuckles greeted that.

## 7: A Job Well Done

*"Lorentz, like Einstein, understood that the 'invariance' of the speed of light required the redefinition of the notions of space and time."*
Location 556 of the e-book edition of "Making Starships and Stargates" by James F. Woodward

Rob Hood wondered just how long Commodore Kincaid intended on pushing her luck. He couldn't deny she was making him nervous. True, so far, she had plausible reasons for the risks she was taking. It still made him nervous.

She'd deliberately committed classic errors of military strategy. She'd divided her forces in the face of the enemy. She'd bluffed depending on her foe to make mistakes, rather than depending on her own strength. She'd overstretched her forces logistically. The least of her sins had been proceeding in the absence of good intelligence.

It could be argued that good enough intelligence was never going to be available. In fact, she'd argued that exact point with Hood in the privacy of her cabin before they'd gone on this latest watch together.

She'd argued that engaging the enemy, taking prisoners, and aggressively scouting had provided information that she'd never have been able to obtain through passive information gathering.

Hood could hardly debate that. He had pointed out that although the cost so far had been very light that she'd risked paying much more. A price neither she nor humanity could actually afford. Her ships, and - most of all - her crews, were all that humanity would be able to afford for sometime. And they were far out on a limb.

Between the *Bonaventure* emptying out her munitions holds and cross transfers between the fleet's fighting ships, those ships now had mostly full magazines. Better yet, since the Humans were relying on standard galactic missile tech, they could replenish their stocks at Far Seat Trade Hub if they returned there. Rob had argued they should do exactly that. He'd argued they should finish their assigned patrol route and return to the Trade Hub. Once there, they could offer to tackle the hidden pirate base Amy Sarkis' scouts had found contingent on the Trade Union fully replenishing the stocks of their fleet.

Kincaid wasn't having any of it.

She had the pirates on the back foot and was in hot pursuit of whoever was behind them. She had no intention of letting them regroup, or worse, get away. She'd decided to take the whole fleet to the system with the hidden pirate base, defeat the remnants of the pirate fleet, and take their hidden base. Immediately.

And so here they were standing in her flag command center waiting to emerge from jump into that system, not entirely sure of what they'd find.

All too soon they felt the familiar gut-wrenching sensation of jump emergence.

The sensors officer reported first. "Ma'am, appears all clear. No enemy near the jump point. Our ships are all intact. There is no active combat. The closest enemy are half way across the system on the direct course towards the enemy base. They seem formed up for battle in front of it."

The comms officer passed on reports from the rest of the fleet which had arrived before the *Bonaventure*. They confirmed in greater detail what the sensors officer had already reported.

"Well, about as good as we could have hoped," Rob commented. He wasn't really happy. He was afraid Kincaid was like a new gambler who was too lucky at first and learned the wrong lesson. He'd pointed out to Kincaid that her hero Napoleon had failed in the end by doubling down on his luck until it finally failed him. She'd conceded the point, but countered she wasn't sure about Napoleon, but that she had little choice. The bar for humanity's entry on the galactic stage succeeding was very high. She had no choice but to gamble aggressively if she was to have any hope of meeting it, she'd asserted.

Kincaid grinned at Rob. He figured she had a pretty good idea of what he was thinking. She looked him in the eye as to say as much. "We gutted them when we sprung their own trap on them." She looked at the tactical displays showing the dispositions of the two fleets. "I'm surprised they're standing and fighting at all. None of this is logical for sensible pirates. I want to know who's behind them, putting them up to it."

Rob nodded. "Suspecting the Lizards is one thing. Confirming that and proving it are two different things."

"Exactly," Kincaid said, "and just to prove a point, I'm going to be careful here and not charge in. Who knows, maybe they've got a surprise or two waiting for us."

"You can never be certain," Rob said.

"Indeed," Kincaid agreed. "Comms," she ordered, "message for the fleet; commence execution of Plan Tippy-Toe. Send confirmation messages to the CAG and Commander Scout Group that they are to aggressively patrol for possible ambushes and traps. Remind Lieutenant Commander Sarkis that it's critical that enemy command elements not be allowed to escape. Request acknowledgment."

"Sarkis and Maddox both know their jobs," Rob said.

Kincaid frowned. "Granted. However, I'm not going to let important priorities go unemphasized because I'm afraid of hurting someone's feelings. Understood, Lieutenant?"

"Yes, ma'am," Rob answered, duly chastened. He'd messed up by appearing to criticize her publicly.

He kept his silence during the hours they slowly worked

their way in-system towards the asteroid holding the pirate base.

Superficially, it went well, although slowly, due to the caution Kincaid had mandated.

The pirates fought hard, even suicidally, but they were inexorably forced back towards their base, their numbers diminishing as they went.

The tension in the command center subsided, but then ramped up again as they approached to within maximum range of the asteroid housing that base.

It was a report from the sensors officer that ended the building anticipation. "Ma'am, a half dozen ships have just exited the pirate base at maximum velocity towards the jump point to system 2358132."

Before Kincaid could respond, the comms officer spoke. "Ma'am, Lieutenant Commander Sarkis reports she has only one scout, the *Cuxhaven*, positioned to intercept the ships fleeing the pirate base. She says the *Cuxhaven* might be able to cripple some of them and keep all of them from escaping, but that's not certain, and it'll probably mean the *Cuxhaven's* loss. She wants your decision on whether the *Cuxhaven* should engage the fugitives or just track them at a safe distance."

Kincaid took a deep breath. Her face remained impassive. It was clear to Rob that Sarkis didn't want to sacrifice the crew of her scout. It was also a simple, cold-blooded calculation, such that if this had been a video game or some other sort of simulation, that the sacrifice of the *Cuxhaven* and her crew was an acceptable cost for the potential gain. Only, even if Kincaid had been a dead cold sociopath, and she wasn't, in the real world, sending your people on suicide missions carried significant long-run cost. So Rob wasn't surprised when Kincaid gave her orders. "Comms, order Lieutenant Commander Sarkis to have the *Cuxhaven* track the fugitives as closely as it safely can," she commanded.

It felt as if the whole command center heaved a sigh of relief. Kincaid looked over at Hood. "We're already asking a lot of our scouts," he said.

Kincaid nodded. "That's true. Also, seeing where they're fleeing to might be more important than capturing prisoners ."

"Not like taking prisoners would be guaranteed."

"No guarantees at all here."

Rob grimaced.

"What?"

"It's going well."

Kincaid smiled. "Don't jinx us."

"I can't help thinking of everything that could go wrong and what we might have missed."

Kincaid sighed. "Yep. If I was just betting money, say my next year's salary, I'd bet that now that their leadership has bailed out, that the pirate fleet's resistance will crumble. Also, that the armament emplaced on that asteroid is minimal. Too short ranged and too light to cause us any problems. But, with people's lives at stake, I'm not going to make that bet. There's not much to be gained by it. So we're going to nibble away at their fleet carefully and take our time methodically reducing the base's defenses."

Rob nodded. This was really all above his pay grade. He settled for responding with the old standby. "Yes, ma'am."

\* \* \*

It had been a couple of blissfully boring and predictable hours since the probable pirate leadership had fled. They'd just jumped out of system and Amy's scout the *Cuxhaven* was about to follow.

Katie couldn't help being rather pleased. She wasn't happy the pirate leadership had successfully escaped, but their capture had always been a long shot. So, she wasn't too disappointed either. For the rest of it, the assessment she'd given Hood a couple of hours before was holding true.

A hard core of pirate resistance remained, but they seemed more intent on delaying her than inflicting damage. Every once in a while, a pirate ship would attempt to defect and flee the action. So far few of them had succeeded. Few of them had had enough of a head start to escape the combination of Bobby Maddox's fighters and Amy's scouts.

Neither had the pirate base weighed in with the long-range weaponry it might have conceivably have had. Katie had surmised that the pirates had probably depended on keeping their base hidden rather than heavily armed, but there'd been no way to be sure. So that was gratifying.

"Ma'am, the pirates appear to be attempting to disengage," her comms officer announced. "They seem to be scattering rather than remaining in a single formation."

"Thank you, Comms," Katie replied. "General message to the fleet: I'm ordering a general pursuit." Katie had anticipated this possibility and the Space Force's newly worked out doctrine covered it in any case. The tight formations and careful dance of the last few hours were done. Katie was surrendering most of her control over her fleet to her individual captains, who would pursue and destroy the fleeing enemy on their own initiative.

With two exceptions. "Comms, special orders for the *Freedom* and *Bonaventure*; per previously disseminated assault plan, prepare to bombard then assault the pirate base."

The next several minutes featured a litany of acknowledgments from the fleet's ships.

Finally, when it was done, Hood who'd been quietly standing beside her spoke up. "I know pirates are as close to vermin as sentient beings can be, but it almost feels like murder."

Katie nodded. "It is. I don't care about wartime legal excuses. It is murder and we should never forget that. But, it's a historical constant that most of the losses taken in a battle tend to be by the losers once they break and flee. I'm not going to sacrifice the lives of my people or our victory in order to let pirates escape and continue their depredations in the future. If they wanted to, they could have surrendered."

Hood grunted noncommittally. "You want me to request the asteroid base's surrender?"

"Please," Katie answered. She didn't have much hope it would, but it didn't hurt to try.

Hood strode over to the comms console and, handing a data chip over to the comms officer, spoke quietly to him. Katie knew that although both Hood and Wootton had learned Snout and the galactic trade language with a basic level of competence that he'd had his pet Snout, Tee-Nah, record the surrender request. Their prisoner-cum-new-ally was simply much more fluent. In particular, his accent was probably a lot more comprehensible. Particularly in the Snout language. Human and Snout vocal apparatus were similar, but not exactly the same.

In short order, the surrender request was transmitted. They didn't have long to wait for an answer. A gray-snouted and worn looking Snout appeared on their video screen and without preamble snapped off a quick few words before terminating their transmission.

Katie looked at Hood. "They're not going to surrender," Hood said. "Didn't give any reason or make any defiant speeches. That's all he said."

"Odd," Katie commented.

"I'll go over it with Ensign Wootton later, but right now I'm as baffled as you are, ma'am."

"Very well. Comms, get me Lieutenant Colonel von Luck."

When von Luck's image appeared, Katie got right to the point. "Colonel, prepare for an assault as soon as the preliminary bombardment is complete. The plan stands as is. Only thing resembling new information is that they refused to surrender. Do your best to get me and Lieutenant Hood some prisoners, despite that."

"Yes, ma'am. We'll be ready," von Luck answered.

"Good, Kincaid out."

Hood looked over at Katie. "More waiting."

"It's my job to remain here, far from the action, and make calm, considered decisions when needed," Kincaid answered in dry tones. "It's your job to stand by my side and provided any needed information or advice. So, suck it up, Lieutenant."

"Yes, ma'am."

And so, they waited while the *Freedom* and *Bonaventure* carried out a pre-planned forty-minute bombardment of the pirate asteroid that elicited exactly zero response. Besides pulverizing the already desolate surface of the pirate rock, it appeared to have little effect. Finally, the assault shuttles were launched and soon marines were being disgorged on the pirate asteroid's surface.

"Ma'am," the comms officer relayed, "the marines report no resistance on the surface."

Shortly afterward, he added, "Enemy base has been

breached and entered. No significant resistance has been encountered."

A little over twenty minutes later, an unwelcome message came. "Ma'am, Lieutenant Colonel von Luck reports the pirate base is much more extensive than expected and he's run out of communication relays."

Katie felt annoyed at that. It was a simple thing they should have thought of beforehand, but had missed. Nothing they could do about it now. She wondered if they'd be able to find comms relays they could use back at the Trade Hub or if they'd have to send all the way to Earth for them. She could try to make sure they didn't have this problem in the future. "Hood, please note this issue. In the future, we'll want to make estimates of the size of target installations and make sure we have a sufficient number of relays."

"Yes, ma'am," Hood answered. "It's possible we could get our electronic maintenance techs to cobble some spare parts up into a few relays, but that's not certain, and it'd take a least a few hours, and like as not we'd not get enough of them."

"Okay, any good news?"

"Yes, ma'am, we can probably get the needed components for more back at the Trade Hub and build as many as we need from them. We don't want to buy finished units from the Galactics. I'd put the odds they wouldn't be bugged at slim to none."

Katie snorted. "I see. Please, put that on your to-do list. You write the orders for me and I'll see they get where they need to go."

"Ma'am," the comms officer announced, "Lieutenant Colonel von Luck reports that resistance so far has been light and disorganized, but fanatical. He's not been able to take any prisoners. He's requesting permission to push forward to the center of the base and out of communication."

"Comms, tell the colonel he has permission to push forward to the base's center and out of communication." Katie resisted the urge to wish him luck.

Hood looked at Katie expectantly.

Katie smiled at him with grim amusement. "I can't do much more here, so I'm going to lead an away party to follow up on von Luck. You will not be on it. It occurs to me that altogether too much of what we know about our little part of the galaxy and its denizens is still stuck in your head. I need a summary of everything your replacement will need to know written down in case something happens to you. I also need you to start analyzing what's happened here. First, send Ensign Wootton and Tee-Nah to the flight deck. They will accompany me. Also, after passing that message on to them and before your other tasks, you should get some sleep."

Hood looked constipated. Katie was certain he wanted to point out her hypocrisy in being will to risk her own life and in continuing without sleep herself. Only he obviously knew it'd be both pointless and inappropriate.

"Understood?" Katie asked.

"Yes, ma'am. Understood," Hood replied.

\* \* \*

The naval part of the battle was over. Katie was finally able to escape her flag command center. She was now going to deal with the mopping up of the pirate's asteroid base directly and in person. She wanted to make sure that she got some more prisoners to question.

Fortunately, Lieutenant Colonel von Luck wasn't present to complain about that. He was still directing the leading edge of the main assault. Katie and the small party with her were following a trail of bodies and wreckage to his current location. Direct communication wasn't possible. He was too deep into the tunnels of the solid iron-nickel asteroid that made up the pirate base.

Despite the destruction, Katie was finding herself surprised at how extensive and well finished the base was. It hadn't been just a rough outpost manned by ruffians indifferent to good housekeeping and their surroundings generally. It seemed it'd been a home, well cared for and loved. Katie was reluctant to apply human feelings to aliens, let alone alien pirates, but that was the sense she was getting.

It wasn't what she'd expected. That bothered her. It likely meant there was something she was missing. Katie was a firm believer that what you didn't know could most certainly hurt you. So it bothered her. That and the fact it made her feel like a homewrecker.

True, the home in question had belonged to bloodthirsty and ruthless pirates, but somehow that didn't make her feel better.

The two spacers leading her party came to an intersection with a broad concourse and signaled a halt while they investigated.

Each of them slunk carefully to one side and down the broad concourse.

Katie, cautiously surveying it from the side corridor they'd come down, was amazed. Despite the scattered bodies congregating in little piles here and there, and despite some of the little trees and plants in the large planters running down its middle being shredded and destroyed, the concourse could have been part of an upscale shopping mall on Earth.

Katie, a lifelong spacer, had never seen any Human space station anything like this supposedly backwater second-rate pirate base. Maybe the upscale part of the Far Seat Trade Hub had approximated it, but Katie had been too preoccupied by other issues to really notice. Now she was noticing and the reminder of the technological edge the Galactics enjoyed was sobering.

As sobering as the fact that this section of a pirate base in a nowhere system was lined with stone that had obviously come from not just a large planet with oceans, but one with life, too. Katie's geology was basic, but she knew the marble all around them must have formed from the tiny shells of a vast number of tiny organisms. And once laid down, metamorphized in a fashion that screamed of plate tectonics and a place that was very old and quite Earth like. A place in which limestone sediments were subducted and a carbon cycle existed.

Fascinating, very suggestive, and probably not something Katie wanted to think about too much right now. She was here to gather first hand unfiltered intelligence, but intelligence of a somewhat more immediately useful nature. Katie turned to the people following her and singled out Ensign Tanya Wootton. Wootton had been uncharacteristically quiet. She was white and wide-eyed, seemingly shocked by the devastation and carnage they'd been encountering. That they had had, in fact, a large hand in creating. "Ensign Wootton!" That got the young woman's attention. "Are you taking all this in? The fact they have artificial gravity and apparently managed to import both plants and marble from somewhere?"

Tanya Wootton stared at Katie like a startled deer for a few moments. "Yes, ma'am! Highly suggestive of a more permanent establishment with more sophisticated and long-standing economic ties than we'd anticipated. I'm recording everything." She held up her tablet, which Katie knew to be a special intelligence version with better sensors and more memory than most such devices.

Katie smiled reassuringly at her young intelligence officer. "Excellent! Just making sure. Like you said, this isn't much like what we anticipated, is it?"

Wootton nodded vigorously. "No, ma'am!" She looked around wide eyed. "It certainly isn't."

Katie looked at another of the people following her. Not one of her officers. Not even a human. The English-speaking Snout "guide" or prisoner, as you cared to put it, Tee-Nah. "Tee-Nah, is this place typical of the bases your people build?"

Tee-Nah looked about lackadaisically and shuffled his feet a little. That was the Galactic equivalent of a small shrug. Their pet Snout seemed at pains to not seem too disconcerted by the destruction around them. "Much nicer than some, but not as nice as others." Another little foot shuffle. "Nice side of average, you might say."

"Thank you," Katie replied. A few minutes later, her scouts returned and indicated they could continue.

On the other side of the concourse from where they'd entered, they found a small pile of bodies and a wounded marine who was holding up a wall. At least none of the bodies so far had been Human. This was the first Human they'd seen who was even wounded. The Human attack forces had caught the Snouts unprepared in small, uncoordinated groups, with only light arms and no armor at all. Katie was amazed none of them had even tried to surrender.

Katie was also surprised to realize she knew the marine who struggled upright and gave her a salute with his good right arm. His left arm was a burnt mess from the elbow down. A glancing blow from a plasma pistol. It could be fixed by modern medicine given a good hospital and most of a year, but unless this marine was on some serious pain killers, it had to hurt like hell.

Returning the marine's salute, Katie exclaimed, "Bloggins! Tommy Bloggins! Fancy meeting you here. Sergeant now."

"Yes, ma'am," Bloggins answered. "Been a while since Mars. Lots has happened, hasn't it?"

Katie looked about. "Sure has. You okay?"

"Yes, ma'am. Just resting up on the way back to Med Bay. The colonel insisted I go back. Is it clear all the way there?"

Katie nodded. "Dead quiet. Just bodies all the way back. Is it a clear run forward?"

Bloggins winced. "Yes, ma'am. You'll hit the colonel and the rest of them before it gets dangerous. The last of them have holed up and we're not sure how to winkle them out without paying a price. Guess I should get on with it."

Katie patted the marine on his good shoulder. "Take care, Bloggins."

The marine nodded and moved off. He moved with the slow, careful precision of a man who'd had a drink or two too many. He was doubtless drugged to the eyebrows. Katie watched him leaving briefly before turning back to her party.

She found Tee-Nah staring at one of the bodies around them. Despite the fact it'd been almost torn in two by a plasma blast, Katie could see it'd been slighter than most of the rest of them. A female maybe? Tee-Nah was tapping his snout in an erratic fashion with his fingers. Katie hadn't been briefed on this gesture, but she had a feeling it signaled distress. She looked at Wootton.

Wootton just gave a tired shrug.

"A problem, Tee-Nah?" Katie asked. "Someone you knew?"

"My sister," Tee-Nah answered. He paused and looked at her briefly before looking away again. "May we spare a few moments, esteemed leader, that I might demonstrate some respect for her memory?"

Katie blanked. She was torn by an urgent need to reach von Luck and take charge of the situation. She wanted prisoners and so far it didn't seem they'd taken any. On the other hand, common decency and the fact that Tee-Nah was a valuable resource she wanted to keep happy dictated acceding to his request. Katie glanced at Ensign Wootton, who seemed to be struggling to keep an expression of eager curiosity off of her face. Apparently, the young woman had enough common sense to realize how inappropriate it was. Small favors. Katie suppressed a sigh and took a deep breath. "Yes, we can spare a few moments."

Tee-Nah nodded. He'd obviously studied Human customs quite carefully. He turned to his sister's remains and head bowed and hands clasped, muttered for a long minute in his own language. Katie noticed Wootton recording it. Tee-Nah finished up with a spreading of his hands and a lifting of his eyes to the ceiling. "What is done cannot be undone," he said, turning to Katie. "I have paid my respects. We may continue."

Katie looked to the senior of her two scouts. He nodded and led the party off down the side corridor they were in, past the pile of bodies and plasma scarred marble of its walls.

Not long later, not much more than five minutes, he paused at a new large cross corridor and signaled a stop with a hand gesture. He seemed more puzzled than wary, and leaving his partner behind on over-watch, moved out of Katie's sight. After a tense few moments, he reappeared and gestured the rest of them forward.

"What is it, Atkins?" Katie asked when she reached him.

The scout, Leading Spacer Atkins, gave an incredulous shrug. "I think it's a lemonade stand, ma'am. Two small Snout kids, I think. They seem to know at least a little English. No weapons and they seem friendly enough."

Katie blinked. A few seconds of contemplation, and it still didn't make sense. Nothing for it but to keep moving. "Tee-Nah, follow me," she said, moving out into the large cross corridor. Sure enough, there was a classic lemonade stand. A big blocky box of a table with a large sign on two supports with something written in large alien script. On the table were glasses and some jugs full of yellowish liquid. Cool yellowish liquid going by the condensation on the jugs. Behind all that stood two small figures. Young Snouts. Already entrepreneurial despite their age and despite this being a war zone.

Apparently, Tee-Nah wasn't the only student of Human culture either. It was surreal. Katie moved towards them, feeling strangely disconnected from what she was seeing. She waved her translator forward. "Tee-Nah, ask them what they're doing."

"Yes, Commodore," that worthy replied, moving past her. He launched into a rapid fire interrogation of the youngsters.

Katie would have been intimidated, but not these kids. They listened out the older Snout with a bland attentiveness. Katie could only imagine they were too young to realize the gravity of the situation.

Shortly, Tee-Nah was done. He shuffled his feet a little and fluttered his hands, too. Katie wasn't sure how to interpret that. He turned to Katie and spoke. "They've set up a refreshment stand. Apparently, they were assigned to study Human culture in particular North American Anglo culture and got the inspiration from that. They say the other children were hostages, but that their parents and other older relatives were killed earlier on board their ship. Hence, these young individuals lost their worth as hostages and were let go to fend for themselves. They say they speak some English, so you may interrogate them yourself. I must warn you they will be angling for a position with you."

"Angling for a position?"

"Yes, they've lost their family and likely all that it owned. They're still young and weak. If they do not find a patron or a new family, they will become disposable victims."

Katie couldn't help frowning. This stunk. Apparently, the galaxy ran on a you-broke-it-you-own-it principle. Who knew? She couldn't really imagine what'd happen to these young aliens if she just moved on and left them to their own devices, but she really didn't need to adopt a pair of young alien children either. Still, maybe they could be useful and perhaps she could do something with that. "You speak English?" she asked them.

The right-hand child nodded vigorously. It, no, make that "she": she was wearing a reddish-white, arguably pink garment, something like a sleeveless dress. She replied in a rush of words, "Oh, yes. We've studied very hard and have a large vocabulary and know many idioms. I think our pronunciation of the words is very good as we watched and imitated a large number of movies. We've chosen mid-century middle American as our baseline, as it is apparently considered classical. Are we nailing it, ma'am? Would you like some lemonade? It's only a silver a glass, and it's the hard stuff. Just what you need to stiffen your resolve in a fight."

"Alcohol?"

"Yes, ma'am, fully compatible with both Snout and Human physiologies." She looked down and shuffled her feet. "If you don't consume too much, of course."

"Of course," Katie echoed, blinking. "I think the hard part is over for us." Heavens, she hoped that wasn't too insensitive. "We need to be more delicate from here on in. I think we'll want to keep our wits about us."

The young Snout girl nodded solemnly. "Yes, our elders never expected to win, so they didn't need to keep their wits about them, just to numb the pain of the situation."

Katie nodded slowly. Sadly, that made sense. "Your English is excellent. Your pronunciation is very good," she said, answering the girl's earlier question. "You seem to be well informed, too. Can you tell me anything about what happened here?"

"Yes, ma'am. The Scaly Ones were cagey, but they didn't pay us much mind. We listened carefully to what they said. We even learned a little of their language." She frowned. "I don't think we speak it so well, though. Their hisses are hard to do and we didn't have hours of their entertainment to use for examples. Their entertainment seemed to be mostly killing things and gambling. Usually gambling on things trying to kill each other."

"Like cock fights?" Katie asked, wondering if the young Snout would recognize the reference.

The little girl's face went blank. She glanced towards her companion. Dressed in blue, they were probably male. Her brother, maybe? He gave a slight nod. "Yes, somewhat," she answered. "But more violent, faster, and bloodier. But they were few here and on what maybe a Human would call a mission, what they called under hunt discipline."

"Hunt discipline?"

"When hunting, they're not supposed to fight each other."

"Interesting. Were the Scaly Ones helping? Or were they giving orders?"

The little girl's snout wrinkled up. She looked like she wanted to spit. "Orders. Bad orders. They treated us worse than slaves or livestock. They had no care for our futures. They thought of us as scared meat with no flavor."

Katie thought that was odd phrasing. "They said that right to your faces?"

"Not to our faces."

"In your hearing?"

"Yeah, the Scaly Ones thought all Snouts stupid but young Snouts really stupid. We let them think that and listened and watched carefully. We pestered them with things to sell until they gave up on trying to chase us away."

So, maybe these kids had overheard a lot that might be useful. Katie glanced at Tee-Nah. He gave a slight nod. Something else occurred to Katie. The young Snout female was speaking in the past tense. "So, have the Scaly Ones all left?" Katie asked.

"Pretty sure. When they chased us away, they were all there and in a hurry to get all the other young ones loaded on their ship. They wanted to get away before you arrived." The young Snout shivered. "They were in too much of a hurry to kill us, but I think they'd have liked to. But it would have delayed them and panicked the rest of their hostages."

"Were they pirates? Rogues? Or were they working for their government, do you know?"

The young Snout gave a very Human shrug. "They were careful to never speak of who they were or were responsible to."

Figured the aliens would have good Op Sec. They might be arrogant, but they certainly seemed disciplined. One last thing, and Katie really needed to move on. "How can I get the last of your elders to surrender?" she asked.

The little Snout covered her eyes with a paw briefly. Then she looked up at Katie, her eyes glistening. "They won't. The

Scaly Ones hold the future of their families and their clans as hostages. They've made believable threats to track down and destroy any that defy them."

And even if Katie's fleet and marines were right here, right now, she had no equally credible threats to make. It was time to move on and hope the young Snout was wrong, but what was she to do with the youngsters? Could she really just leave them here? And what about later? She looked at Tee-Nah.

Tee-Nah looked back and then at the youngsters. He spoke briefly to them in their own language. He nodded before turning to Katie. "With your permission, Commodore, I will adopt these children and take responsibility for them. Their command of your language and culture will be of value to us."

Katie heaved a sigh of relief and nodded. "Good, let's go." Hopefully von Luck hadn't yet killed all the other Snouts on the station and hadn't gotten any of her people killed doing it.

This was turning out to be an unholy mess. Sure they'd achieved a lopsided tactical victory. Katie was particularly grateful for the low losses her people had suffered. Only strategically what she needed was to get to the people who were behind it all. And mostly here on this base, what she had were dead ends.

Taking this base wasn't the endgame she'd been hoping for.

## 8: I Want It All

*"[A]n extraordinary idea occurred to him, a stroke of pure genius: the gravitational field is not diffused through space; the gravitational field is that space itself."*
Page 7 of "Seven Brief Lessons on Physics" by Carlo Rovelli

Katie still had plenty to do, but she'd been up too long already. She knew she wasn't at her best. She was tired and frustrated, and she'd been too busy, and too much in public, to fully digest the events that had happened in the last day. The space battle to take the system had been tense enough. The assault on the pirate base had been worse.

The space battle, contrary to all reasonable expectation had gone as planned. Even the assault by her marines on the pirate base had nominally been, by any conventional criteria, a phenomenal success. And the cost, always tragic to the individuals affected, had nevertheless been minimal. A handful of marines killed by bad luck as much as anything and a few more badly wounded, and that'd been it.

True, they'd failed to capture many prisoners, and failed to determine who was behind the pirates and where they were based. The battles themselves, though, had gone much better than they had any right to expect.

She ought to be feeling elated to have gotten off so lightly. Only she wasn't and now that she was finally back in the privacy of her cabin, and about to get some well-deserved rest, she could afford to indulge her feelings and analyze exactly why.

She went about the act of relaxing in a deliberate and careful fashion. Stripped off the old uniform and shipsuit she'd been wearing for the better part of the day. Cleansed herself. Put on a clean shipsuit and having poured herself a drink and opened a snack, stretched out in what might be the fleet's only armchair. Heavens, she'd lost track of her privilege. None of her subordinates enjoyed the privacy and comfort she did. Of that much, she was sure. And the excuse for that was that she needed to be in shape to make the important decisions as well as possible.

Okay, time to test that theory.

She wasn't happy. Why? Well, because she'd hoped this was going to be the triumphal end of her mission and she'd be able to get back to Earth and the Solar System with the fleet it needed to defend itself.

Only this wasn't the end of her troubles, and that wasn't going to happen, and there was no clear path forward.

She didn't even know who all the players in this high stakes game were. The pirates she'd faced weren't simple criminal entrepreneurs. Somebody had organized them with malicious intent. Intent to remove Katie and humanity from the board. Katie wasn't sure who. She suspected the Lizards, or at least a faction of them, but she had no proof. She wasn't even sure of it herself. Obviously, whoever it was had some agents back at the Trade Hub, and she wasn't at all sure the Trade Union wasn't involved. Ostensibly, they were allies, but they gave Katie an itchy feeling between her shoulder blades. Whatever the case, she wasn't finished here until she had some answers to her questions.

Katie took a sip of her drink and stared at the wall of her cabin. There were no answers written there.

Okay, let's break it down finer and see what she had.

She'd completed most of the itinerary the Trade Union had given her. She could claim she'd not only done all they asked, but more. She'd eliminated a major pirate base with what were apparently most of the pirates in the region. Yeah, her and the Earth fleet.

Only, she couldn't prove it, but it seemed to her that the pirates had just been catspaws. Of some faction of the Lizards. Katie felt it was probable that the Lizards didn't have rogue factions. Her sense was that this was the main Lizard government up to no good. Again, there was no real unambiguous evidence she could bring back to either the Trade Union or her own government.

Her door buzzed. Katie got up and went and answered it. It was Amy.

"Sorry, if you were trying to sleep, but I figured you'd want my report as soon as possible," the tired-looking Scout Leader said.

"Come in," Katie said.

After they'd both sat down, Amy got right down to it. "A handful of ships fled in a variety of directions. Fewer than I'd have expected. With what those little Snout kids told us, I think I know which way the Lizard ship with the hostages went. Probably the bunch the *Cuxhaven* is following."

Katie smiled grimly at her friend. "Good news, and good work."

"Thanks," Amy replied. "Just doing my job."

"Doing it well."

"Leaves you with a bit of a decision."

"Do we follow them with the entire fleet, or do we declare victory and go home?"

"Yeah."

Katie puffed up her cheeks and huffed out a breath. "Tough one. I'm going to sleep on it. The fleet needs the time to reorganize anyhow. I think you know which way I'm leaning."

"Yeah, our Katie isn't one to quit or leave a job half done."

Katie nodded. "I'd like to think so, but we do have competing priorities to balance."

"Just the same, you'll be wanting me to send at least an additional pair of scouts after the Lizards, right?"

"Right. As many as you can spare without compromising their efficiency." Katie checked her chronometer and fleet status dashboards. She got up and, activating her console, tapped out a series of commands. "I'm calling an orders group in the main conference room at Zero Five Hundred. I'll give my final decision then."

Amy got up, her drink only half finished. "I'd better get my people on their way and get some sleep then."

"Good idea," Katie agreed, showing her to the door.

Amy turned as she left. "I say we track these guys down and finish it."

Katie had never seen Amy so determined. She smiled wearily. "I agree, but I'm still going to sleep on it."

Amy nodded and left.

Katie climbed into her sleeping pod.

Mere minutes later, she was asleep.

*　*　*

The Huntmaster was not pleased. He would have liked to have been able to soothe that feeling of displeasure in a traditional Grotto of Decision. Alas, the nameless hidden base of the Forward Stalking Ambush Group had a Decision Grotto that catered to less traditional sensibilities. True, it was dark, cool, and damp, but its center was dominated by the bright colors of a holographic display of the nearby stars and the installations and ships present in their systems. Practical, but annoying.

In particular, the bright red symbols representing the Human fleet that now overlaid the system in which the Snout pirates had had their base were greatly irritating the Huntmaster.

The Humans were not supposed to have made it so far. Furthermore, they were supposed to have taken far heavier losses.

A cough interrupted his gloomy reverie. "Fat prey, Huntmaster."

"And a clean kill, Foremost Stalker."

The local commander moved to peer at the star display. "The jumped-up monkeys have proved to be quite the tricksters. It will not serve them in the end. In the end, it is necessary to fight."

"True, but it is also our role to see the fight cleanly favors our hunters. We used the Snouts to flush out the tree dwellers and, as we could have expected, they have shown themselves to be sneaky ambush predators."

Foremost Stalker hissed. It was an expression of disgust. "Tree dwellers. They all try to avoid fair fights." Most of the Great People's home planet was composed of dry plains, but a planet is a big, varied place and it had its strips of forests on certain coastal plains and at certain altitudes in certain mountain ranges. Like most sentients, the Great People were adaptable generalists who'd escaped their original ecological niche. They'd found a way to make use of those forests, but it hadn't been an entirely pleasant experience for them. The sub-clans that lived in them had a reputation for being odd and tricky. Ironically, they were disproportionately represented in scouting forces like that Foremost Stalker commanded. Foremost Stalker was himself, like most commanders, from a central plains clan.

All this occurred to the Huntmaster, as he contemplated how to reply to his subordinate. "As must we, unfortunately. Our position among the stars remains precarious."

"Are these infamous elder races really so fearsome?"

"Our best information indicates they are beasts whose lairs we'd be fools to enter. We, of course, are always sniffing the wind for better information. As you should well know." It was part of Foremost Stalker's job to seek out and gather exactly such information.

Foremost Stalker dipped his head in acknowledgment of the rebuke. "As you say, Huntmaster. These Hunting Grounds among the stars are both new and immense and yet strangely crowded, but that is no excuse for not learning everything about them. Under your eyes, I redouble my vigilance."

"Well said," the Huntmaster replied. "It is a difficult task to be aggressively sneaky. Be assured I recognize that. Be assured too, that I share your assessment regarding the Humans."

"Huntmaster?"

"They will have to fight. They cannot hide up in a tree indefinitely and they do not dare return to their home system leaving the 'pirate' problem unsolved. Neither can they leave that system underdefended indefinitely. Someone will eventually take advantage. So they must fight, and better sooner than later, but they cannot win that fight."

"So, the Humans are a problem that will resolve itself as we watch from hides in the grass?"

The Huntmaster gave a slight clatter of his teeth. That all the players in this great game faced dilemmas of their own was cause for some amusement. Real, if limited. "That would be amusing," he allowed, "but we dare not assume it, or that they'll fail in a timely fashion without complicating our hunt in the process."

"But it'd be wiser not to rush in to fight the whole herd and the scavengers following it on our own and in the open?"

The Huntmaster flicked his tongue in approval. Foremost Stalker was a not unworthy student. "Just so. We must show ourselves but briefly and partially so as to misshape our competitors' perceptions of the hunt."

"And when they misstep and lunge at empty space or prey beyond them?"

"Then you may tap the tree dwellers on the nose. Then you may teach them salutary caution."

"Leaving them impaled on the horns of their dilemma."

"Just so."

* * *

Rob Hood hadn't had much sleep the last few days. He hadn't been risking his life like others, but he hadn't got much sleep. He'd been busy gathering information and trying to actually make sense of it. With a lot of help from Wootton. They'd come to conclusions about the current situation in humanity's corner of the galaxy.

They weren't comforting ones. They meant Rob was having to give the presentation from hell.

Well, at least he had a spiffy new room specifically designed for it. The *Bonaventure*'s "Main Command Briefing Room" was an impressive place. It was a mini-amphitheater with a small stage up front where Rob was standing. He had a huge wall-filling screen behind him and in front of him, between him and his audience, there was a large, three-dimensional display. It was showing the local region of space. The volume being represented was a huge rectilinear slab tens of light years on each side. Over a hundred light years on each of the longer sides.

Mastering the controls to that fancy display had sucked up almost a half hour of his precious time. It annoyed Rob. Still, a slick presentation with pretty bells and whistles had more impact than a dry monologue without them.

His audience was just settling in. Commodore Kincaid herself was front and center. Tanya was way at the back and almost lost in the dim lighting. She gave Rob a quick thumbs up.

Not exactly correct military demeanor, but Rob appreciated the sentiment. He gave her a slight nod of acknowledgment.

Also present closer to the front were Commander Fritzsen, the flag captain, and Rob's boss, Commander McGinnis, who was sitting next to Fritzsen. McGinnis was good people. She asked a lot, but she was hands-off while being careful to make sure her people had everything they needed.

Rob could see Lieutenant Commander Sarkis and Lieutenant Commander Maddox, too.

They both consulted Rob quite regularly about what he thought was coming down the pike operationally. Amy Sarkis, in particular, seemed to value his input highly. Rob appreciated that and did his utmost to be as helpful as possible.

Lieutenant Colonel von Luck, who was also present, had gone out of his way to thank Rob for his reports and to affirm that they'd been very useful in planning and conducting the assault action just completed.

That was immensely gratifying.

Rob could have hoped everybody would be as happy with the coming presentation. He wasn't optimistic.

Time to bite the bullet.

"Ladies," Rob made a slight bow towards Commodore Kincaid and her friends, "and gentlemen," a different bow, "allow me to apologize in advance," he announced. "If it seems like what I have to tell you will require us to commit the fleet to three, maybe four, courses of action, none of which are mutually compatible, it's because that's exactly the case."

He stood erect at parade rest and gave his audience a toothy rictus of a smile. "No joke. I'm glad I'm just a middle rank intelligence weenie and not a senior commander like you folks, because I don't know how you're going to square this circle."

Having captured his audience's full attention, Rob turned to the schematic that now filled the wall behind him. Essentially, just a top down 2D representation of the local star field with some symbols and blocks of text in various colors scattered about. Rob hoped it avoided the wall of text effect. Sadly, every individual in the room had too much information coming at them. Of necessity, they prioritized what they paid full attention to. What Rob had to say was important, and he'd done his damnedest to ensure it'd penetrate the skulls of the decision makers here.

Rob waved a virtual pointer at a block of text in bright red near the top of the screen. "As you can see, we have been given three missions that are all supposed to be our top priority."

Subdued snickers greeted Rob's casual sarcasm.

"I think we have a fourth, unstated mission," Rob continued. "We have to get back to the Solar System before somebody realizes it's undefended and decides to take advantage."

Despite the dim lighting, he saw nods of agreement.

"Our primary mission is to follow the patrol route given us by the Trade Union. Dealing with any pirates we encounter on the way."

No news there. Still, it'd needed saying.

"That might seem an obvious point, but Ensign Wootton and I assess it as being critical in the light of some background facts. The Galactics, and the Trade Union especially, are a mish-mash of species and cultures. Common cultural understanding cannot be assumed. In response, the Galactics and the Trade Union are rather picky about adhering to the exact letter of agreements they make. They're not prone to accepting reasonable interpretations."

Rob paused. He wanted this point to sink in. "Our very successful engagement with the pirate fleet and our taking of their base might be considered to have dealt with the pirate threat to local civilian commercial traffic. But our assessment is that the Trade Union, being both a civilian organization and legalistic in its outlook, won't see it that way. We don't think they'll see us as having met the terms we agreed to."

The silence that greeted this statement seemed rather expectant to Rob.

"We can't recommend that you consider our patrol obligation as having been met. We should complete the rest of the given itinerary."

That did get a reaction, if only some uncomfortable shifting of bodies.

"At the risk of repeating myself, let me sum up. The Trade Union has a tradition that contracts are inviolate and not subject to interpretation. There's no being reasonable. You're expected to do precisely what you agreed to do in every detail."

Reluctant nods greeted that.

Rob looked at his feet before looking back up. "That said, our second mission is the most urgent."

He looked in the direction of Amy. "Lieutenant Commander Sarkis' scouts are already pursuing it. We've got to trace the fleeing pirate ships back to whoever was sponsoring them. Controlling actually. Taking people's families hostage does seem rather more like controlling."

That got a slight humorless laugh from someone. "Fact is, those scout ships are needed by the fleet if it's to move safely, and, in turn, the scouts need the fleet for backup if they bump into serious opposition. We have to work together. And we believe that the scouts can expect serious opposition, eventually. Assuming they don't lose the fugitives first."

That resulted in some unhappy grunts.

Rob took a breath. "This issue gets us back to the Trade Union and how our perception and theirs differ."

He inspected the bland, fixed faces before him

"We're convinced that not only are the individuals behind this latest spat of pirate activity Lizards, but that the Lizard state is, in fact, responsible for instigating it."

Rob looked at Kincaid. She gave a short, sharp nod.

"Only we're basing that on what a small number of captured Snout individuals have told us."

Rob's audience looked grim.

"This will not convince the Trade Union. We need more.

We need to capture ships with both Lizards and hostages on board. We want prisoners who can give testimony."

Someone snorted. Nothing they knew about the Lizards indicated that any of them would allow themselves to be captured alive.

Rob ignored the wordless comment. "We need to find the base they've been operating out of. We have to capture it intact to provide evidence of what it was used for and to link it back to the Lizard state itself."

The faces before Rob were blanker than ever.

"A tall order. I don't know how it can be met. Perhaps it can't, but the cost of that is that the pirate problem won't go away. Which means trouble trading with Far Seat, an ongoing threat of attacks, and likely further requests for patrols by the Trade Union that we'll have a hard time mounting. We don't really have the resources and every time we go on patrol we'll be risking an attack on the Solar System. That's the situation as we understand it."

Kincaid and some others nodded, accepting his point.

Rob took that as permission to continue. "That's not the worse of our problems. So, the third issue we need to deal with. If the Lizards really are hostile, we're going to have to take them on directly. This may be a lousy time to do so, but the balance of power isn't going to get better."

That moved his audience to an epidemic of fidgeting and unhappy noises.

Kincaid looked around. She spoke out clearly. "Enough. The man warned us he had bad news. Let's not shoot the messenger. Carry on, Lieutenant Hood."

Rob swallowed. "Yes, ma'am." He pointed at the holographic display between him and his audience.

"As you can see," Rob continued, "the Solar System is pretty much directly down-arm from Far Seat Station and like it pretty close to the mid-plane of the Galaxy. The Solar System is only fifty light years above the plane in a thin disk that's only five hundred light years thick. I know you all know this, but it bears repeating." He briefly flared the little light representing humanity's home system for emphasis. He marked Far Seat with a bright yellow symbol. Allowing a moment or two for that to sink in, he then triggered the display of the systems known and believed to be the ones occupied by the Lizards in bright red. "The Lizards are further off the plane than we are and to the galactic south, but further up-arm."

"They've got us flanked," von Luck said.

"That's right," Rob confirmed. "And the Trade Union's link back to the 'civilized' stars of the middle powers and the elder races, too. Even if they're not hostile, which is a big assumption, they're not just a major threat to ourselves, but to everyone else in the sector, including the Trade Union."

"War is it, then?" Commander Fritzsen asked.

Rob shrugged. "All we know is that they're a threat we have to do something about. We're not sure that the Trade Union recognizes that threat. We're not sure it matters either. They seem to habitually outsource military action. And failing that, they just pack up and pull out."

"Hard on those of us they leave behind," Lieutenant Commander Maddox said.

"The name says it all. They're a union of traders," Rob replied. "Not a state. Not a military organization. Not even an organization that has a military of its own. The fact is that empire and military conquest over interstellar distances don't seem to be practical long term."

"Unfortunately, we've got to get through the short term and we don't have the strategic depth to retreat and wait it out that the Trade Union does," Kincaid said.

"Yes, ma'am. That's our assessment."

"So, I've got three goals, each enough for our whole fleet, one probably impossible, and I have a fourth goal of getting back to the Solar System as soon as possible to defend it. Is that correct, Lieutenant Hood?"

"I think that about sums it up, Commodore."

"Very well. Thank you."

"Yes, ma'am."

* * *

Katie had just finished reviewing Rob Hood's presentation with Amy. They'd only given the copious backup documents he'd provided a quick scan, but they appeared to support his conclusions. Katie wasn't surprised. She trusted Hood, not only to be honest, but to know his job.

She looked around her office. It mightn't seem large to anyone who wasn't a spacer, but to Katie, it still seemed huge. Only it looked like now she was getting to earn her perks.

Amy certainly seemed to be enjoying them. She was kicked back in a well-padded chair with her feet up on Katie's desk. Pretty close to lèse-majesté in Katie's mind. It was amusing. Katie suspected it was intended to be. Amy made a point of enjoying life no matter what it threw at her and she liked to share her good mood.

Amy noticed that Katie had finally surfaced from her deep dive on Hood and Wootton's work. "So, in a few hours, I'm going to need new orders for my scouts."

Katie gave Amy an attempt at a quelling stare. It didn't have much effect. "It looks like I need a plan to do the impossible in order to save the Human race and a few other alien ones, too. Might take me a whole hour."

Amy laughed. Lightly. "Yeah, it's a lot to ask. Only here's something to think about that ought to cheer you up. This is what you've worked your whole life towards. And that despite even your friends," here Amy pointed to herself, "sometimes thinking you were crazy. Just a little bit. You thought we'd find ourselves in a tough place as soon as we inevitably ventured out into the wider galaxy. You thought somebody was going to have some tough, important decisions to make, and you thought you'd be the best person to make those decisions. Pretty damned crazy if you ask me. But you were right and here you are now."

"I guess so," Katie replied, "but I don't think I knew what I was letting myself in for."

"How could you?" Amy asked. "Only Katie, I think you were right again. I can't think of anyone better suited to do the right thing right now than you. Yeah, it's going to take a miracle, but you're the best miracle worker we've got. Okay?"

It was Katie's turn to laugh. "Okay."

Amy removed her feet from Katie's desk, and sitting up, looked at her friend seriously. "You know you don't have to accept Hood's conclusion that you have to take the initiative and pull off a miracle. You could just finish the patrol route the

Trade Union gave us as quickly as possible and bugger off back home pronto. Nobody would blame you. Even if you do find it plausible, you have to admit Hood's assessment is at best speculative. Also, I'm not sure tracing the pirates back to the Lizards and then engaging them in an all-out war is a good idea. In fact, I think most people would say it's a damned bad idea."

Katie bit a thumb thoughtfully. She wasn't most people, that was for sure. "That sounds reasonable, but when humanity is facing extinction, I don't think nobody blaming me for it is going to make me feel better."

"Bit melodramatic, don't you think?"

"No. No, we've been over this. Over it again and again. That's exactly what we're facing. When a small primitive group makes contact with the wider universe, it doesn't tend to work out well for them. They're lucky if they avoid being wiped out. I intend to see we beat the odds."

Amy smiled wanly. "Just playing devil's advocate. Guess I better go off and check on how our search is going. I'm going to take the *Lockhaven,* which has what's probably my best crew, out and see if I can catch up with the *Cuxhaven.* Take over the direct pursuit. One way or another, we'll find whoever is behind this."

Katie nodded. "Right. I'll work up something formal to put on the record, but that sounds good."

"Right then," Amy said, swinging upright. "Later," she said as she exited Katie's cabin.

After she'd left, Katie leaned back and sighed. That was the first step. First of all, they needed to put an end to the pirate attacks and that meant tracking down the instigators and supporters of them. The local Snout clans may have been not just defeated, but all but annihilated, but there was no lack of desperate factions to take their place given the right encouragement. And if it turned out it was the Lizard state responsible, and Katie had no doubt it would, then they'd have to be taken care of. That was going to be difficult.

She'd cross that bridge when she came to it. Only first she had a more immediate problem; she didn't want to leave Amy's scouts unsupported, but she also had to continue the patrol she'd been assigned.

The obvious solution was to split her fleet. Something any military strategist could tell you was a classic mistake. Any enemy with a clue would use the opportunity to concentrate against one of the weaker parts of the split force.

Katie had thought she'd had lots of experience being overwhelmed by difficulties, but pushing on, nevertheless. Only thinking of it, she realized that however difficult the hurdles she'd had to jump had been, those hurdles had always been defined by others, or by circumstances. Even when she'd taken the initiative in the heat of battles, her objectives had always been clear.

That wasn't so now.

Katie liked to read history, mainly military history, in her limited spare time. She'd had a busy career. The build-up to the First World War by the British Navy and how it'd been handled had struck her as maybe germane to the problems she expected to face. She'd read a famous saying about how the British Admiral, Admiral Jellicoe, was "*the only man on either side who could lose the war in an afternoon*". She'd thought that rather melodramatic. She was repenting of that feeling now. The moral burden of making decisions on one's own that could lead to the destruction of one's country or the extinction of one's species was rather heavier than she'd anticipated.

But she'd fought hard to be in the position to do so, and now it was her job to man up.

If the opportunity presented itself, it was her job to confront the Lizards and defeat them decisively and quickly. There was no doubt of that.

Only first Amy's scouts had to find where they were operating from.

## 9: The Calm Before the Storm

*"Another consequence of Einstein's theory was that nothing could travel faster than the speed of light. In fact, no object with mass could even reach that speed because to do so would require an infinite amount of energy. Remarkably, nature had a speed limit that was completely determined by Maxwell's theory of the electromagnetic field and depended only on the elementary properties of electricity and magnetism."*

Page 267 of "Faraday, Maxwell, and the Electromagnetic Field: How Two Men Revolutionized Physics" by Basil Mahon and Nancy Forbes

Each new system was a gut ache. Only part of that was physical and the unfortunate side effect of FTL transit. Most of it was due to fear and worry.

"Okay, ma'am?" Jim Windsor asked. Lieutenant (junior grade) Windsor was the engineering officer of the SFS *Lockhaven*.

"Just the usual queasiness, Jim," Amy answered. A wild flip upside down combined with at least two weird rotations jammed her stomach somewhere up between her eyes. Amy barfed.

Barfed right into the handy bag installed below her chin like a bib. Unfortunately, this unpleasant little evolution had become somewhat routine. Amy really hoped the little ship's captain wasn't holding back on her behalf. Their lives might depend on the *Lockhaven* being as difficult a target as possible.

FTL exit points were predictable and ships were vulnerable just after exit. It took time for ship's crews and systems to adjust and acquire a picture of their new location. Time during which they were vulnerable.

Amy already felt guilty about how she was using the *Lockhaven* more often and on the more important, read riskier, missions than her other scout ships. Not that she was giving any of her scouts an easy time of it. Still, she really didn't want to be the weak link that they had to compensate for, thereby further endangering their lives. "You'd have to pay for a ride like this at the circus," she commented after expelling the remnants of her lunch and as she wiped the edge of her barf bag before sealing it.

"Back on Earth," Jim said. They all wondered how things were going back home on the Mother Planet and if anything like normal life continued there.

"Yep," Amy replied.

"Yes, ma'am," the engineering officer replied in a distracted way. His job wasn't as critical as the captain's, who was piloting the ship, or the co-pilot's, who was on the sensors trying to determine if they were alone or targets, but he was supposed to be monitoring the stress the captain was placing on the *Lockhaven* and its systems. Especially the engines. It required a degree of attention.

Amy let her crew get on with their jobs, and refrained from distracting them further.

After what seemed an eternity, but was, in fact, less than an hour, Sally van Tol, Lieutenant (junior grade), on sensors finally announced, "Nothing local I can see. We're clear. Recommend steady course towards system's south ecliptic pole."

"What's that in relation to galactic directions?" Amy asked.

"About thirty degrees off of straight galactic south and

roughly up-arm, ma'am," van Tol answered.

"Towards Lizard space."

"Yes, ma'am."

Amy grinned. "Well, well," she commented. Up to now, her fear had been that she'd lose track of the fleeing pirates.

The sensors officer nodded in agreement. "Yes, ma'am, doesn't look like the bastards are going to give us the slip. We have to be close to wherever they're going."

"Yep," Amy replied, her grin becoming somewhat forced. "That's good. Don't want to jump the gun, but looks like we've done it. Done the first part anyhow." Amy turned towards the little ship's captain in the pilot seat. He could afford a few spare cycles now that he wasn't busy jerking them all over the sky. "Captain, sorry, but this is going to complicate things for you. We don't want to lose our prey, but you're going to have to start exercising extra caution."

"Yes, ma'am," the captain replied. "If they can't shake us, the worm's likely to turn. Try to take us out guessing we don't have much support close behind us."

"And they'd be right about that."

The captain just nodded. "And even if they don't turn on us, what do you think the odds are their home base is undefended?"

Amy snorted. "Somewhere between nil and none."

"Joy. Guess that's why they pay us the big bucks," Jim the engineer interjected.

They all snickered at that. It was at times like this that the old joke bit. No amount of money was worth the stress and danger. Only duty kept them at it.

"We have to find their home base," Amy said.

"But then we bugger off back home, pronto, right ma'am?" the engineer asked.

"Oh, yes, we have to find their base and report back to the fleet. Getting killed isn't part of the mission."

"That's nice."

"Isn't it?"

\* \* \*

Shadowguide didn't like anything that dimmed his wits. It was therefore immensely ironic that he spent most of his time in establishments that profited by selling products that did just that.

Worse, although he was in them for the other people who frequented them for the purpose of learning what they might happen to know, he did not truly enjoy either the company of most of those individuals or find most of what they had to say interesting.

Shame is not a useful emotion for a spy, but Shadowguide regretted his feelings in the matter. They did not make his job easier. Moreover, he recognized that they were unfair. He prayed to the myriad gods he no longer truly believed in for the strength to be a better person.

And for all that, he still regretted that he was in a bar, pretending to sip a cheap drink, in the company of people he'd have a hard time respecting even if they'd been sober. He'd hoped to be a scholar when he was younger. He'd have preferred to be spending his time in a quiet library.

Only he had a job that needed doing.

Right now, that job entailed buying drinks for the chief accountant of a small local trading company based out of Far Seat Trade Hub. The accountant in question was a Swimmer by the name of "Babbling Brook." Shadowguide wasn't sure how he'd come by the name. The Swimmer method of bestowing names was baffling even to most Swimmers, but Babbling Brook's name certainly fit. He liked to talk. He liked to drink too. Most of all, he loved gossip. Excessively.

Very convenient for Shadowguide.

Right now, the hot topic of gossip was what the Human fleet was up to. They'd been a surprise. Most new species did the minimum the Trade Union asked. This typically resulted in some skirmishes in which both sides took as much as they gave. But now first the Scaly Ones and then Humans had proven unusually aggressive and effective both and it had the kibitzers of Far Seat in a tizzy.

Babbling Brook was close to bouncing up and down in his seat. "The Human leader has turned out to be very clever. Very tricksy. She's all but wiped out the local Snout pirates. Nobody knows what to think. You might think the Trade Union pooh-bahs would be happy about that."

"You might," Shadowguide agreed, priming the pump.

"Only they might be a worse threat than the pirates," Babbling Brook said breathlessly.

"They seemed friendly enough when they visited," Shadowguide said.

"Oh yes, friendlier than the Scaly Ones." Babbling Brook gave a dramatic shudder. "Cold and nasty, that lot. Give me the creeps. Give lots of people the creeps."

"They were well disciplined."

"Oh yes, well disciplined, a military virtue, I understand. I was never good at history. Still, what happens when their masters let them off their leashes? Me and all the other traders, just simple business people, we worry about that."

"They're not the easiest people to understand."

"Might be they're stone cold killers just biding their time. That's what worries us."

"More than the Humans?"

"The Humans can be friendly enough, but they're even less predictable. I'm told they don't even always get along with themselves. Most species that aggressive blow themselves up before reaching the stars. Could be the Builders who stumbled into their system messed us all up. No, nobody knows what to expect from the Humans."

"Can't be that bad."

Babbling Brook looked into his drink and shuddered again before taking another big gulp of it. "Don't know, but the Humans and the Scaly Ones both, that's got us all antsy. Every trader and trading group I know of is pulling back and trying to hide themselves and their assets somewhere safe as best they can."

Shadowguide made a point of not smiling. Babbling Brook had finally given him some actual information. Shadowguide dipped his head in the universal sign of agreement. "So, they're thinking it's going to come to a head sometime soon. Nobody can stop doing business for too long."

Babbling Brook gave a twitch. "Just so. We can smell the storm coming. We can just hope it blows over without destroying too much."

"Does anyone care who wins?"

Babbling Brook gave an exaggerated sway back and forth. It was what the Humans would have called a shrug. "Some. Not much. I kind of favor the Humans. Less predictable, yes, but friendly sometimes at least. It might work out if they were to come out on top. Only guess there's not really much chance of that. Nasty but efficient, that's the Scaly Ones." He shuddered once more and gulped yet more of his drink.

Shadowguide swayed a small shrug of his own, then tsked. "Well, hard to say what's going to happen yet. Guess we'll just have to wait and see."

"Yeah. Guess so."

Shadowguide wondered if there might be something he could do to tip the scales a little in the Humans' favor. The ideal outcome would be, of course, if the Scaly Ones and Humans managed to cancel each other out, and the Humans were in the weaker position. Also, like Babbling Brook, he found the Humans more congenial. Maybe there was something he could do.

Not much to be sure, but maybe a little.

\* \* \*

Katie, Amy, and their entourage threaded their way through the crowded passageways. They were on the way to the viewing gallery overlooking the *Bonaventure*'s flight deck.

Katie had been keeping Amy company all day. A briefing of her scout group had been followed by a stint watching the beginning of operations from its command center. And watching and being present was the sum total of what Katie got to do.

Turned out high command sometimes amounted to an extended morale building and PR campaign. Having made the decision to basically split her fleet, Katie found that she didn't have much to actually do other than try to encourage the men and women of Amy's scout group, who were bearing most of the burden of that decision.

Katie had sent her only cruiser, the *Freedom*, and all of her destroyers off to finish following the patrol route mandated by the Trade Union. She'd sent half her frigates and two-thirds of her corvettes to accompany them. So going by numbers and size of ships, she could honestly say she'd used most of her fleet to finish the requested patrol.

The Galactics didn't have humanity's tradition of wet navy carriers that were the main element in strike groups. To the Galactics the *Bonaventure* might appear as a lightly armed support element.

A support element for Amy's overstretched scout ships.

Katie had been on the committee that had advised Admiral Tretyak on what sort of ships the new Human interstellar fleet should have. She'd strongly argued for them to have FTL capability despite not invalid arguments that this was an inefficient use of resources. All the same, she'd seen the capability as necessary to their popping into a system ahead of a main force and reporting back. She'd not envisioned them being used on extended multi-system patrols. The little ships were just too cramped and lacking in the amenities for prolonged deployments to make that a good idea. And yet that was exactly how she was using them.

The scouts that were pursuing the fleeing pirate forces and those scouting ahead of the main fleet were all based on the *Bonaventure*. They were many systems away from their disparate areas of deployment. She was asking a lot of both the scout ships and their crews. She wasn't sure how long they'd be able to endure the consequent operational stress.

She was doing her best to help. Good food, and lots of rest time when not deployed, were two things she was making sure of. She'd made it clear to the entire ship's crew that the happiness and health of the scout crews was everyone's top priority and that nobody was to harass them with non-scout duties. Even cleaning and maintenance parties had been briefed on how to not disturb resting crews.

She was herself wandering about, showing her face and providing concrete evidence of how important she considered their efforts.

Not hard work. Rather boring. Being able to talk to the crews more would have been nice, but they didn't need the distraction. Her job was to be seen, to be supportive, not to interfere.

"Heads up," Amy, next to her, muttered, "we've reached the viewing gallery."

Katie grunted. One of her many flaws was a tendency to daydream when not busy. One that Amy was well aware of and was compensating for. Thank the heavens for good friends.

There was already a small group in the viewing gallery. It was Tee-Nah and the two Snout youngsters he'd acquired on that Snout pirate base. Ensign Tanya Wootton was with them. Doubtless she was enjoying the process of milking the youngsters about Snout culture.

Wootton looked up from talking to one of them. Startled, she spoke in haste. "Sorry, ma'am. We'll leave right away."

Katie grinned. "Not necessary. I'm glad you're taking care of our guests. We're all on the same side now."

"Yes, ma'am." The ensign looked uncertain. "Ma'am, I'd like to put Kaa and Gee in school with our kids."

"Kaa-Nah and Gee-Nah," Tee-Nah added rather stiffly, it seemed to Katie. "But yes, this is a good idea if the highly esteemed commodore would allow it."

One of the side effects of having both male and female Space Force members was that sometimes they formed families and sometimes those families grew to have children. Ideally, only one member of a couple would ever deploy at a time and those children could enjoy a proper childhood somewhere safe. Unfortunately, the world was not ideal. The *Bonaventure* was big enough to provide accommodations for children whose parents could not make other arrangements. Those accommodations included the modern equivalent of a traditional one-room school. Would adding a pair of young aliens to the mix be a big stretch?

Katie looked at Amy and got a slight nod. "I will talk to the school staff," she answered, "and see what can be done."

Ensign Wootton grinned widely. "Thank you, ma'am!"

Tee-Nah just nodded. He was becoming quickly proficient in Human body language.

"And now," Katie said, "I have to stand at the viewing window and provide moral support to our scout crews. You're all welcome to stand there with me."

"Thank you, ma'am," Wootton answered, waving her young charges forward. "You're really working them hard, aren't you?"

Katie smothered a sigh. "That I am."

"Guess it's necessary."

"Yep," Katie agreed. She didn't add she hoped it was enough.

* * *

Once again, the Huntmaster found himself using his local commander's garish holographic display to get a sense of how their operations were proceeding.

He was not displeased.

An aggressive youngster on their first hunt might be. Without direct experience of anything other than squabbling with their siblings in the creche, they might see the Human ships spreading out towards the Great People's space and think this meant the Humans had the upper hand.

But the Huntmaster had long aged past such simple assessments. He knew that the best time to strike at an enemy was when, having overextended themselves, they were off balance. Even better if you could induce them to commit the tactical error of attacking prepared defenders at poor odds. If somehow an ambush could be arranged, that was better yet. If you could somehow create all three conditions, a victory of legendary proportions was possible.

So, no, the Huntmaster was not displeased. It was best to not count one's prey down before pouncing, as the saying went, but the situation seemed to be shaping up as planned. And the plan was intended to meet all those conditions.

"It grates," his local commander, Foremost Stalker, said, "to fall back before these tree dwellers. It will be a relief to finally spring our trap."

The Huntmaster dipped his snout in agreement. "True, but we wish to harvest their whole herd, not just take their weaklings for a meal. We must wait until they're wholly within the jaws of our trap."

It was Foremost Stalker's turn to dip his snout. "True too. These tree dwellers are most impertinent and must be dealt with. Having lured them down to the ground, we must not let any of them escape to plague us in the future." He gestured at the star display with a claw. "They venture far too close to our home stars. If allowed to penetrate further, they'll show the traders at Far Seat and those lurking up-arm where our hunters hide. We could triumph in this struggle only to compromise ourselves in future more important ones."

The Huntmaster allowed himself a flick of the tongue. Foremost Stalker deserved to see that the Huntmaster was pleased with him. The Huntmaster put the sentiment into words. "Yes. It is good you see this. The Humans are not to be trifled with, but they are prey that think themselves predators as they will soon learn."

"And, we must dispatch them cleanly without wasting time so as to get on with the more important hunt."

"Just so."

## 10: A Bad Moon Rising

*"We've seen that Einstein's equations of general relativity seem to allow for the possibility of faster-than-light shortcuts and backward time travel. However, we've also seen that there appear to be severe restrictions on the actual realization of wormholes, warp drives, and time machines, especially when we consider the laws of quantum mechanics."*

Page 218 of "Time Travel and Warp Drives: A Scientific Guide to Shortcuts through Time and Space" by Allen Everett and Thomas Roman

Katie had thought she was dodging politics by taking on the anti-pirate mission.

And yet, here she was at a get-together where neither the food nor the people were what they seemed to be. Katie detested stupid little snacks and idle chit-chat with equal passion.

Well, at least most of her fleet had made it back to Far Seat Trade Hub intact. She'd accomplished one of her main goals. The Trade Union had expressed formal approval and deemed her anti-pirate patrol a success. They had waived docking fees and were even paying to resupply the Human ships. Most of

Katie's crews were getting some well-deserved shore leave. Katie would have preferred they spend the time resting up rather than getting drunk in bars, but you can't have everything.

Neither the crew of the *Bonaventure* nor those of most of the scout ships she hosted were getting to enjoy shore leave. Most of the little scout ships were busy tracking down fleeing pirates and trying to find more of their bases.

A job made easier by the fact they no longer had to scout in front of the main patrol and could concentrate on that task. That was one thing allowing an easier operational pace. The other thing allowing it was cause for some concern.

The trail that had seemed to point directly toward Lizard space had taken a sidewards step. A step towards the vicinity of Far Seat as it happened. It suggested operations uncomfortably close to the jugular of local trade. Amy and the *Lockhaven* had already detected one probable base only a few jumps away from Far Seat. A profoundly disturbing discovery.

"Far be it from me to give advice to the esteemed Human commander or to attempt to decipher your specie's emotions," a voice came to interrupt Katie's thoughts; it was "Far-farer-for-profit," "Far" for short, who was Katie's local liaison and translator, "but aren't you supposed to be mixing, getting to know people, and buttering them up? Are you unhappy about something, despite a very successful patrol?"

Katie gave Far a hard, unhappy glance. She knew he'd see it and also knew he'd never admit that. Far might be helpful as a guide and translator, but there was no doubt he was a spy for the Trade Union. That was annoying. It was also annoying that he was turning out to be so very observant. It was downright irritating that he was also right about what she was supposed to be doing here. She decided to play it straight. "It was a good start. I took some chances and got lucky. It could have gone bad. That bothers me. Still, as we say, water under the bridge."

"Water under the bridge? This means something that's happened and now there is nothing that can be done about it? With the implication, there is no point worrying about it?"

Katie studied her Climber liaison. "You're either real quick on the uptake or you've been studying hard, Far."

Far bobbed his head. Katie could tell he was amused. Good for him. "Well," he said, "it could be both."

"What is really worrying me is that what we discovered suggests our problems are only beginning. Somebody organized and was supporting those pirates. They weren't just independent entrepreneurs. Those somebodies appear to have all been Scaly One individuals, and they fled somewhere taking hostages with them."

"Pirate gangs tend to be motley collections recruited from all sorts of species. It doesn't mean much. Being a certain species doesn't automatically mean being a puppet of some government."

Katie had been impressed by just how non-motley the pirates she'd encountered had been. She didn't see much point in directly contradicting Far though. "Maybe," she said, "it makes sense you Galactics would think so. Species seem to spread out and break into a lot of fragments once they get out among the stars. But the Scaly Ones seem to be well disciplined and coherent both. If they didn't have a strong control over their individual members, you'd see more individuals doing business out here." She frowned. "You'd have an easier time recruiting spies, too."

Far shuffled his feet in a Galactic shrug. He clearly wasn't going to comment on that. "Perhaps they're conservative and xenophobic both, and their people are afraid of venturing out into the wider galaxy. That's common for species new to the stars."

"Maybe," Katie replied, "but we both know that in a large population, there are always a few outliers. In any case, we Humans, as divided as we have been on a species level, have a lot of experience with strong states exploiting less tightly organized ones. They often liked to dissemble about their operations. Using secret agents to stir up trouble. Sending them in but denying responsibility if they're caught. Calling them volunteers or criminals acting on their own. I think the fact these 'pirates' fled towards Scaly One space is telling. That my scouts have narrowed down one of their destinations to a place between Scaly One space and Far Seat, and quite close by, concerns me greatly."

Far flapped his hands in a gesture Katie didn't recognize. Some form of equivocation, no doubt. "I understand your concern. I doubt my superiors or many others would. None of this proves anything. Bases close to where prizes are to be found are to be expected. There is really not much you can do other than follow those still fleeing. And if you lose them, it proves nothing. If they enter Scaly One space, you can't follow them, and it still proves nothing. Criminals go where they want. In the end, you're still empty-handed despite great efforts. Best not to waste your time. You don't have much time, do you?"

It was Katie's time to shrug. She couldn't very well tell Far the Solar System was virtually undefended, and she had to return as soon as possible. She guessed that he guessed as much, but it'd be irresponsible to make it official. "It is true I can't prove anything and that I'd like to return to Earth sooner rather than later."

"So why worry?"

"It's not knowing that worries me. I'm not sure it's accidental."

"It's a big galaxy."

"And rather nasty."

"That's not news."

* * *

Rob found it altogether too easy to relax around Commodore Kincaid. He was glad for the presence of Ensign Tanya Wootton. It made a good excuse for keeping the proceedings at least semi-formal.

They were in Kincaid's cabin briefing her on the situation.

The information and opinions they were about to present to her were critical. Kincaid had decisions to make. They'd probably determine not only the fate of their little fleet, but that of the entire Human species.

Rob felt like a pompous idiot thinking that even in the privacy of his own mind. Only, stripping out all his emotions and being as objective as he could, that's what his analysis told him. Didn't help that Tanya, who - for all her youthful enthusiasm - was dedicated to intellectual honesty, agreed.

"Lieutenant Hood, you're very pensive," Kincaid said.

"Surely the news isn't that bad." She sipped a drink. She'd offered them all drinks. Rob had the weird feeling one of her friends had told her this was standard when staging an ostensibly informal meeting.

Rob fidgeted. This sort of thing wasn't something he was used to. But it was clear Kincaid wanted them relaxed, so she could talk with them in a direct, honest manner. She wanted to know what they thought without anything held back. Well, he could try to oblige. "You know this is a historic meeting?"

Tanya perked up. Apparently she'd been heads down and hadn't thought it through.

Kincaid sighed. "If there are any future historians to write about it, sure, I expect so."

Tanya failed to contain herself. "Wow, that makes perfect sense." A sense of wonder infused her words.

Kincaid smiled. "Welcome to the big leagues, Ensign Wootton."

Rob realized they were drifting off topic. "Unfortunately, in the big leagues, there's never enough time to explore all the issues you'd like to," he said.

Tanya blinked. "Yes, sir," she responded.

Will wonders never cease? Rob wasn't sure he'd ever heard that ubiquitous phrase drop from her lips before. "Sorry," he said. "But I'm afraid it's future historians who'll get to study it at leisure. Just imagine the silly stories they'll tell."

Tanya giggled. Caught herself, and glanced at Commodore Kincaid in alarm.

Kincaid was simply amused. "Gallows humor," she commented. "I have to be serious and optimistic in public. Here with just us present, we can relax a little. But Lieutenant Hood is correct on both accounts. This is an important meeting, but we can't get hung up on that. You need to tell me what you think is going on and maybe suggest what to do about it."

Rob nodded. "I suspect you have a pretty good grip on the situation and plans to deal with it. But that you'd like to make that understanding explicit."

"I always inspect my suit seals before going on a space walk," Kincaid replied. "It pays to be careful."

"Straight out. We're going into a head-on fight with a foe that's expecting us and has had time to prepare. They've got their home base close by for support. We're alone and way out on a limb even if Earth had more to provide. They can survive a defeat. We can't."

Kincaid's lips quirked. "Doesn't look good, does it?"

"No, and they understand that. They probably don't know we know that they understand that. I'm guessing you plan to use that somehow."

Kincaid snorted. "Spies. You all live in a fun house of mirrors. But you're right. I think they think we're walking into this fat, happy, and dumb. And I plan to use that. First, I want to hear what you and the ensign think."

Rob took a deep breath. "So, from what Lieutenant Commander Sarkis' scouts tell us, we've located the secret Lizard base they've been supporting the pirates from."

"Close to Far Seat," Tanya interjected. "Too close. They're planning something bad."

"No doubt at all that it's the Lizard government behind it?" Kincaid asked.

Tanya looked at Rob. He nodded. "We've no doubt, ma'am," she answered. "Only it's all circumstantial based on our understanding of the actors involved. I don't think it'd stand up in a court of law. And we don't think it'll convince the Trade Union either. They're dedicated to not wanting to believe it because doing something about it would be bad for business. Also, worse comes to worse, they pull back up-arm and let the middle powers handle the upstarts."

Kincaid laughed.

Tanya looked at Rob, who shrugged. "Ma'am?" she asked.

"Sorry, Ensign," Kincaid answered. She wiped her eyes. "But it's startling how close our assessments are. Also amusing how similar situations result in thinking beings acting much the same. When it comes to the geopolitics, these galactic aliens are acting exactly the way human beings would. Which is not only amusing but a relief. It means we're not lost at sea. We've got a good chance of understanding what's going on and manipulating it to our advantage."

"Yes, ma'am. That's quite optimistic, ma'am."

"The stakes are high," Kincaid admitted, "but in my experience, when you know what's going on and the other guy doesn't and you're willing to act decisively, well then, the odds tend to favor you."

"I see," Tanya said. She looked down. She looked up at Rob, who gave her a slight nod. "About that, ma'am, we thought about it and although the safest course of action right now might be to return to Earth after sharing our suspicions with the Trade Union, we think that would be a mistake."

Kincaid gave another disconcerting smile. Rob could tell that she was one step ahead of them in their analysis, but she could have been less smug about it.

"Why is that?" Kincaid asked.

Tanya fidgeted. Finally, she spoke. "These considerations might be above our pay grade," she said, "but we didn't think our briefing would be complete without them."

"Go on."

"We don't think the Trade Union will take our warnings seriously."

"Okay, and if the Lizards make a move on them, how's that our problem?"

"Like the name indicates, the Trade Union is composed of traders. They don't much care who's running things as long as they can make a profit. In fact, they'd rather not have to be bothered with it. At best, it's a distraction. At worse, it's extra overhead. They're sort of benignly indifferent to us."

"But the Lizards are different."

"Yes, ma'am. Classic empire builders, but more xenophobic and genocidal than anything than humanity ever managed to come up with. We think they potentially make the Assyrians, Mongols, and Nazis look like nice guys."

"Okay, but does that make them our problem? They're on the other side of the Trade Hub from us. Can't we let the Trade Union and middle powers up-arm deal with them?"

Tanya grimaced. "It's complicated, ma'am. We ran a lot of different scenarios on the simulators, though. Left alone, the Lizards will almost certainly defeat or marginalize the Trade Union, locally at least, and get control of most of the resources available in this part of space. Also, we're not certain of our analysis of their demographic biology, but we think it's likely they'll drastically increase their population, taking over as many habitable worlds and stations as they can without compromising local productive capacity."

"So they'll be significantly stronger. And you think they'll come for us?"

"Yes, ma'am. We think so. Strategically, they think the way any Human conqueror would. They won't want to leave a potential threat in their rear while they deal with the main one. Even if we're not threatening them, they'll want to take us out while we're still weak."

"Well, that doesn't sound good."

"Honestly, ma'am, we think they're so genocidal, so prone to dividing people into predators and prey with themselves as the only genuine predators that they'll try to extinguish us as a species. If we let the Lizards run riot, we'll be lucky if a few of us survive as slaves."

"So, to sum up, you think we have to take them on and now, but that the odds really aren't very good."

Tanya looked very unhappy. "That's right. The odds aren't good, but all our calculations are that they're as good as they'll ever get."

"Solutions?" Kincaid asked, looking Rob's way.

"Kind of fishy how we were lucky enough to locate that well-hidden secret base," Rob said. "We think it's probably an ambush."

"And?"

"And, to use a Human analogy, they'll let us get close enough to see the whites of our eyes so that their initial surprise attack has maximum effect."

Kincaid gave another infuriating smile. "Potentially an opportunity for us."

"We have some ideas."

"Good, so do I. Let's get down to brass tacks."

After all the portentous talk about the strategic situation, working out the dry mechanics of possible tactics was a relief.

Retail death and destruction, rather than wholesale.

\* \* \*

Katie looked around at her senior officers. They filled the

*Bonaventure*'s main conference room.

Also present were support element leaders and various staffers. The staffers included Lieutenant Hood, Ensign Wootton, and Tee-Nah. She might need them to answer questions.

They were all here for the penultimate meeting before the final formal orders group for the upcoming operation. This was the last chance for any serious amendments to her basic plan.

"Your attention, please," Katie said. The room quieted. "All right, you've all had a chance to read the plan."

This elicited murmured affirmatives.

Katie smiled grimly. "Good. I know it's a long, complicated document and that I've kept all of you extremely busy."

She stood up and turned to the display screen filling the wall behind her. "But whatever other concerns or priorities you might have, nothing is more important than getting this plan right."

She paused and tried to read the room. She wasn't a mind reader and she couldn't be sure what they were thinking. "We're all busy, and we're about to be busier, but I can't emphasize this enough. Getting this operation right is not only the most important thing in your lives, it is likely the most important thing in the existence of the Human race. And, that's because the existence of the Human race depends on it. Ladies and gentlemen, there is nothing more important."

"Commodore, no offense, but a lot could go wrong with this plan. If the stakes are so high, should we be risking it at all?" Oddly enough, it was the normally affable and laid back "Bobby" Maddox who'd dared Katie's wrath to ask that question.

Katie smiled gently. "A good point and a better question. I'm glad you asked it, Lieutenant Commander Maddox. "

"You're welcome, ma'am," Bobby replied. That got a few snorts and snickers.

"Long story short, the Lizards and Trade Union both are still underestimating us. That presents a positive window of opportunity. On the negative side, if we just retire to the Solar System, we're not just surrendering the initiative to the Lizards, we're allowing them to get stronger, both absolutely and relative to ourselves."

"I see, ma'am," Bobby said.

Katie was grateful to Bobby for giving her a chance to make some vital points. She was also grateful that no one asked why she assumed the Lizards were an enemy they'd have to fight. All of Human history suggested it, but, no matter how convinced of it she, Hood, and Wootton were, the formal case was very subjective. She was glad she wasn't being asked to make it. She should, however, finish answering Bobby's questions.

"You're welcome, Lieutenant Commander Maddox," Katie said. "I should elaborate, though. Our odds are better now than they're likely to be in the future. That doesn't translate to their being particularly good. We need a quick and complete victory against an opponent that's at least as strong as us and more experienced. We're going to have to take the maximum advantage of surprise, of the fact that we understand them better than they understand us, and that they're underestimating us. Our plan is to deceive them into making serious tactical errors and to then exploit those tactical errors to the maximum. That leads to a complicated plan that makes some serious assumptions. My staff and I have gamed out all the options. We believe the plan I've devised is the best possible. Bear with me as I review it one last time before formally issuing orders. If you have questions, do speak up."

Katie's speech received quiet murmurs of assent. Gratifying, but she'd meant it when she asked to hear any objections. Not that she expected any. It just wasn't the Space Force tradition. In the past, publicly questioning a senior officer had tended to be career limiting. She hadn't had time to overcome that. Still, she doubted that any officer without her reputation and past successes would have had much success selling her plan. It was like Bobby had pointed out risky. But, the best she could think of.

"Okay, to summarize," Katie said. "We've spotted the location of the base from which the pirate attacks were being organized and supported. With suspicious ease as it happens. It turns out to be distressingly close to Far Seat Trade Hub, barely three or four jumps away. Rather brazen, if you ask me."

Light laughter. Looked like she was carrying her audience.

"Even more arrogant that they apparently think we're dumb enough to walk into an obvious trap."

Not so many chuckles. Nobody likes being disrespected.

"Our plan is to turn the tables on the arrogant bastards."

Quiet anticipation greeted that.

"The Lizards have a habit of sneaking up on their prey. That's what they mistake us for."

Angry grunts were the response to that. Being disrespected is one thing, being treated like a victim by predatory bullies is another.

"We're going to make them pay for that mistake."

Katie paused and did her best pugnacious Winston Churchill imitation. This wasn't just a calm, rational presentation of a plan. It was also a pep talk.

"What the Lizards don't have is any experience with fighting a foe as strong as they are. In particular, they have no experience of enemies who use deception against them to attack. We're going to be a new experience for them."

Katie gave a big predatory grin.

"Not a good experience for them. Not one I intend to give them a chance to learn from."

Someone coughed. It sounded like a suppressed laugh. Good.

"Thanks to our flogging off parts of good old Mother Earth to various groups of aliens, we now have electronic warfare capabilities that we believe are superior to those of the Lizards. We're going to make full use of that fact to fool them into seeing what they expect to."

Katie looked around to see if her point was sinking in.

"Once again, Lieutenant Commander Sarkis' scouts are going to play a key and risky role," Katie looked at her old friend. "Sorry, Amy."

That got some laughs.

"They'll be the first to enter the target system. They'll sniff around very cautiously, first to give the impression we're timid and unsure of ourselves, but also to make sure there are no sensor platforms or scouts placed to get a good look at us once our main fleet enters the system."

Pausing for breath, Katie saw she had everyone's rapt attention.

"After the main fleet, destroyers, and corvettes, and then the *Freedom* in company with the *Bonaventure* enter the system, the scouts will deploy in force to get a solid look at the moon the 'hidden' base is on."

Katie took a deep breath.

"We expect the Lizards to hold fire except for perhaps some light ineffectual fire from their base proper. They will want to appear to be only lightly defended so as to suck us into an ambush. If we're mistaken about that, we may lose some scouts and we'll have to systematically reduce the base with a careful staged frontal attack."

Katie looked around to see everyone was looking grim again.

"But we believe they'll try to ambush us, and we intend to look like we're walking into it. This is where our superiority in electronic warfare will come in. We're going to make it look like our entire fleet is moving to take station over the enemy base. As our scouts return to the main fleet, we'll launch a massive long-range bombardment to confuse the Lizard sensors."

Katie saw heads nodding at this.

"Under its cover, the main fleet will go into stealth mode. The scouts will turn back and start pretending to be the main fleet. They'll be mixed in with plentiful missiles, mines, and long-range drones."

A pause for breath.

"By this point, the Lizards ought to be convinced we're both timid and rather incompetent. When the jaws of their ambush spring shut on our supposed '*main fleet*', it should be a complete surprise. A very unpleasant surprise for them."

Katie turned and looked at the graphic behind her. It showed the expected position of the opposed forces and with the expected losses to the enemy displayed in a luridly red font.

"Those precise numbers are speculative," she continued, "but the Lizards should be hurting. Surprised and disorganized, too. While they're still that way, the main fleet will move in, engage, and finish them off. Questions?"

There were none.

"That's the plan," she said. "Let's make sure it works."

* * *

The Huntmaster wasn't one to rail at what couldn't be changed. If he had been, he'd have cursed the Galactics who'd thought it wise to sell the Humans advanced sensor technology in exchange for planetary real estate that was strategically worthless.

It left him all but blind in advance of a critical clash. The Huntmaster wasn't young or naïve enough to believe any plan ever went completely as expected. The bards and chroniclers might pretend otherwise, but he knew better. It was vital to be able to watch events as they unfolded and to adjust as needed.

The problem was that the tree dwellers had sensor technology as good as anything the Great People had. Hence, if a Great People scout could see the Humans, the Humans could probably see the scout. And secret bases aren't supposed to have extensive scout screens, or really any at all. It would be as grass waving where there was no wind, a sure indication that a hunting party was present. A sure method of spooking one's prey.

And so, the Huntmaster was forced to rely on a few passive sensors concealed on what astronomical bodies were available. He was a prisoner of his own deception.

"The tree dwellers plunge heedless into our trap," Foremost Stalker commented.

The Huntmaster stared at the star display in their hidden base's Decision Grotto, pretending to be absorbed in the data being presented while he gathered his patience. "So it appears," he finally said.

"I'm almost disappointed that we'll probably annihilate their entire force without a serious struggle," Foremost Stalker replied. "I understand, esteemed Huntmaster, that they are unfamiliar prey, almost predators, and very tricky, but the force we have here is twice as strong as everything they possess without counting the hidden batteries. What trick could possibly prevail against such odds?"

"None that I can think of," the Huntmaster conceded, "but

remember, this is just the beginning of our hunt, not its end. If the tree dwellers somehow manage to inflict injury in their death throes, it could greatly complicate our efforts against the Trade Union and those behind them up-arm."

"But I do not believe that you think that likely."

"No, but I do not like this hiding low and blind in the grass and waiting, either."

Foremost Stalker clattered his teeth in amusement. "Surely, this is a splendid day on which I get to counsel my master to have patience."

The Huntmaster gave a slight tooth clatter back. It was amusing. "True, but I will still be glad when this is done."

\* \* \*

Fighting the nausea of jump emergence, Katie snapped out an order. "Sensors, report!"

The sensors officer gulped audibly, but soldiered on. There was only the slightest pause as they consulted their instruments before they reported. "All clear, ma'am. No enemy, mines, or obstacles nearby."

The comms officer spoke up. "Commander Wong reports the same, ma'am. For all the *Freedom* and the rest of the fleet have been able to see, this could be an empty system."

Which meant the enemy Katie was sure in this system was remaining well hidden. The *Bonaventure* was the last of the fleet to have arrived. The rest of the fleet had had time to do as thorough a scan of the system as was possible without straying too far from their entry jump point. "Thank you, Comms. Thank you, Sensors."

"You could still have the scouts do a systematic search of the entire system," Hood standing beside her said. It was his job to act as her devil's advocate. "Just because Lieutenant Commander Sarkis' scouts located the probable hidden base's location doesn't mean there aren't other surprises hidden here. Even a small M3 system is a big place."

Katie shook her head. "No, we'll stick to the plan. We want to seem fat, happy, and dumb if in a timid way. They have to know we suspect where their base is. Otherwise, there's no reason we'd be here with our whole fleet."

Hood nodded. "Makes sense, ma'am."

"Glad you you think so." Katie took a breath. "Comms, message to commander scout group, copy the fleet; execute preliminary reconnaissance in strength of suspected enemy base."

"Yes, ma'am," the comms officer replied before repeating back and sending the message. Seconds later, Amy's scouts began to accelerate in-system towards the gas giant whose moon they'd identified as hiding the enemy base.

"So it begins," Katie said to Hood. "Now we wait."

Even a small system, with an M class red dwarf primary, presented distances that were a challenge, even given tech so advanced it resembled magic. FTL just didn't work that effectively over relatively short distances crowded with astronomical bodies and their moving and overlapping gravity fields. That, coupled with the chance of encountering some space debris in a catastrophic fashion, meant that purely natural complications required a degree of caution when moving around in a system. Slow, hour-consuming, patience-trying caution.

Katie supposed she should count her blessings. The enemy could have ambushed her or left a minefield around the entry jump point. They hadn't. It was all still going according to plan.

But that meant having to wait.

Katie didn't like waiting. She liked action.

## 11: Ground Zero

*"The procedure led to a result that perfectly reproduced what was measured (and therefore must be in some fashion correct) but clashed with everything that was known at the time."*

Page 14 of "Seven Brief Lessons on Physics" by Carlo Rovelli

A couple of hours had passed and Amy's scouts were approaching the gas giant, whose moon was of interest. The scouts spiraled in, carefully checking out each of the many bodies orbiting the giant gas ball. They didn't want to find themselves unexpectedly within range of some enemy battery hidden upon one of the fractured collections of rock and ice.

Katie knew these were sensible tactics and tried hard to set an example of patience for her staff. She looked over at Hood. He didn't seem to be faking his patience.

Hood looked back. "It won't be long now. It's not likely they'll allow any of the scouts close enough to get too good of a read on them."

"I hope we're right about their not wanting to show how strong they are. I'd rather not have any of our scout ships become flaming datums."

"Amen," Hunt responded. "Only there's only so much we can learn without poking them, however cautiously. Like somebody said, some risks are necessary."

Katie snorted. "True, but it doesn't make me feel better about having to bet other people's lives."

Hood looked pensive. "Personally, I'm glad you feel that way. I'm also glad it doesn't stop you from making the necessary decisions. It improves the odds most of us will get out of this in one piece. Anyhow, won't be long now."

Less than half an hour, as it turned out.

"Ma'am, the *Tanshang* reports a small missile salvo launched from the vicinity of the suspected hostile base," her comms officer announced.

The message the comms officer had passed on had been on its way even as they'd talked earlier, but, as Einstein had asserted, space and time imposed limits. You can't have everything happening all at once in just one place. Katie knew that, but it still freaked her out that the events she was just hearing about had already played themselves out.

"Thank you, Comms."

"Yes, ma'am. They're launching decoys and taking evasion action."

"Good."

"The scouts are aborting their search and falling back on the main force."

"As per plan," Katie said.

Finally, some tens of minutes later, the report they'd all been waiting for came. "Ma'am, the *Tanshang* reports it has evaded the enemy missiles and is now falling back on the main fleet."

"Excellent," Katie responded. She glanced over at Hood, who was intently inspecting the command center's large displays. They were showing what the *Tanshang* had been able to see.

Hood looked at her. "That missile salvo was what we could have expected from a small base with minimal defenses. The *Tanshang* didn't see anything to suggest otherwise either."

Katie thought about that. The expected Lizard pirate support base had been right where expected. When "discovered", it'd displayed just the complement of weaponry appropriate to a hidden base that had relied mainly on remaining undetected.

If heavier weapons platforms existed, they were well hidden. Wouldn't it be disappointing if it turned out there just weren't any?

Katie snorted.

"Share the joke?" Hood asked.

"I was just thinking how disappointing it'd be if this turned out to be what it looks like, a small minimally defended base intended as a cutout for the people really behind the pirates."

Hood didn't look amused. "I know you'd like a decisive battle, but I don't think I'd mind that."

Katie quirked an eyebrow.

Hood flashed a thin smile. "The plan's not bad," he said, "but there's too much we don't know for sure. There is some chance it could be decisive in the wrong direction. That'd be a catastrophe."

"So, you understand the need for taking the risk, but you're not happy about it?"

"Exactly."

* * *

They were hours into the operation. It'd taken a couple of hours for Katie's scouts to reach and uncover the hidden enemy base.

It'd taken almost another couple of hours for them to fall back to the main fleet.

It'd been long enough for both Katie and Hood to take a short break. It was going to be a long day.

Now the next part of Katie's plan was beginning.

Her main fleet had gone into stealth mode. It should be invisible. Her scouts had formed a fake fleet that should have replaced it on the enemy sensors.

It all appeared nominal as her people tracked the progress of the fake fleet towards the anticipated ambush point. In addition to the scouts pretending to be much larger ships, that fake fleet was composed of a varied plenitude of decoys and nasty surprises for anyone that attacked it.

They hadn't seen any sign of that ambush Katie felt sure

must be waiting, but their own deception seemed to be holding up.

So far, so good.

Katie's eye fell on one discordant note. Ensign Tanya Wootton was beavering away at an auxiliary sensor console. She'd wheedled the position out of Katie based on the good work she and Hood had done. Katie had been feeling grateful.

Katie had not only allowed Wootton the use of the console, she'd agreed to have one of Amy's scouts drop a full-service and extremely expensive sensor suite on the far side of the moon the Lizard pirate base was located on.

It seemed to Katie that Wootton was more interested in documenting the upcoming battle than in contributing to winning it. That sensor suite would be more useful in tracking fleeing enemy ships after the battle had been won than in actually winning it. Could be it'd be useful in planning future battles.

It was that future beyond this particular battle that spoke to Hood's ongoing doubts.

Katie looked at Hood. "This is a necessary risk. We have to give the Lizards a bloody nose. We have to convince them to back off. We also have to convince the Trade Union that the Lizards are a threat they need to take seriously. Otherwise, we're in an untenable situation."

"We'd have to figure out how to be in two places at once," Hood said.

"Exactly. We'd have to somehow defend Far Seat Trade Hub and the Solar System both. So, the risk here is worth it."

"Yes, ma'am," Hood said.

Katie couldn't help thinking she hadn't done much to reassure him.

At any rate, there didn't seem to be much more to say.

Another hour and the fake fleet was more than halfway to the decision point. The real main fleet slowly trailed in its wake as closely as it dared. It wouldn't be much longer.

The storm broke sooner than expected, just before the fake fleet entered the zone of anticipated ambush.

In an unanticipated way.

"That's strange," Ensign Wootton announced to the whole

command center. "Commodore Kincaid, ma'am, my sensors are picking up multiple quakes on the pirate base moon."

"Dozens of them, I imagine," Katie responded patiently. "They must have been hiding their weapons platforms somehow."

"No, ma'am," Wootton replied. "Not dozens. It's hard to tell, but it looks like hundreds of separate seismic events."

Katie felt a chill run down her back. Her guts could be misleading her, but this was one risk she dared not take.

"Comms, emergency broadcast to the entire fleet!" she announced loudly. "All units. Immediate retreat with all possible dispatch to exit point Omega. Operation is aborted. Expect a fighting withdrawal."

Startled faces glanced her way.

"Comms, further orders for the CAG. He is to launch every available fighter to screen the withdrawal of the Scout Group."

Bobby had had his fighters on standby. It was mere tens of seconds before they felt a series of shivers through the *Bonaventure's* hull as she launched her fighters.

It takes long minutes for events to propagate over interplanetary distances and maybe the Lizards were surprised enough to grant them a few more before all hell broke loose.

A few quick requests for confirmation, and the main fleet was accelerating back out of the system in a ragged formation. It looked like Katie had managed to convey her urgency to her ship's captains.

A few more minutes and her comms officer spoke. "Scout Group confirms it's dropping stealth and making maximum acceleration for the jump point, ma'am."

"Ma'am, I can verify that our scouts are altering course," her sensors officer interjected.

Katie nodded. It was a quick response to an order none of them could have expected.

Her relief was short-lived. Turned out there had indeed been Lizard weapons platforms, and ships too, waiting in ambush. A lot of them. There had to be twice as many Lizard ships as there were Human. Katie's fleet was badly outnumbered. "Sensors, you seeing what I'm seeing?"

"Yes, ma'am," the sensors officer replied. He sounded

shaken. "It's a mess out there. Most of our sensors are overwhelmed and our software isn't keeping up. I'm not sure what we're seeing. Between all our surprise packages going off and some really incredible fire output from the target moon's surface, it's hard to make anything out for sure."

"I can see that," Katie said, putting a smile into her voice as if this was all merely an amusing show, "but give me your best estimate."

"A lot of fire being put out from that moon, ma'am," the sensors officer responded. "It seems to be mostly beam weapons and short-range missiles, so that's good." He sounded surprised he had a bit of good news.

"Our scouts?"

"Hard to tell, ma'am. It's not like they're trying to be easy to track and there's a lot of noise in that area. Enemy ships are lifting from the moon and out of distant stealth. A lot of them, ma'am. Sorry, ma'am, our tracking software is optimized for less than sixty-four major targets and there's more than that."

Katie faked a smile. "Well, going to have to take that up with procurement." That got some surprised chuckles. "But more than twice our numbers, than?"

"Yes, ma'am," the sensors officer replied. "But half of them look like they're probably smaller than one of our corvettes and not much bigger than one of the scouts. Nothing that looks as large as the *Freedom* or the *Bonaventure*. That's about all I've got right now."

Katie nodded. "Thank you, Sensors." She surveyed her command center. They were all calmly going about their jobs, almost as if everything hadn't just gone to hell in a handbasket. "Good job all, keep it up and the Lizards are going to be severely disappointed by the results of their little surprise."

Nothing to do now but wait. Katie was happy she'd insisted Amy stay on the *Bonaventure,* commanding her Scout Group from a distance rather than accompanying her scouts personally. Right now, it wasn't at all clear how many of the scouts, if any, were going to survive.

It was most of an hour before the answer to that question began to become apparent. A stern chase is a long chase.

Also, it was clear that with the Lizard ships dispersed, and many of them having to buck the little moon's gravity to get into the fight, they had been at a disadvantage even before the manifold surprises, missiles, torpedoes, and mines mixed into the fake fleet along with the scouts had exacted a heavy toll on them. Slowed them down enough to let most of the Human scouts escape.

Whittled them down significantly. Although it turned out that almost half of the Lizard ships had been fakes, too. Katie wondered why. Were they decoys or an attempt at psychological warfare?

In any event, it looked like the Lizards had only outnumbered Katie's fleet by two to one at the start and that they'd lost about a third of those numbers. Mostly their smaller ships, but Katie had a fleeting temptation to turn around and give them a real fight.

Only it'd most likely turn into a brawl that was costly for both sides and the Lizards had a nearby base to do repairs at and get supplies from, whereas the Humans only had the *Bonaventure*.

Katie hated to run. But it was the prudent thing to do.

It was a relief when they hit the jump point and got away intact.

It was more of a relief after they exited jump, and found that the Lizards had declined to follow.

Made conventional sense. After all, a fleet coming out of jump was at a severe disadvantage if someone was waiting for them.

So, tactically, the whole exercise had been a draw. In fact, they'd inflicted more damage on the Lizards than they'd taken. Only they hadn't destroyed the Lizard fleet or taken their base. They'd fled in the face of superior strength.

Strategically, it was little short of disaster.

* * *

Katie was emotionally gutted. Beyond feelings or even being depressed. They'd made it out of the "target" system. But only barely.

They'd expended most of their ammo stocks and lost several scouts. All the larger ships had escaped. Without damage that couldn't be repaired in the field.

Tactically, they'd pulled off a minor miracle.

Strategically, it was a major defeat. If Katie couldn't figure out how to ameliorate its effects, perhaps a catastrophe. It was too soon to tell.

She was too weary. She needed rest. So did her people.

"Okay, folks," she announced with a firmness she did not feel. "That's it. Set up a skeleton watch. Get some rest. That was good work under tough conditions. I appreciate it."

She looked over at Lieutenant Hood. "You too."

"Yes, ma'am," Hood replied. "We couldn't have known. Given the odds, you did well." He turned and left.

Katie waited a little while before making her way back to her cabin. Like all of her people, she needed rest. But she couldn't stop thinking about what had happened. Hood was right; given the odds, she'd done well.

Still, emotionally, it'd been a shock. The crews of the scout ships they'd lost had been real people. Ones they'd miss. One of the lost ships had been the *Lockhaven*. Amy would be feeling the loss of all her scout crews, but of that one in particular.

Back in her cabin, Katie contemplated her sleeping pod, knowing she should climb in and do her best to sleep.

She couldn't make herself do it. She needed rest, but she needed to process what had happened more. She couldn't sleep until she had.

They'd escaped largely intact. That was good. They'd taken a bite out of the Lizard forces. That was good, too. Not only had the Lizards been weakened by that, but the fact they'd been gathering large hidden forces close to Far Seat Trade Hub had been revealed.

It could be argued Katie had intruded on a Lizard base. But that base wasn't in Lizard-claimed space, and they'd fired first. Politically, that would count with the Galactics.

She'd forced the Lizards to show their hand.

One other good thing was that Hood and Wootton had correctly predicted that the Lizards would attempt an ambush. That suggested they had a good grip on how the Lizards thought and operated.

Thinking of Wootton, Katie needed to reward her for her

vital early warning. It'd saved all of them from probable annihilation.

Katie shuddered at how close-run a thing it had been. How essentially accidental. Life and death, the very survival of one's species, shouldn't hang from such slender threads.

But Wootton's sensor package that Katie had only deployed as an incidental indulgence had made all the difference.

Maybe the next time her luck wouldn't be so good. It gave her the willies.

They needed more information on the Lizards. No longer having to be circumspect for political reasons, she'd deploy Amy's scouts more aggressively to ferret it out.

So, there were some good things to have come out of the battle. But it was disturbing that they'd come so close to utter disaster. And a relief they'd escaped in such, rather undeserved, good shape.

They now knew for a fact too that the Lizards weren't just rather creepy, that they were indeed up to no good.

Sadly, the fact that the Lizards had at least one fleet stronger than anybody else's also couldn't be escaped. There was no putting lipstick on that pig. Maybe the Lizards, having been exposed, would decide to fold their hand, go home and leave everyone in peace. Maybe, but Katie wouldn't bet a plugged nickel on it. Having to resort to overt aggression might complicate their probable plans for dominating the local bit of the galaxy, but nothing Hood and Wootton had told her suggested it would cause them to slink off home.

Which was too bad. A direct clash probably meant a planet devastating total war humanity would lose. Some sort of bluff was the only thing she could think of that might work. However, given how they'd just turned tail and run in the face of what was likely only a portion of the total available Lizard space forces, it was kind of hard to see how that could work.

It remained a conundrum.

But, at least now, Katie felt able to sleep on it.

\* \* \*

Their jaws had snapped shut on empty air. Their claws had grazed their prey and drawn little or no blood. Worse, they'd incurred significant injury in the course of their wild, ultimately unsuccessful, lunge.

The Huntmaster felt a rage like none since his distant youth.

He'd fought hard over a long life to contain that rage. It'd been useful when he was very young and somewhat more scrawny than his siblings, but much more vicious. As vicious as he'd been, he'd never been stupid. So he'd taught himself to value cold calculation over vicious rage and had believed he'd succeeded.

And now the tree-dweller descended Humans had reversed the achievements of a lifetime.

No, the Huntmaster was not pleased. Not pleased, and very angry.

His subordinate, Foremost Stalker, was also present in this local Grotto of Decision. Foremost Stalker was not a being notable for his abilities of subtle observation. But even he had apparently observed the Huntmaster's anger. Foremost Stalker was being uncharacteristically quiet.

The Huntmaster clattered his teeth in grim amusement. "You have the scent of this prey, Foremost Stalker? You see the mistakes I made?"

Foremost Stalker looked away and dipped his snout. "Forgiveness, Great Huntmaster, but in my blood, I feel different. I planned and led the ambush, and it was I who failed to wait quite long enough to spring it. It was I who failed to heed your warnings that these cursed tree-dwellers were typically full of tricks, not mere prey, but in part predator."

This time the Huntmaster's tooth clatter indicated a more genuine amusement. "You take too much on yourself, young leader of forward stalkers. I could have overridden your plans at any point. We both failed here, despite neither of us being stupid or unschooled in the ways of the hunt. No, sadly, this suggests an issue with how the Great People see our world."

"It sits poorly on the stomach."

"Indeed, it does. But, *better a sore stomach than an empty one and starvation*', as the old saying goes. We must make do with the game the world offers us."

Foremost Stalker dipped his snout again in further

agreement. "Must the Humans divert us from our true goals then?"

The Huntmaster looked away and gave the display of the local stars and the various forces there present a long stare. "So it appears. I cannot see how to avoid it. Can you?"

Foremost Stalker gave their holographic strategic display a long look of his own. As if they hadn't already both studied it intensively. "No, Huntmaster, I cannot. It is truly a lesson in patience. We must take care of the Humans and the local Trade Union before we dare begin the pursuit of our true prey. We dare not pursue the tree-dwellers into the thicket, either. We cannot be sure of what tricks they have. We must flush them out somehow."

The Huntmaster dipped his snout in assent. "Truly, but they cannot hide from us indefinitely, either. Sooner or later, they must come out and face us again."

"Sooner would be better."

"True, and it is that we must maneuver towards."

Foremost Stalker flicked his tongue. "I will enjoy herding them."

"Good."

\* \* \*

Rob looked around the small office he shared with Tanya Wootton. It felt dim, dingy, and overcrowded. They'd filled it up, plundering every source of information they could find, looking for vital facts that might help Kincaid in her quest for victory.

They'd paid scant attention to being tidy.

Rob was proud of what they'd managed to learn, but it hadn't been enough. He felt disappointed.

"Edison used to say he never failed; he only learned what didn't work," Tanya said.

Rob gave her a quizzical look. Tanya wasn't normally that sensitive to people's feelings. "It's a good point," he answered.

"But?"

"Wishful thinking is a mistake. Right?"

Tanya smiled wanly. "Right."

Rob gave a sharp nod. Damn, this was hard. "People didn't die as part of Edison's finding something that didn't work. Our experiments are more expensive. We can't afford to run too many. Each one might be the last one possible and might cost humanity its future. Edison had a lot more upside and limited downside. Still, your point stands. We can't give up because of one failure. So, what do you think we learned?"

Tanya looked thoughtful. "We assumed the Lizards were like us. We assumed if they were being sneaky, it was because they either had to be or because they wanted plausible deniability. We assumed that if they were strong enough to attack us and the Trade Union outright, they'd just do so and not futz about stalking us in secret."

"Yep," Rob said, "we made a lot of assumptions. All based on our own Human history, despite the fact we knew theirs was very different. We knew they were ambush hunters who habitually stalk their game and yet we expected them to act like a Human great power. Humans will try to intimidate each other. Even the Mongols, ferocious as they were, would accept surrender."

"Whereas the Lizards mean to eat us alive after catching us unawares."

"Yeah, it's kind of scary and disappointing all in one," Rob said. "I mean, I kind of admired how rational and straightforward they were."

Tanya nodded. "The Lizards are win-or-lose everything. Honest, maybe, but not nice."

"So, we didn't think we might be attacking more than a kind of special forces base using pirates to stir up trouble. We didn't expect such a major naval force to be hidden there."

"I didn't," Tanya admitted. "I'm embarrassed."

"Me too," Rob said. He grinned. "Have to say I'm disappointed you didn't expect better of me."

Tanya had the grace to blush. "Sorry."

"No problem. Question is, what did we learn?"

Tanya gave a contemplative nod. "Well, looks like we're fighting the whole Lizard race, so we need to find out how strong they are. Was that force at the secret base all they have?"

Rob sucked his teeth. "Doubt that."

"Okay, but we need hard data. We need to carefully scout

out their space."

"Scout group is already stretched, but I can't argue with that."

"We outed their plans, too," Tanya added.

"Given what we know of them, they're not going to pull back to try another day, are they?"

Tanya frowned. "No, their reaction to failure tends to be to double down."

"Damn, have to give Kincaid a heads up. What about the Trade Union?"

"They're not going to be happy, and unless I completely misunderstand them, they're even less prepared to deal with what the Lizards are up to than us."

"Ouch."

"As a study in how disruptive agents can completely alter a stable system of long standing, it's fascinating."

"Too bad we're on the short end of the stick."

"Yes."

Rob took a breath. "So, to sum up; we can't expect the Lizards to give us much time. They're playing for keeps and likely have superior force. They're at a similar tech level but have had longer to build up and evacuate vulnerable industry and population from their home world. The Trade Union is likely to be of little help at best and at worse might be a serious distraction."

"Baseline. It could be worse. You'd better talk to Kincaid ASAP and tell her what she needs to help us find out. Get those scouts out. Soon, because the Lizard tradition when their prey detects them is to strike hard and fast."

"Ouch."

## 12: When At First

*"A theory based on a bizarre model was bad enough, but one based on no model at all was beyond comprehension."*
Page 211 of "Faraday, Maxwell, and the Electromagnetic Field: How Two Men Revolutionized Physics" by Basil Mahon and Nancy Forbes

It was now a couple of days after the debacle with the hidden Lizard base. Katie was in her cabin and in a funk.

She wasn't alone. Amy and Hood were present too. They were helping Katie evaluate the strategic situation and come up with a new plan.

Katie was chewing over a report Hood had just given.

Apparently, most species, if they survived reaching the stars at all, ended up as a remnant of what they had been scattered among the stars. Those stars being not so much cruel as completely indifferent.

Those remnants were the lucky ones.

It didn't look like humanity would be so fortunate. Humanity had had the bad luck of reaching the stars not too long after the Lizards.

Dealing with just the wider galactic community alone would have been difficult, but probably doable.

The Lizards made it a whole different ball game.

Katie sighed. "Well, Lieutenant, your report paints a pretty bleak picture."

"I'm sorry we didn't have better news, ma'am," Lieutenant Hood said. "It doesn't improve, I'm afraid. Lieutenant Commander Sarkis' scouts are gathering more intelligence on just what sort of threat the Lizards pose. It's proving to be a difficult and time-consuming business. But they've managed to build a basic picture. It doesn't look good."

Amy elaborated, "The Lizards hold several systems. All of them with forces larger than our fleet. They're also closer to their bases. They block all the known direct routes to the Lizard home world."

Katie heaved a sigh. "Doesn't look like we have a clear way forward," she said. "I'm tempted to withdraw to the Solar System. It would mean letting them come after us at a time of their choosing, but I'm not sure there's any alternative."

Hood looked unhappy. "Ma'am, with all due respect, from what Ensign Wootton and I have discovered, there's no doubt that they'll do just that, and sooner rather than later. They won't wait for us to build up good defenses. They'll attack and in overwhelming strength. And, ma'am, they'll not settle for just defeating us and they have no tradition of slavery or even domestication."

"Does that mean what I think it does?"

"If you think it means they'll try to exterminate us, yes, ma'am. And, ma'am, I think they'll probably succeed."

Katie had guessed as much. She'd hoped she was wrong. She looked at a grim faced Amy. "Any thoughts?"

"Not really," Amy replied. "Other than pointing out Lieutenant Hood is only human and could be wrong, the most I can offer is that I'll push my people to pull out all the stops trying to find some weakness in the Lizard defenses we can use."

Katie digested that. Trying harder wasn't a promising plan. "Thanks, Amy. I hate to ask for more sacrifice from your people, but it is vital. Only..." She paused.

Amy waited a moment before asking, "Only what?"

"Only we need to do more than work them harder and ask

them to take more risks. We need to give them a better idea of what to look for."

Amy nodded. "Makes sense. Ideas?"

Katie looked at Hood. "I need a chink in their armor. Find me one."

Hood looked blank for a second. "You don't ask for much, ma'am. You're positive you want to attack?"

"I am. Concentrated the Lizards are stronger than we are. If we go on the defense, they get to concentrate where ever they want to. Standing on the defense is a non-starter."

Hood took a deep breath. It was obvious he knew Katie was right. But also that any sort of direct, conventional attack was suicidally impossible. He rallied. "You need to attack while their forces are still dispersed, somewhere where they're weak, and find a vulnerability that's so severe that they'll surrender when you exploit it. Theoretically, if you could manage to meet their forces piecemeal and achieve local superiority in successive battles, you could beat them that way, but it's unlikely we could sustain such a campaign."

"A reasonable assessment," Katie said. The situation stank, but an accurate assessment of a problem was the first step in solving it. "Also, any drawn-out campaign will give them a chance to react. We need to catch them by surprise and decisively beat them before they can react. We need to find a chink in their armor behind which there's a severe vulnerability."

Hood laughed. It sounded hollow, more startled than amused. "Again, you don't ask for much, ma'am."

"Again, only what I need," Katie answered. "Think of it as catching a bigger tougher, bully off guard, getting them down on the ground, and putting your foot on their throat."

"Rather graphic, but I see what you mean. Could you elaborate on what a 'chink in their armor' or a 'severe vulnerability' might look like?"

Katie smiled. "Well, if you were to discover that their home system was defended only by a death star that had a fatal flaw that a well flown fighter could exploit, that'd be great."

Hood chuckled. "I think that's unlikely, ma'am, but we do need a way to get to their home system and some idea of what's there, don't we?"

Katie sighed. "Yes, to be serious, the ideal 'chink in their armor' would be some sort of back door way into their home system. Additionally that the home system was only lightly defended and there was some serious vulnerability there we could use to force them to surrender. Not very likely, but that'd be ideal. Anything approaching that'd be great."

Hood looked pensive for a few seconds, then grinned. "You know, it might not be as insane as you think."

Katie blinked. "Say again?"

"It mightn't be as crazy an ask as you think."

"I want to hear this."

"Well, ma'am, we don't have any solid recent information on what's going on inside Lizard space right now. But we do have records of how they reacted on first contact."

"Okay."

"They reacted very aggressively. The records suggest they realized any hostile presence or fighting in their home system was a threat to their home planet. They went all out to establish strong forces in all the surrounding systems they could reach."

"Okay, but how does that help us?"

"It suggests they decided to invest heavily in a forward defense. They probably have most of their forces in their frontier systems."

"So, if we can punch through or sneak past that outside crust, we might find a soft interior."

"Yes, ma'am. And, even better, they did this before getting good FTL from the Galactics. The systems they occupied were ones they could reach using only the primitive FTL they developed themselves. They may have missed some dim nearby, but not too close, systems. Ones their home system, Assherraskill, is now reachable from with our current FTL tech, but weren't with their original FTL capability. Ones they aren't aware of and aren't guarded."

"Really?"

"Yes, oddly enough for a star-faring race, the Lizards, or at least their current dominant culture, aren't into exploration for its own sake."

"So, there might be a back door route into their home system, which might be poorly defended."

"Yes, ma'am, even better, if it exists, it's likely composed of small, unoccupied, and infrequently traveled systems."

"We might be able to achieve complete surprise."

Hood grinned. "Best case, their forward defense forces don't even realize we're attacking before we take their home system."

Katie laughed. "That would be ideal." She looked Amy's way. "Seems unlikely we could be so lucky, but I'll put Amy and her scouts to work looking for this possible back door." Amy nodded. Katie continued, "It'd be a game changer if we found one. Thanks, Hood."

"It's mostly speculation, you understand? It's possible there's no such back door route."

Katie nodded. "I understand, but that's my problem and Amy's, not yours. You and Wootton, I need to find some vulnerability we can use to induce surrender."

"Not sure the Lizards understand surrender. On the other hand, nobody's ever seen any Lizard young, so that suggests they never entirely evacuated their home planet the way we're doing. That might mean they're vulnerable there. But that's a pretty thin reed to lean on."

"It's what we need."

"Okay, ma'am, guess we better get right at it."

"That's the spirit, Lieutenant Hood," Katie answered. "You're dismissed. The sooner you solve this problem, the better. Days not weeks."

"Yes, ma'am."

Katie looked at Amy. "You followed all that?"

Amy nodded. "Yes, I think my people might prefer long-range exploration to skirmishing with Lizard scouts. But long-range patrols will require some preparation."

"Like I told Hood, days not weeks."

"Yes, ma'am," Amy replied. "I'll get right to it."

Katie waited until Amy had left before slumping down in her chair.

She felt as bleak as ever.

Determining the preconditions they needed to win didn't

make them any less unlikely.

She supposed highly improbable was better than outright impossible.

* * *

Logically, several days and catching up on her sleep hadn't changed the dire situation Katie faced. But she didn't feel quite so crushed by it. Duty required she do her best and inspire her people to do the same. In Katie's mind, that didn't mean pure stubborn defiance of the odds. It meant devising some plan, however wild, that might give them a chance.

She was in the *Bonaventure's* conference room. She and Hood, his boss Colleen, and Amy, who'd had the job of finding a way past the Lizard defenses, had fleshed out the plan she'd brainstormed earlier.

They hadn't solved the puzzle yet, but they had identified what the solution had to look like, and what puzzle pieces they needed to find. Amy and Hood were in the process of trying to find their pieces.

They also had a plausible sounding story for the rest of the fleet's command structure. Whatever the plan they worked out, it would need some selling. They needed something that didn't sound like the desperate grasping at straws that their plan really was.

Katie needed to trust that Amy would find an opening, a "back door" ideally, and Hood and Wootton would find some worthwhile target she could strike at through it. It was now Katie's job to prepare the fleet to undertake that strike. It was essential they strike hard and without any missteps.

This was going to be at best an all-or-nothing effort against heavy odds.

If they failed, they were done for. Probably the Human race along with them.

No pressure.

Katie looked around and smiled. "Attention, please," she declared in a voice that carried and cut through the low murmur of conversation. She gave them all, her entire staff, the captains of the *Freedom* and the *Bonaventure*, Bobby the CAG and Amy her Scout Group leader, and all her squadron commanders and key members of their staffs, a few seconds to quiet down. "So, I trust you've all had time to read your briefing papers and are suitably appalled."

Quiet, surprised chuckles greeted that.

"Ladies and gentlemen, it's just the sketchy start of a risky plan and there's no denying that."

Nods and murmurs of agreement greeted that.

"However, we don't have the numbers we need to defend everything that requires it. It's not an option. Despite the odds, we must attack."

Reluctant nods in response to that. It was an obvious observation, but not one anyone liked to make.

"Also, my intelligence people tell me that the flip side of the Lizards' extreme aggressiveness is that they're not used to other people taking the initiative against them. They can hand it out, but we don't think they're going to turn out to be so good at taking it."

Silence.

"It's a no-brainer that we need to take the battle to them. The rest is just details."

"Lieutenant Commander Sarkis' scouts are working overtime to identify weaknesses in the Lizard defenses. Commander McGinnis' analysts are busy identifying the best pain points for us to hit."

Turned out that it was possible for people to look skeptical, but reluctantly hopeful. Katie understood that despair can act as a numbing agent in hopeless circumstances, and the sudden advent of hope could be painful. She wasn't going to allow her people the comfort of that numbness. She needed them sharp and doing their utmost.

"Once they've completed those tasks, we're going to need to strike hard and without hesitation. I don't expect we'll have much room for error. I need you and your people completely ready. Understood?"

Nods and exclamations of "Yes, ma'am" greeted that.

"Good. Let's get down to brass tacks."

Damned if Katie didn't half believe herself by this point. Her people, miracle of miracles, seemed to. It was scary the faith they had in her ability to do the apparently impossible.

By the time the briefing was done, it looked like she'd

managed to convince a group of intelligent military professionals that they really had a chance to win this war, not just the duty to try.

One miracle down.

Only two or three more needed.

It was a start.

\* \* \*

Shadowguide was detecting signs of panic at Far Seat Trade Hub.

Perfectly understandable, anyone not feeling very worried and making plans to bug out to safer realms up-arm, was either stupid or not paying attention. Much the same difference in Shadowguide's mind.

Of course, this was all tempered by the facts that the authorities naturally wanted to avoid that panic and that there were many for whom bugging out simply wasn't an option. In the first case, those authorities might be making plans for their own evacuation, but by no means did they want others clogging the exits. In the second case, well, there's no point getting all worked up about things you can't change.

Shadowguide himself somewhat straddled the two categories. He could in technical fact commandeer transport back up-arm. He had an emergency back up bug-out plan in the form of a interstellar freighter sitting at a small mining station further in-system from Far Seat.

However, spies are not chosen for a lack of daring, and neither Shadowguide's superiors, or Shadowguide himself, would find it easy to forgive him for bugging out in the midst of the most interesting developments on the Frontier in many centuries. Millennia probably. So, Shadowguide would remain on scene until his safety was in clear and imminent danger.

The current scene was a stool at the bar of an establishment in which he was not exactly a regular, but in which he was well enough known to not attract any particular attention. Fact was that drunks, or even the mildly tipsy, are fine sources of information for patient eavesdroppers. A fact even the Humans, who hadn't struck Shadowguide as being particularly good at information gathering, seemed aware of. Apparently, they even had a tag for it in one of their ancient languages. *"In vino veritas*". In wine, truth. Indeed.

This current establishment catered to a mix of types but mainly lower-tier members of various administrations. Likely, none would be privy to solid facts, but they did have eyes, ears, and a sense for the mood of their bosses. It was a necessity for servants of any sort, however labeled.

Right now, it was too early for many of them to be present. Being early and quiet was part of blending into the surroundings. It was rather boring and did lead to a certain degree of woolgathering.

Shadowguide was reduced to conversing with the barkeep. "Business been good?"

The barkeep, a Varkoid - nobody troubled them - grunted. "Numbers been down. Station admin and the Trade Hub and all the larger trading companies are quietly going nuts over the news about the Humans stirring up a hive of the Scaly Ones."

"That bad?"

"Not so much. A lot of them might be too busy to spend long hours here, but when they do, they drink a lot."

"Bit nervous then?"

The barkeep shuffled his feet in a *"Who knows? Who cares?"* gesture. "They've got soft and complacent sitting at their nice safe desks in a nice safe Trade Hub and a little goes wrong and they start running around in circles."

"Well, the Scaly Ones or the Humans alone would have made for a bit of excitement. Both of them at once, getting into fights, that is unusual."

"Sure, and maybe they'll try to throw their weight around some, but in the end, the galaxy is bigger than any of us, and nobody profits from random destruction. It'll all work out."

"After a while."

"Sure."

\* \* \*

One of Amy's scouts, the SFS *Tetbury,* had just come in hot. Her captain, LTSG Sean Murphy, had left his co-pilot to handle shutdown and requested an immediate meeting with Amy.

Amy was on tenterhooks. She couldn't resist the urge to pace back and forth across the deck of her scout group command center, but she hoped she was managing to keep her nervous tension out of her stride. The *Tetbury* had been out for a long time. Amy had sent her by a roundabout route to the far side of Lizard space. Lieutenant Murphy had news, either very good or very bad. Amy could barely wait to learn which.

Murphy arrived on Amy's deck breathless. He took a moment to pause and compose himself. He strode up to Amy. "Ma'am, I have important news." He glanced towards her little day cabin's hatch. It'd provide some privacy.

"Very well, Lieutenant," Amy replied. "I'll take your report in my day cabin."

As soon as the hatch to the cabin had closed behind them, Murphy blurted it out. "A whole series of red dwarfs, and a couple of brown ones to boot, ma'am, and I didn't attempt the final jump into the Lizard home system, so I don't know what might be waiting there, but it's a back door in."

Amy smiled. It was good news. Also, Murphy hadn't paused once for breath during that whole run-on sentence. "Good news. Congratulations. Details?"

Murphy grinned. He held up a data chip between thumb and finger. "It's all here, ma'am."

Amy took the chip. "The commodore is going to want to see this pronto. Well done. Make sure your crew gets some rest. Take a couple of days' leave. I expect the commodore will want to speak to you herself, so stand by. Stay sober. You're dismissed for now."

"Yes, ma'am," Murphy replied, snapping off an entirely unnecessary salute.

Amy laughed and returned it. "Damned good work, Murphy."

"Yes, ma'am," Murphy said, grinning as he spun on his heel and left.

Amy opened a channel on her comms device. "Katie, we need to talk. ASAP."

## 13: Once More Unto the Breach

*"Physicists and philosophers have come to the conclusion that the idea of a present that is common to the whole universe is an illusion and that the universal 'flow' of time is a generalization that doesn't work."*
Page 59 of "Seven Brief Lessons on Physics" by Carlo Rovelli

Katie was in her cabin and had been about to go to sleep when Amy appeared. She looked almost breathless and certainly excited.

Katie sat her down before asking, "What's up?"

Amy held up a data chip. "Murphy on the *Tetbury* found you your back door."

Katie grinned. She didn't fully feel that happy. She didn't trust how desperately she wanted to believe that Amy's scouts had found the first key to unlocking a solution to their problem. Also, rationally she believed her back door assault on the Lizard home world was the way to go, but emotionally it'd be so much easier to withdraw to the Solar System and leave its defense in the hands of Tretyak. She knew that was fatigue and stress talking, but the feeling was real for all that. So, no, the grin was a bit of an act, but it was an act Amy deserved. It was tremendously good news. "Okie-dokie, no excuse not to follow protocol. Let's put that thing through the scanner."

Amy shrugged and handed the chip over. "Can't imagine how Murphy could have a compromised chip, but sure can't hurt. Haven't looked at it myself, though. Can't wait to see what he found."

Katie smiled and nodded. "I'm trying not to get sloppy in my excitement myself." She put the data chip in the isolated little computing device with hard wired programming that existed solely to check data chips for being infested with malware. "Even if the stars all align our way, we're going to have to be precise in our execution for this to work."

Amy laughed. "Oh? Is the great, daring, and bold Katie Kincaid getting cold feet?"

"Is that any way to talk to your superior officer?"

"Maybe not, but my friend and partner in crime, sure."

Katie tried not to smile and failed. She looked at the chip scanner. After some electronic dithering, it returned a green result. "Anyhow. Looks like your chip is safe. No surprise. Let's see what we have."

"Murphy is solid. He said a bunch of small systems, even some brown dwarfs, and that they didn't attempt the jump to Assherraskill, the Lizard home world, itself - but if he says they found a back door, I'm willing to bet my firstborn they did."

Katie, busy inserting the data chip into her standalone computer, nodded absentmindedly as the data from it appeared. "A very, very roundabout back door that'll leave us on the far side of Lizard space from both the Solar System and Far Seat," she said quietly, almost to herself. "But, yeah, you're right, this looks like what we were looking for."

"Happy?"

Katie grinned for real. "Getting there."

* * *

Being back on the home world, in a Grotto of Decision free of modern annoyances, soothed the Huntmaster's soul some.

It needed it.

Once again, the Huntmaster found himself, along with the Great Chief-King, Princess, and Triumvirate's recording Scribe, waiting for the Great Broodmother's arrival. Her petty political games in the face of troubles affecting their entire species angered him. An anger that, of course, he could not afford to indulge. He needed to ensure that as much as possible reason prevailed in the Triumvirate's deliberations. Neither his feelings nor his political standing counted against that need.

When the Great Broodmother arrived, she did not waste time on pleasantries or even the bare minimum of politeness. "Your hunt failed," she declared, flipping her snout at the Huntmaster.

"The hunt is in progress. That the prey has turned and drawn blood is all the more reason for caution," the Huntmaster replied, evenly, neither dipping nor raising his snout, and gazing casually past the Broodmother's head. He would be civil and respectful, even if she couldn't be bothered.

"My broodlings will starve while you search for your courage."

"*I* would not presume to tell another how to manage the responsibilities they're assigned by long tradition, and long success," the Huntmaster said, "but perhaps if you'd tailored your production of young ones to the resources we have this would not be a problem. The aliens among the stars are a threat we can manage, but if we miss our strike, they could end us. End us. End your current broodlings and end the possibility of any future broodlings."

The Broodmother hissed and flipped her snout in disdain. She stepped forward in a manner that might be thought threatening if such a thing was possible. The Huntmaster had years of fighting and could end her with a single slash of her throat. Only such an attack on a mother was as unthinkable as a mother threatening a full-grown male. Or violating the peace of a council. The Huntmaster could only blink in puzzlement at the Great Broodmother.

The Great Chief-King spoke. "Peace. Great Broodmother, you mistake the Huntmaster's prudence for lack of courage. Huntmaster, your blood runs too cold. For a Broodmother, the death of her children for any reason other than valid sibling competition is an unacceptable cause of pain. The broodlings exist and they need sustenance. The final chase has started and must be run to the end."

The Huntmaster turned slowly to his old huntmate, despair roiling his stomach. "We speak of a hunt, as is natural to those of us of the Great People," he enunciated slowly. "It shames me that I have not clearly shown my colleagues on the Triumvirate that this is no hunt we're engaged in. This is something else. It is not a matter of running down prey and risking some young males to secure what our broodlings need. This is a competition for our continued right to exist. All is at stake. The Great People are indeed great, but we are small and weak against the powers that rule the galaxy. They are not so much prey, or competition, or fellow predators as forces of nature. They are as storms, or floods, or a sun grown too strong, but powerful to a degree that only our most ancient myths speak of. I say again, this is not a hunt, it is a pit competition with the continued existence of the Great People as the stakes. Heed me, or our bare bones will bake in the desert sun."

The Great Broodmother snorted in disgust and stepped back with a flip of her snout. "His blood is not cold, he has no stomach."

The Huntmaster's vision turned red with rage. It took all his will to remain still.

"Enough!" the Great Chief-King declaimed. "The Huntmaster may be mistaken, but he does not lack for stomach."

The Huntmaster huffed. "Again, I counsel that we let this prey stumble, weaken, and fall behind the herd. Else we will tire and be trampled, and surely, not only will the broodlings suffer, but all will be lost."

The Great Broodmother said nothing but looked to the Great Chief-King.

"We must trust in our instincts and close in for the kill," the Great Chief-King finally said. "It is not possible to plan every hunt and competition down to the last detail."

The Huntmaster looked around the Grotto. It was evident neither the Great Chief-King nor the Great Broodmother were inclined to changing their minds. What the Scribe thought he could not tell. He wondered exactly how the record of this meeting would read and if it mattered. The slightest of nods from the Princess decided him to give it up for now. It was an indication from a very canny individual that at this point in his hunt, the wind wasn't blowing his way.

He could only hope that he was either wrong or another opportunity to sway his colleagues would arise. For now, he needed to do as they wished.

"I will order our scouts and fleets forward," he said without inflection. "We will pin the Human fleet and pounce. That done, we will tackle the rest of the herd."

"Finally," the Great Broodmother said.

She'd managed to get the last word.

\* \* \*

Once again, Katie was in the *Bonaventure's* main conference room, about to give a presentation.

At least it was going to be short and sweet.

Based on Amy and Murphy's news, her little fleet was about to depart on a campaign she had no doubt would determine not only humanity's future but that of the local galactic sector.

The room was much less crowded than the last time. Everybody was busy preparing for the coming maneuver. Many of the attendees were only present virtually.

"Ladies and Gentlemen," Katie declaimed. The room quieted. "Major news I wanted to give to you personally. Also, I want to make sure we're all on the same page here. We want this to go off without a glitch."

Nods and murmurs of agreement.

Katie grinned. "One of Lieutenant Commander Sarkis' scouts, the *Tetbury* under Captain Murphy, has found us our back door."

More murmurs. One heartfelt *"Thank God,"* too.

Katie took a deep breath. "I thought about giving a stirring speech about how important the campaign we're about to embark on is. But we have a lot to do and I think you all know what's at stake here. I'm going to cut right to the chase. I'll tell you the plan, answer any questions, and that'll be it."

Katie took a quick breath and launched right into a high level account of their planned maneuver. The first part was the trickiest. Their first goal had to be to break contact with any Lizard scouts that might be watching and essentially disappear. So the first step was to find and destroy all the Lizard scouts keeping tabs on them. The second step would be a long tortuous trek through minor and poorly mapped systems. A journey that needed to be executed as quickly and unobtrusively as possible. It was essential that there be no stragglers or breakdown of any of their vessels. Katie made it clear that each captain needed to check with their engineering staff that they were fully prepared and not take anything for granted.

Speed and precision of execution were essential to the success of this operation. Katie figured that with new, but now worked-up ships, and the best crews humanity could find, that it ought to work out. She didn't intend to leave that to chance, however.

Katie glossed that over. "Once we've reached what we're calling System Omega, one jump from Assherraskill, the Lizard home system, we'll have more work for the scout group. The second trickiest part of this little evolution. "

That elicited a few chuckles.

"In order to maintain surprise, we haven't scouted out Assherraskill yet. Amy's scouts will do a deep stealth check of it to see what's actually there. We hope we'll still be able to obtain a degree of operational, if not tactical, surprise. Complete surprise, of course, would be ideal."

Katie, after a slight pause, continued. "In any event, it'll be of vital importance not to linger in System Omega any longer than absolutely necessary. To reduce planning time, my operations staff have worked out a set of plans for various scenarios, most of them centered on a quick deep penetration to orbit over their home world. Our intelligence staff," Katie nodded to them, "believe they have identified several vulnerabilities that will induce a Lizard surrender, but they are still working on refining that."

Colleen and Wootton just smiled and nodded at suddenly being the center of attention. Lieutenant Hood grinned and gave a thumbs-up.

Katie smiled indulgently. "As you can see, they're feeling optimistic. As ship's captains and officers, you'll be responsible for making sure the fleet can move quickly on short notice.

Whatever our targets, it's critical we strike swiftly. Doing this means careful, intense prior preparation on the part of us all. I want you ready to go with no delay within minutes of my giving the orders."

Katie looked around. "Questions?"

It took a few moments for someone to work up the nerve to pose a question.

That someone proved to be Commander Wong. "Commodore," he said, "how realistic is it to expect absolutely no problems on a long deployment of the entire fleet? We all know there are always unpredictable problems popping up with a ship."

Katie nodded and smiled. "You're not wrong," she answered, "about problems popping up." She smiled wider and held up a finger. "I disagree with the idea that most of them can't be predicted."

She looked around and saw skepticism on many faces.

"No offense, but except for myself and Lieutenant Commander Sarkis, most of us are command track and have no background whatsoever in engineering. I understand why. Believe me, I wouldn't wish my experience on anyone and I don't think Lieutenant Commander Sarkis would either. But, it means most of you just have to take whatever your engineers tell you on faith."

"Surely, you're not suggesting we can't trust our engineers?" Wong asked.

"You can trust them to do their honest best for you," Katie replied. "Only that of necessity requires making judgment calls for you based on technical considerations you're not able to fully understand. And, many of those calls are about whether a piece of gear that's functioning adequately but is showing signs of possible issues is worth taking offline and tearing apart. If they do that, they can't be sure they'll be able to find out what's wrong, let alone be able to fix it. So, they tend to leave well enough alone."

"Okay," Wong conceded. He didn't look happy.

"Worse than that," Katie said, "any time you take a piece of machinery or system apart, there's a chance it won't work as well when you put it back together. There's a chance it won't work at all. Every time you disassemble something, you're giving Murphy an opening. Smart working engineers don't like fixing things that aren't broken."

Nobody in her audience was pleased by Katie's message.

Again it was Wong who bit the bullet. "What are you saying exactly, Commodore? Are you suggesting our engineers are aware of problems they haven't been telling us about?"

"No, I'm not," Katie answered. "But good technicians, and good engineering officers, are going to be aware of possible problems that haven't yet risen to the level that it's worth bothering command about. You don't want to hear about it every time Leading Spacer Smith figures auxiliary power generator number two is running a little rough, or figures Ordinary Spacer Whats-his-name wasn't very tidy about how they wired a light in a storage space. Also, some problems are illusive but not really worth getting worked up about. I understand, Commander Wong, that every once in a while the water on the *Freedom* tastes a bit funny. That right?"

Wong blushed. "Yes, but it's harmless. The mineral balance tests as being a bit off, but it's not harmful. My technicians have already wasted days looking for the problem with no luck. They're keeping an eye on it. How did you hear about it?"

Katie took a deep breath. "I know it's irregular and amounts to jumping the chain of command, but I took the liberty of reading the engineering reports for all of your ships. In the case of your water, Commander, I'd be willing to bet that the problem is a filter in your secondary water purification system being installed backwards."

Wong frowned. "My technicians are all extremely well qualified and motivated."

Katie smiled. "I know, but the job of changing filters goes to the most junior and least experienced of them, and probably someone who was station or planet born. Sadly, there's nothing in the world that can make having to change filters fun or very interesting. They wouldn't be human if they didn't get bored and occasionally make mistakes. If I'm right about the problem, please, don't go too hard on whoever made that mistake. If that's what happened, the real problem is that it's possible to put the filter in wrong and we'll write reports and send them to the Design and Procurement Bureaus both. Anyhow, we both know it's not a major problem. I was just using it as an example."

"Yes, ma'am. Do you have other issues you plan to flag? What are you expecting us to do?"

"I've already directly flagged any issues to your engineers. Basically, I've directed every engineering officer in the fleet to handle any possible incipient problems now, and not wait for anything to actually break down. You will observe that order is already part of the plan for Operation Shenandoah, and they should have already been aware of it. I merely emphasized its importance." Katie looked around at her subordinates. "It is possible that this may result in some ships not being ready to depart with the rest of the fleet. That is preferable to a breakdown enroute to Assherraskill. Any ship not ready in time will be left behind and will return to Earth when able. No one privy to the details of Operation Shenandoah will remain with such a ship. It'll also have all its logs and records purged of information on the operation. Understood?"

Bobby Maddox spoke up, "Understood, ma'am, but that's draconian."

Katie nodded. "It is, but it's necessary."

"Any good news?" Susan Fritzsen asked dryly.

"Yes," Katie replied. "I know it's a lot to ask. But the truth is, we're in a sweet spot for this to work. Our ships are new. Not so new we haven't had time to work out the initial kinks. But new enough that parts wearing out isn't a problem yet. Also, only power generation systems and the interplanetary drives are critical. We need the FTL drives too, but they're really black boxes we can't do much with and very reliable fortunately. So, people, make sure your engineers all know the generators, the power distribution systems, and the interplanetary drives have to work and you've done your job. Feel free to make me the boogie man. Okay?"

Nods of agreement greeted that.

"Very good, Commodore," Susan Fritzsen answered, "but could you expand on another point?"

"Of course, Commander Fritzsen."

"This plan says that in the event of one of our ships, or a

civilian ship encountered on the way, not being able to keep up, that those ships will need to be destroyed without leaving any traces. What exactly do you mean by that?"

Katie tried not to grimace. "Exactly what it says. We cannot afford to be slowed down by one of our ships or by a captured ship. If a ship can't keep up, we'll evacuate the crew and scuttle it. We won't be able to spare much time, but we'll try to take as much cargo as we can off of any merchants. Then we'll drop them into a convenient gas giant or sun."

"And if a civilian ship doesn't want to co-operate?" Lieutenant Colonel von Luck asked.

"Then we cripple it and send in your marines to capture it if we can," Katie answered. "Otherwise, we use our firepower to destroy it. We do our best to vaporize the debris."

Grim silence greeted that.

"Any more questions?" Katie asked.

Nobody answered.

Finally, they were done. "Dismissed," Katie announced.

One more step on the road done.

\* \* \*

The fleet was assembled. They'd made an effort to conceal the fact. They wanted to disappear from the ken of the galaxy. The Lizard leadership in particular, but also that of anyone the Lizards might be able to question. All the same, being ready to go on a minute's notice had been their priority.

Katie was waiting in her flag command center. Waiting for the report that would trigger her sending out that notice.

They'd been patrolling the systems around and between the secret Lizard base and Far Seat Trade Hub.

Now they were concentrated in a binary system that consisted of a K class orange star and small M class red star. Given the complications of jumps from systems with multiple stars and the fact that this one had no usable asteroids and its few planets were useless balls of ice and rock, this was an infrequently visited system despite its relative closeness to the Trade Hub.

Given the additional fact of the tensions between the Lizards and everyone else, Katie figured it was a good bet they'd not get any unwelcome visitors who might report on her fleet's doings.

The Lizards had been strangely quiescent. Katie wasn't willing to bet on that continuing. Her scouts had assured her that there'd been only one small Lizard scout tracking them. It seemed almost too good to be true, but Katie had no choice to bet it was. The report she was currently waiting for, the one they were all currently waiting for, was that that Lizard scout had been taken out. That they could depart on their long flanking maneuver unseen.

"Tense, just waiting, isn't it?" Amy asked.

Katie gave her friend an annoyed look. "Yes, that's true."

Amy smiled. "Just like the fact that we both hate waiting while other people get on with the job. And yet you ordered me to hang back here with you. For good reasons, so suck it up."

Katie just shook her head. "You're incorrigible."

"Yes, but seriously, Commodore Kincaid, ma'am, I've got every faith in the *Tanshang* and her crew. It won't be long. They'll get the job done. I almost feel sorry for the Lizards given the advantage in electronic warfare we have. They won't know what hit them."

Katie nodded. "I don't doubt it, but there's always a chance things will go wrong. It's my job to be prepared for that."

"And you're as prepared as possible. Don't worry. It'll just age you prematurely."

As commander, Katie had to maintain some dignity and the flag command center was a semi-public place. She suppressed her urge to laugh. Instead, she gave her friend a thin smile and a shake of the head.

As it happened, it wasn't all that long before the comms officer spoke up. "Ma'am, the *Tanshang* reports full success. All mission objectives met."

Katie felt a predatory grin stretch her face. "Good. Thank you, Comms. General Dispatch: we are go! Execute Operation Shenandoah. I repeat, we are go!"

The mood in the command center was electric. It intensified with the beginning of a low rumble throughout the *Bonaventure*'s hull as she ramped her engines up to full power. They were going to make their run up to their first jump as quickly as possible. The quicker they departed, the less the chance they'd be detected.

By the time they reached jump, the mood had subsided, but spiked as the gut-twisting sensation of jump entry hit.

They'd gotten away clean, to all appearances unobserved. They'd broken contact with the enemy.

They'd completed yet another step on their journey to victory.

A victory their species needed.

## 14: Some Surprises

*"As soon as there is heat, however, the future is different from the past."*
Page 52 of "Seven Brief Lessons on Physics" by Carlo Rovelli

"Ma'am, unknown jump emergence from jump point near zenith. That's roughly toward the Trade Hub," Katie's comms officer announced.

It never rains, but it pours.

They'd already been in this K7 system a couple of hours longer than Katie would have liked. It was a pretty useless system with a close-in gas giant precluding any useful terrestrial worlds and no asteroid belts to speak of, but its primary was still larger than those of most of the systems on their route and therefore more likely to be on somebody else's path. And Katie did not want to encounter somebody else. It'd already been bad luck that the *Pansy* had chosen this system to discover its interplanetary drive units had never been mounted correctly.

The *Pansy* was the newest of her nine corvettes and now it appeared its completion had been somewhat rushed. Too rushed. Apparently, both the installers of her interplanetary drives and the inspectors who'd signed off on them hadn't been careful enough.

Katie had been waiting for a report on just how severe of a problem this had created. And now what she'd feared had happened. Someone had found them while they were trying to surprise the Lizards by taking a back door route to their home system.

"Comms, message for the CAG. Launch all fighters and the ready scout," Katie ordered. "Intercept unknown ship. It can't be allowed to exit the system."

Surprise was essential to their plan. They couldn't let the news of their end run through a back door into the Lizard home system get out.

"Ops, give me odds on intercepting that ship," Katie demanded.

"Ma'am, even if they spot us and react in the next few minutes, we'll be able to kill them before they can decelerate, reverse velocity, and get out through the jump point they entered by. I'm still calculating possible jumps to other nearby systems based on the parameters for a Lizard scout, but based on preliminary sensor readings it looks more like a merchanter. Probably Swimmer make."

Katie nodded. That was good news. "Thank you, Ops," she said. The operations officer had anticipated her most likely request. It would take a little more time to get a full answer. "Update me as soon as possible."

"Yes, ma'am," the ops officer responded in a distracted tone.

It seemed longer, but it was only minutes before the operations officer spoke again. "Ma'am, I've calculated paths to jump points for the half dozen most likely nearby systems. Used stats for a Lizard scout. And it's close for a couple of them, but we should be able to obtain kill intercepts for all of them. I'll keep working the problem, but it looks more and more like a merchant anyhow and it still hasn't reacted to our presence either. It's still accelerating in-system."

"Very good, Ops," Katie answered. "Sensors, Comms, I want to know first thing when that ship shows signs of realizing we're here." She turned to Hood standing beside her.

"Translation?" she asked.

"Ensign Wootton or Tee-Nah would be better," he replied.

"Comms, message for Ensign Wootton. Report to the flag command center," Katie ordered.

Wootton had arrived, and close to twenty minutes had passed, and Katie was starting to consider hailing the unknown ship, when the comms officer announced, "Ma'am, the unknown ship, apparently it's a merchant called the '*Something Ventured*', is calling us."

"Put them on the main display, Comms."

A sleek looking Swimmer appeared on their main screen and rather lackadaisically rattled off something in the galactic trade language.

Wootton translated. "Ma'am, he says he's Captain Swims Up Creek of the *Something Ventured*. That it's a peaceful trading vessel. He's happy to comply with any orders you might have, and awaits them eagerly."

"Eagerly?"

"Well, ma'am, that's what he said. Really, he seemed more resigned than eager."

"Okay, thank you, Ensign. Please, prepare a message that politely requests he plots a zero velocity rendezvous with us. He should prepare to take on an inspection team."

"Yes, ma'am."

"Comms, send that message as soon as the ensign is done."

Shortly later, the sensors officer reported. "Ma'am, the *Something Ventured* is changing course as requested."

"Good. Thank you," Katie answered.

It was an unwanted complication and delay.

It could have been much worse.

* * *

Katie was trying her best to be diplomatic. Political even. As important as the current Operation Shenandoah was, if it worked - and that was a big if - it was still going to be necessary to deal with a variety of alien factions. She didn't want to unnecessarily offend any of them.

And so it was that she'd invited Captain Swims Up Creek to the flag command center to watch the evolution in progress.

She'd taken him and his crew prisoners. She was trying to treat them like honored guests, but they all understood they were prisoners. She'd also seized his ship, the *Something Ventured*, and was about to send it and the bulkier and less valuable half of its cargo into the local K7 sun.

Swims Up Creek had considerable reason to be very unhappy with Katie. If he was, he wasn't showing it. Maybe that was natural and merely prudent when he was the prisoner of an unfamiliar alien race that held his life and that of his crew in their hands. Or maybe he was just that philosophical and understanding. Maybe some combination. Katie didn't know, but she was doing her best to assuage any hurt feelings.

The command center's main screen was showing a closeup of the *Pansy* and the *Something Ventured* lashed together.

Improperly installed, the *Pansy*'s interplanetary drives had sheared part of their mountings. It was something that couldn't be fixed short of a long stay in a well-equipped dockyard. There was no such dockyard nearby and even if there had been, they didn't have the time.

The *Pansy* and the *Something Ventured* were both about to meet a fiery end that would leave no trace of their existence once the fleet departed the system.

The *Pansy*'s captain, Lieutenant (senior grade) Torres, had been a lot more unhappy than Swims Up Creek about this. He hadn't openly expressed that unhappiness to Katie. She'd nevertheless assured him that the problem didn't reflect poorly on him or his crew. It was an issue that couldn't have detected anywhere short of that dockyard they didn't have.

Katie's reassurances might have helped Torres feel a little better, but she doubted anything could completely remove the sting of losing one's command. It didn't help that Katie didn't have another ship to give him. She'd dispersed his crew throughout the rest of the fleet and assigned him to Colleen's intelligence group, along with a strong hint to Colleen to keep him as busy as possible. It wasn't ideal. Katie sighed.

Her reverie was interrupted by a burst of chatter in trade galactic from Swims Up Creek. She looked at Ensign Wootton, who was hovering nearby and tasked with translation. Katie understood a smattering of words and phrases in the galactic trade language and she suspected Swims Up Creek understood more English than he let on, but Wootton not only provided better translation, she added a layer of plausible deniability should it be needed.

Wootton took only a second or two after the chattering ended to translate. "Captain Swims Up Creek says that it is a sad sight that we're watching."

Katie nodded. Then it occurred to her the Swimmer mightn't understand the gesture. "Tell him that I agree, but it was necessary. Regardless, it is right and proper we watch and appreciate the consequences of our decisions. Tell him I regret the price he and his crew have had to pay. Say that I'd like to make it up as best I can."

Wootton blinked and thought for a moment before slowly starting to chatter at Swims Up Creek. When she was done, Swims Up Creek shuffled his feet in the standard for a galactic shrug and, looking at Katie, chattered back at Wootton.

When he was done, Wootton dipped her head and then translated. "He says he appreciates that, but what is done is done and cannot be undone. Still, actual pirates would have not treated him and his people so well. He says a license to trade with Earth and some introductions might help compensate him and his investors. He asks if you could put in a kind word for him."

Katie made a point of not sighing and keeping her face blank. The Swimmer merchant captain was a slippery character. She wasn't sure exactly how well he understood human expressions and body language. Swims Up Creek, for all his co-operativeness and apparent affability, was likely only not a smuggler by the dint of there not actually being any local law. His turning up in such an unfrequented part of space spoke of a strong desire to avoid anything resembling authority. Still, he was being co-operative and might prove useful in the future. "Tell the captain that I'd be glad to speak of him and his desire to trade with those responsible on Earth."

Wootton translated that and then Swims Up Creek's gratitude. Then silence prevailed for a short time while they waited.

Finally, the *Pansy*'s reaction drives flared a deep, bright, sustained blue as at her computer's command they pushed her and the *Something Ventured* on their final trip to their end in the local sun.

Katie couldn't help but feel a certain melancholy at that. A melancholy very tempered by the fact they could finally continue their mission. "Comms, general orders for the fleet. Proceed to jump point."

She smiled. It could have been much worse.

It'd been less than a day and they were on their way again. Undetected so far.

*  *  *

There'd been complications, but no showstoppers before their entry into System Omega.

Katie knew that was a minor miracle she ought to be grateful for.

Standing in her flag command center, watching her people work quietly and competently, she counted her blessings.

As far as Katie could tell, they'd managed to completely escape being tracked. Somehow they'd managed to break contact with the Lizards. With everybody, really. Right up until their entry into System Omega, she'd have been willing to bet anything that nobody had any idea where her fleet had gotten to. That the Human fleet had effectively disappeared from the galaxy as far as the Lizards and everyone else could tell.

It suggested a certain laxness or a blind spot on the part of the Lizards, but it was also a testament to the professionalism of her crews.

That the breakdown of the *Pansy* and the appearance of the *Something Ventured* had been handled so quickly and effectively was a further demonstration of their skill and dedication.

Katie did appreciate that.

But when they'd reached System Omega, she'd received a profound surprise.

There'd been a message buoy waiting for them.

Not much more than a big metal can with a low power transmitter announcing its presence. It'd contained a single piece of hardcopy and a collection of data chips.

Nobody other than the marine bomb squad, Katie herself, and the close group of advisers Katie was about to meet with, knew even that much.

Katie had simply declared it Top Secret intelligence and ordered that no one talk about it. Of course, there'd be speculation despite that, but hopefully they'd just imagine that Katie had a secret source of information she wanted to protect.

That was even true, in a way.

Only she had no idea who'd provided the intelligence on those data chips. The note with them had simply read: *"Commodore Kincaid; some useful information. A friend."*

Very useful information if it was accurate. It had detailed the deployment of the Lizard forces right up to a day ago, and provided some insight into their plans. It'd also provided a detailed chart of Assherraskill and its defenses. Not just where the static ones were, but detailed patrol schedules and sensor surveys. Seemed Lizard sensors and home defenses were somewhat antiquated if extensive. So, Katie could count on having a substantial edge in electronic warfare. Even better parts of the sensor net went down periodically for maintenance, and the unknown informant had provided a maintenance schedule.

Katie would have given her back teeth to know how that information had been gathered. She wouldn't have minded knowing how her unknown benefactor had known where her fleet was going to be, either. That was very worrisome.

The intelligence, if true, was priceless. But thinking about who might have originated it gave Katie the willies.

In any case, she'd shortly have some indication of how reliable it was. She'd sent a single scout through to the Lizard home system using the information provided. It should be returning and verifying the accuracy of that information soon.

She didn't have long to wait. It was mere tens of minutes later that her comms officer announced, "Commodore, the *Cuxhaven* has returned and is narrow-beaming us its report."

Katie grinned and nodded. Had to keep the show up.

"Excellent. Please route it to my day cabin and request that Commander McGinnis, Commander Fritzsen, and the Galactic Intelligence Section meet there ASAP."

"Yes, ma'am," the comms officer replied.

"Thank you," Katie said as she turned and left.

She found Hood and Wootton, her grandly labeled "Galactic Intelligence Section," already waiting outside her cabin. They must have been waiting for the report. She hoped they had good news. She smiled at them anyhow. She'd seen enough peacetime Space Force bureaucracy to appreciate their eagerness.

"As eager as I am to hear your report, we'll wait for the others to arrive. Then meet inside where it's secure," she told them.

"Yes, ma'am."

It wasn't long before Colleen and Susan appeared.

Katie quickly reviewed the *Cuxhaven*'s report. It looked like the intelligence their unknown helper had provided was accurate. That was one positive data point. She silently showed the report to the others.

Hood spoke first. "So far, it looks good, but we haven't committed the fleet yet."

Susan grunted at that.

Colleen was unusually forward. "We both know you don't think it's a trap."

"True," Hood admitted, "but I'd hate to be wrong. Probably this is some agent from up-arm with vastly superior tech, tracking both us and the Lizards, deciding that for the time being it's the Lizards who are getting too big for their pants."

"So," Katie said, "maybe in the future they'll decide differently, but for today and maybe tomorrow, we can trust them."

"Probably," Hood conceded.

Wootton raised her hand.

Katie smothered a laugh. "Yes, Ensign?"

"All the data confirms what Lieutenant Hood and I already thought was true. The parts we didn't know, like the patrol patterns, the *Cuxhaven* seems to have confirmed. Also, that information they gave about how to make the emergency jumps from anywhere more controllable is both priceless and has to be from someone with tech superior to what's common locally. Finally, ma'am, if they'd wanted to damage us, they didn't have to set up a fancy trap here."

"Thank you, Ensign. That makes sense. Susan, what do you think?"

"It could be a trap. Still, I think we have to do this."

"Hate to give out unverified information. We haven't tested this new way of using the jump drives at all, but we don't have time to do that. Might as well be hung for a sheep as a lamb. I'm going to order that data package promulgated to the entire fleet." Katie had anticipated doing this, and it was the work of a few keystrokes to do so.

"Guess that means we're going ahead with the strike," Wootton muttered, forgetting to be deferential.

"Yep," Katie answered. "Already issued the orders for that and won't be changing them."

"Might be the horse has already left the barn and I don't mean to carp, ma'am, but that jump tech info is incredibly sensitive," Hood said.

Katie smiled. "Teach your grandma to suck eggs, Hood. I made it abundantly clear that all of that data and its origin were extremely sensitive and the tech info in particular. Only the engineering staff that will absolutely need to use it in an emergency are to see it. I was very colorful in my language about just how secret it was to be kept. Burn before reading. It never happened. It never existed."

Hood nodded. "Glad to hear that, ma'am."

"That just leaves the question of what to do once we've secured the high orbitals over Assherraskill planet," Colleen commented.

"Our unknown benefactor had some advice about that," Katie said.

Susan grunted again.

"It made sense, ma'am," Wootton ventured. Hood nodded in agreement.

"It did. Apparently you and they, whoever they are, agree that surrender is not a mainstream Lizard concept."

"But that's what we want, isn't it?" Colleen asked.

"It is," Katie confirmed. "The alternative is genocide and some combination of a showdown in Assherraskill system and a prolonged campaign to mop up the remnants of their Space Force. That's bound to be costly and besides, Earth is still vulnerable."

"Simplest thing is to blast the planet back to the Stone Age and run back to defend Earth as fast as we can," Susan stated grimly.

Wootton looked horrified by this. Even Colleen seemed disquieted by the idea. Hood was merely grim.

"Our goal will be to force a surrender," Katie said. "Both our unknown benefactor and our own folks here seem to believe it's possible if we play our cards right."

"I still find it hard to believe that their whole species depends on only a half dozen breeding centers, all located on their home planet, to support its population," Susan said.

"It's odd by our standards," Wootton replied, "but it's politics, you know. They're a highly hierarchical, centralized, and rationally efficient society and their broodmothers would lose power if they let reproduction be decentralized. There are a very few small emergency breeding centers, but mostly females surrender their eggs to the broodmothers and that's the last they see of them. The whole business of breeding and egg laying is seen as burdensome tradition by most of them and an impediment to a successful career. It's a different biology and a different society."

"Sure is," Susan answered. "All I ask is you keep Plan B firmly in mind, Katie."

"Will do," Katie replied. "I'd still prefer to weasel a surrender out of them somehow, though."

Susan just nodded at that.

"Anyone else have any thoughts they'd like to share?" Katie asked.

None of them did.

"Okay, that's it then. We're all going to have a long day tomorrow. See you all on the other side."

Susan snorted. Hood chuckled.

* * *

Back in the Decision Grotto of his Forward Stalkers, the

Huntmaster found his tongue sour in his mouth. As little as he trusted departures from tradition, he had to admit to himself that the gaudy three-dimensional display of the local stars and the ships among them desecrating the Grotto's middle was useful. Unfortunate that it couldn't tell him what he needed to know. The Human fleet had disappeared from the ken of the Great People.

Hence the sour taste on his tongue.

"I have flung our ships wide to all corners seeking to flush out the fleeing Humans. We will find the cowardly tree dwellers and feast upon their flesh," Foremost Stalker announced.

The Huntmaster had to admire the courage of his leader of what the Humans would call scouts. He'd correctly determined just how angry the Huntmaster was. And identified the cause too. The prudent course would have been to remain quiet and not make himself a target for that anger. Instead, he'd put himself forward, attempting to reassure the Huntmaster. Perhaps well intended, but mildly insulting. "Any suggestions besides scattering our hunters to all corners of the wind?" the Huntmaster asked.

Foremost Stalker blinked. He dipped his snout. To have been asked his opinion was a great compliment. But he must have wondered at the manner of asking. The Huntmaster had been unusually blunt. Foremost Stalker paused to think before speaking. "I believe it is most likely they seek to hide in their favorite home tree. I suggest we aggressively probe their home system. On the other claw, it is not beyond the realm of possibility that the jackals at the Trade Hub convinced them that there is strength in numbers. The scavengers may have congregated there or nearby."

The Huntmaster snorted, then dipped his snout to reassure his subordinate. It was a claw twisted in the wound of the current situation that both Foremost Stalker and the Great Broodmother had earlier counseled a more aggressive stance. If he'd taken their advice earlier, he would have had more eyes on the Human fleet and more stalkers deployed around them. Perhaps the Human fleet would have stumbled over one of those and not evaded his claws.

Only whenever the Human scouts had met his stalkers one to one, they'd prevailed.

More dust in the Huntmaster's throat. Still, it was as clear as an opponent's silhouette on a ridge crest. The Great People needed to change and the Huntmaster among them. They were not the apex predators on the galactic scene, not even their small local part of it, that they had been on their home planet. Foremost Stalker might be brought to see that with time, as might the Great Chief-King even, but the Huntmaster could not see the Great Broodmother ever changing.

The Huntmaster was convinced wisdom dictated prioritizing the safety of the Great People right now. That meant they should keep most of their hunters back around Assherraskill. Only a few, scattered stalkers should be deployed further out. Those stalkers would be tasked with detecting any threats or opportunities. When either was found, perhaps then carefully timed limited lunges by the Great People's main strength might be justified.

Dust in his throat.

There was no hope now of that plan being adopted. The others didn't believe he'd been aggressive enough before. Now he was being forced to lunge in all directions without even being sure where his prey was. Leaving the home nest undefended in the process.

All the same, the only thing worse than a blind hunt was a timid one. Half-hearted efforts could only fail.

The Huntmaster flipped his snout up. "Yes, let's leave no thicket unsearched, no tree unshaken. And if we've lost track of our enemy's hunters, at least we know where their nests are."

"Indeed, Huntmaster," Foremost Stalker said, "are you going to order assaults on them?"

"You will need to sniff out the Human system first. But, yes, prepare couriers to each of the Hunting Packs. I have orders for them. The final chase has begun."

\* \* \*

It wasn't the seediest bar on Butt End, but it was in the running.

It was full of dockworkers without work and crews whose

ships were docked, waiting for the storm to blow over.

Nobody knew where the Humans had gone and the Scaly Ones seemed to be everywhere, poking their noses into things that weren't any of their business. They were stopping short of murder and piracy, but they did stop every ship they came across and asked questions nobody had answers to. Nobody knew what the Humans or the Trade Union were up to.

Shadowguide found this all very amusing. That the Humans appeared to have disappeared made him mildly hopeful.

The opinion of others was somewhat divided. "You figure the Humans have abandoned us?" a Climber dockworker down bar asked some sort of Swimmer crew member.

The Swimmer swayed back and forth, the interspecies common galactic equivalent of a shrug by one who was seated, "Naah, figure the odds always favored the Scaly Ones over the Humans and we all knew the Trade Union officials would flee at the first hint of any danger. Tell you what, I'll give two gold for three that the Humans come out on top of this mess."

The dockworker blinked. "Generous odds. What do you know that I don't?"

The Swimmer crew member bobbed its head in amusement. "Nothing I imagine. Only it's a bet I can't lose. Do you think if the Humans lose, either of us will be around to settle the bet?"

The dockworker horked whatever it was he was drinking. Shadowguide figured it was male, it had a solid build, and Climber females tended to be homebodies. "Good one," the dockworker exclaimed. "Guess I'll save my gold for drinking."

Shadowguide was, for a change - enjoying his own drink instead of simply pretending to, while, in fact, eavesdropping. He'd done what he could. He'd put his thumb on the scales hard. He figured the Humans had at least a fifty-fifty chance of prevailing now.

His gift of technological information would come in for some criticism on the part of some of his sponsors back up-arm. They wouldn't be happy with the tech edge he'd given the Humans. They'd be even less happy if the Humans lost and the Scaly Ones somehow captured that information from them.

Only life was full of risks no bureaucrat was qualified to understand.

Shadowguide could only hope the Human leader was discreet and didn't spread the knowledge too widely amongst her people or use the tech unless an emergency required it. She wouldn't have to worry about Scaly One spies. They were too direct for those sorts of shenanigans, but again he had to hope she took precautions against the capture by her enemies of the advanced knowledge of FTL he'd provided. His research told him that it was standard Human practice to do so, but that the quality of their execution varied across time and organization.

No point worrying about it now. The bet was placed and couldn't be taken back.

Any chance of keeping a whole section of the frontier from falling into the hands of barbarians who were both aggressive and efficient was worth taking.

He just wished the odds were better.

\* \* \*

A wave of nausea hit Katie as the *Bonaventure* emerged in the Assherraskill system.

Not just her either. All around her in her flag command center, the normal low-key buzz and action of her command staff going about their business paused. It took a few seconds for everyone to recover.

It was a few more seconds before her sensors officer spoke up. "Commodore, everything in-system appears as expected. Just the old static defenses and a single cruiser working up. I'm afraid it's not at dock. It's not far away, though. Doing trials, I imagine. Jump point sentries, all as expected. Civilian traffic, all as expected."

Katie nodded. "Thank you, Sensors."

As the thump, tremble of the air group launching vibrated through the *Bonaventure*'s hull, she looked over at Lieutenant Hood standing beside her. He in turn, looked over at Ensign Wootton working at the console she'd been given.

Hood nodded. "All as expected. Looks like we're sticking with plan A."

"You think we're riding our luck?"

"Ma'am, when it comes to command, I've got some

experience herding electricians and intelligence geeks, and that's it." Hood tapped his rank insignia. "Despite these, I really don't know much about military strategy except what I've got from a few history books."

"But?"

Hood looked around. He didn't seem comfortable discussing this in a semi-public spot. "But, ma'am, nothing we've seen indicates the Lizards understand the concept of surrender."

Katie smiled thinly. It wasn't an amused or happy expression. "The alternative is genocide and fighting a mopping up operation against forces that still outnumber us and have nothing to lose."

"Yes, ma'am. Glad it's your decision."

"Yes, it is," Katie agreed. "And I'm deciding to take the whole fleet, minus small detachments to surprise the jump point guards, right to Assherraskill planet and force a surrender. The Lizards might be murderously aggressive, but they are rational. I'll explain it to them carefully."

Hood gave a slight nod. "If we catch the jump guards before the event horizon of our arrival reaches them and they can escape to call in reinforcements, we might, if we're lucky, have a day's window for that."

"And only a very narrow one of a couple of hours if we don't."

"And military traffic is semi-predictable and their civilian traffic light, but we just can't be sure how long we can keep the lid on."

"So we'd better get on with it." Katie turned away from Hood. "Comms, general dispatch, execute Alpha."

"Yes, ma'am!" the comms officer responded, unable to keep the excitement out of his voice.

They were committed.

## 15: Checkmate

*"The point is that by the time our nervous systems are mature, experience, of the personal or the evolutionary kind, has given us a lot of instinctual knowledge of how the physical world behaves. Whether hardwired or learned at a very young age, the knowledge is very difficult to unlearn."*
Page 4 of "The Black Hole Wars" by Leonard Susskind

Even with drive technology they'd have considered magic just a few short years ago, the run in was long. Katie suspected the information their unknown benefactor had provided might make FTL jumps within star systems possible. She didn't dare experiment now. All the more because she strongly suspected that their unknown benefactor would appreciate discretion in using the help he'd provided. So, light speed remained a hard upper limit within star systems light-hours in size. And, practically speaking, they had to settle for average transit speeds that were a fraction of that hard limit.

Katie had ordered her flag command staff to use those hours to rest. She needed them at their best for the final climatic battle that was coming. She'd followed her own orders and gone to her cabin to try to sleep. Given how keyed up she was, she'd been surprised at how quickly she'd fallen asleep. When she'd been woken, it'd felt like no time at all had passed.

A quick shower and meal, and a new uniform, and she was back in her command center. Hood was close by, and Wootton was at her console. Katie wasn't sure the young woman had actually followed orders and left.

Their ultimate goal here was to dominate the orbitals around Assherraskill planet and force the Lizards to surrender, but there were a number of steps to achieving that. They'd know if the first one had succeeded soon.

Less than an hour later, her comms officer reported. "Ma'am, Alpha Detachment reports they've destroyed the guard ships at jump point Alpha. The enemy failed to get a warning out."

The whole room breathed a sigh of relief.

Katie thought that premature. They had another couple of jump points to go. However, it was Katie's job to project an air of calm confidence. "Thank you, Comms," she said evenly.

It was tens of minutes, forty-two if anyone was counting, and about five minutes longer than expected when the next report came. "Ma'am," the comms officer announced, "Gamma Detachment reports they've destroyed the guard ships at jump point Gamma and that the enemy did not get a warning out."

Ouch. Gamma was early, but Beta Detachment should have reported second. Katie kept her demeanor and tone impassive. "Thank you, Comms."

It was a tense few minutes before the next message arrived. "Ma'am, Beta Detachment reports they've taken out the enemy guard ships at jump point Beta and that the enemy didn't manage to get a warning out."

The relief in the room was palpable. Katie resisted the urge to show hers. "Good. Thank you, Comms," she said.

"Well, that wasn't only the first step, it was the trickiest, too," Hood, standing next to her, said softly.

"Quiet, you. You'll jinx us," Katie replied. She sighed. Hood's comment wasn't welcome. But he was doing his job, part of which was to provide her with a second perspective and a reality check when necessary. "Just joking," she said. "Still, I would have thought negotiating their surrender was going to be more, shall we say, delicate."

It was Hood's turn to sigh. "So far, the Great People, as they call themselves, haven't had to choose much between their instincts and what is in their rational self-interest. It's impossible to say what they'll do when rationality dictates something that offends their every instinct. To tell the truth, I'm not sure we shouldn't pound them back to the Stone Age. They're never going to be safe or easy to deal with."

Katie gave the man a twisted smile. "Ever hear of a Pyrrhic victory, Lieutenant Hood?"

"You can pay me now, or you can pay me later," Hood quipped.

"This is not exactly a visit to the repair shop, but I'll take your advice under consideration," Katie replied with a degree of mock pomposity.

Hood smiled.

They gave up the conversation and waited. They were going to have enough drama today as it was. Also, they both knew it was Katie's decision, and she'd made her mind up.

They had only a few hours, a countable number of minutes - one hundred and forty-seven to be precise if everything went exactly according to plan, before they reached the Lizard home planet and the main act began.

Things did not go exactly to plan.

Only about thirteen more minutes had passed when the sensors officer spoke. "Ma'am, that cruiser is changing course. It's heading back towards the Lizard planet." He paused to fiddle with his console some. "Looks like they're aiming for a point between us and the planet."

Katie looked over at Hood.

Hood grimaced. "A Human commander might have made for jump point Alpha, thinking to overwhelm our detachment there and get a warning out to the forces in their other systems. The Lizards are communal egg layers and protecting the raisers of their young and their nests is their priority. Their own lives are secondary."

"They can't win," Katie said.

"True, but they can try to slow us down, can't they? All our ships except the *Freedom* are lighter. If we meet them head on, they're going to take a chunk out of us."

Katie nodded. "Maybe. We can't afford to lose time. So, we're about to find out."

Hood gave her a grim, resigned look. As well he might.

"Comms," Katie said loudly, "general dispatch for the fleet. Maintain velocity with minimal evasive maneuvers. Prepare to engage enemy unit. Fire as soon as you're within effective range." They'd miss the missiles and gun rounds wasted by that later, but Katie was only so willing to sacrifice her people.

It was barely ten minutes later that the first missiles and gun rounds began to reach out from her leading scouts. There might be a golden BB among them, and they'd help further constrain the enemy cruiser's options. Sadly though, this wasn't a battle of maneuver, it was a high-speed, head-on game of chicken with both sides guaranteed to lose.

Katie, Hood, and most of the rest of the room watched the big display that filled one whole wall in front of them. It was an antiseptic display of colored lines and symbols crawling towards each other. The projectile track lines reached out marginally faster than the ship symbols. There were many more friendly symbols, but the enemy was producing their fair share of projectile tracks. They must be emptying their magazines like there was no tomorrow. For them, after all, there wasn't.

A symbol flashed red. "Ma'am, we've lost the *Allentown*," the operations officer announced.

The *Allentown* was a scout ship. Had been a scout ship. An acceptable loss, coldly reckoned. Only for Katie there were no acceptable losses, only unfortunate but necessary ones. "Thank you, Ops," she coolly acknowledged.

It wasn't long before the next loss. "Ma'am, we've lost the *Aster*. The *Rossiya* reports significant damage, but it hasn't affected its propulsion."

"Thank you, Ops," Katie replied. The *Aster* had been a corvette. The *Rossiya* was a country class destroyer. She hoped its weaponry was intact. It'd formed a significant portion of her already limited bombardment capacity.

Fortunately, as it came closer, the Lizard cruiser switched its focus to the *Freedom*. It likely considered the cruiser the biggest threat. It fired its missiles as soon as it was within effective range. None of them made it through. The same couldn't be said for the storm of projectiles it fired, but most of those missed, and the *Freedom* was built to take it.

Finally, the news came. "Ma'am, the enemy cruiser has been destroyed."

"Thank you, Ops," Katie replied. So, it could have been worse, only one scout and one corvette completely destroyed, one destroyer functional but in severe need of repairs, and only light damage to all other units. But Katie wasn't happy. She'd lost irreplaceable people and expended ammunition she'd need to take down the planet's static defenses and then pose a credible threat of bombardment. The Lizard cruiser's sacrifice hadn't been entirely in vain.

"You did what you had to," Hood, next to her, murmured.

Katie gave a slight nod. And if the intelligence they'd been given on the static defenses was as accurate as the rest of it had been, they should have no problem taking them down. Not even doing it on the hurry. Sooner or later, the out-system Lizard forces would tumble to what was going on back home. They had to drive the stake through the beast's heart before that.

Normally, a fleet of maneuverable ships would have no trouble taking down static defenses without a maneuverable force of their own. Normally, it'd take time and very careful attacks from outside the range of those defenses. Such attacks would incrementally wear down critical parts of the defense. Eventually, it'd start to crumble and then start to dissolve.

Only Katie didn't have time. She was having to rely on very long-range ballistic attacks precisely targeted based on intelligence far more accurate than could normally be expected. At least, they all hoped it was.

The reality proved tense. The fire plan had been worked out in detail while they were still in the Omega System. Katie had no useful decisions she could make. She ordered the fire plan's execution when they were at the appropriate distance, and then all she could do was wait and watch.

It was a long hour and some more units took light damage as a result of last gasp, desperate efforts by the static defenses, but it went eerily close to plan.

And finally they were in orbit around Assherraskill. The planet lay at their mercy.

"Comms, general broadcast to the planet asking to speak to their Supreme authority," Katie ordered. She knew the authority in question was a triumvirate, but that she could expect to speak to its chairman whose title translated as something like "Chief-King." She hoped they had a translator of their own. Wootton had some command of the Lizard language and had created the general broadcast message, but the ensign didn't seem very confident of her abilities.

The response came in mere minutes. The Lizard command must have been waiting. A very beefy and rather dignified looking velociraptor analog appeared on the main screen and produced a stream of hisses and grunts. A skinnier, rather shifty-looking Lizard appeared in an inset window on the display and spoke in sibilant English. "The Great Chief-King asks what you want."

Well, that was to the point. "We want your surrender," Katie answered. "By that, we mean you give up all your aggression and withdraw to the five systems in which you have populations on habitable planets. You will also, under our supervision, destroy most of your armed space ships, retaining only a small portion of smaller ships for defense against pirates. Exact details to be negotiated later. All your FTL ships will be restricted to travel between your five inhabited systems. You will allow Trade Union and Human traders access to Assherraskill. You will also allow periodic inspections by Trade Union and Human delegations based on armed vessels. Those are our terms."

Wootton rendered a largely preprepared translation of Katie's answer and they waited for an answer.

The Great Chief-King flipped his snout and replied in a series of hissing barks.

The translator tilted its head and blinked before speaking. "The Great Chief-King is not familiar with this idea of surrender. He does know that the Great People are not ones to stand frozen in fear like some helpless herd beast. Do your worst and in the end it'll be the Great People that feast. This talking is at an end."

With that, the Lizards broke the connection.

Katie kept her face impassive and turned to Hood. "Your thoughts, Lieutenant Hood?" she asked.

Hood heaved a sigh. "Not unexpected, I'm afraid. It's not impossible that a demonstration will let their more rational side come to the fore."

Katie nodded. They'd discussed this in detail earlier. Not being sure how the Lizards would respond, they'd explored a variety of scenarios. In an ideal world, Katie would have ordered a set of progressively more severe bombardments against ever more critical infrastructure until either the current leadership changed their minds or they were replaced by more reasonable beings. Unfortunately, that would take time. They didn't have that time.

Katie had the choice of a set of options, all of which made her sick to her stomach. From a cold, purely strategic zero-sum, it's us or them, perspective, the best option was annihilating the Lizard race. Genocide.

Incredibly to Katie's mind, almost the entire reproductive capability of the Lizard species was concentrated in a mere half dozen breeding centers on the planet below.

At first, she hadn't believed Wootton and Hood when they'd told her this. "That's insane," she'd said. "No intelligent species would allow itself to be that vulnerable."

Wootton had just stared at her. Hood had heaved a deep sigh. "It's political, and you know Human history isn't that different. The rulers and the already powerful always seek to concentrate anything valuable as much as possible, the better to control it. That it makes society overall much more fragile and vulnerable to failure isn't their main concern. Their own power is. It's just that between Lizard biology making reproduction more a matter for the wider community and their having a longstanding much greater concentration of political power, they've consolidated the process of having children and raising them to a much greater degree than us. Even our communists didn't go so far in giving the state complete centralized control of the raising and educating of the young."

Later, the intelligence from their unknown benefactor had

confirmed what Hood and Wootton had told her. It still boggled Katie's mind, but they'd constructed scenarios on the assumption that this was true. Given that the Lizards were longer lived and fit for more of that lifespan, they had a commensurately slower rate of reproduction. At the very least, losing their current reproductive centers would mean losing one generation and it might take another to rebuild those centers. Their society might break down entirely or it might just suffer a setback for a century.

And that would be just from destroying the breeding centers. If Katie went further and destroyed the infrastructure and also the concentrated herds of meat animals that the population of Assherraskill depended on for life, she would be committing outright genocide. Most of the Lizard population of egg-laying females still resided on their home planet. Again, for reasons Katie failed to understand. The Lizard population would completely collapse without them and the remnants would be left to the mercies of an indifferent galaxy.

Katie sighed. She didn't mind the world knowing she wasn't happy with this. "Comms," she declared, "general dispatch, execute bombardment plan Omega Minus Two." She'd hit all but one of the breeding centers, but she'd restrict her initial response to that. So, they'd not be responsible for genocide, merely the mass murder of babies. Great.

Forty minutes later, her comms officer reported what they could all see on the main display. "All units report they've completed their Omega Minus Two tasks, ma'am."

They waited for the Lizard response. It took less than twenty minutes. Katie had been willing to give them an hour.

The figure that appeared front and center in their display wasn't the Great Chief-King. It was a slighter, but still very dignified individual.

"Female," Wootton commented. "Young, but high-ranking," she added.

The translator from before was in the same frame behind and off to one side of the high-ranking young female.

To Katie's surprise, the young Lizard woman spoke in English. "The Great Chief-King is gone," she said. "I am his heir. Both the Great Broodmother and her replacement died in your attacks." She gestured towards the translator. "The Huntmaster remains. We speak for the Great People. We accept your surrender terms."

* * *

Katie was alone in her cabin. She was supposed to be getting the same rest she'd ordered all her people to get. It'd been a long day. Tense, and worrisome with the highest stakes, even if it'd worked out in the end better than they had any right to expect.

They'd been lucky. Extremely lucky.

Katie ought to be feeling elated. Failing that, she ought to be relieved. She ought to feel extremely relieved.

She didn't. Mostly, she felt hollow. Hollow, with a thick, permeating feeling of aghast, appalled, horror.

They'd been very lucky.

Now that she wasn't busy running the whole show as best she could, she could see that. And it scared her. She needed rest, true, and, true also, once she'd had that rest she'd feel sunnier about it. Only first she needed to, at least partly, digest what had just happened.

The cost of it had been less than they had any right to hope for.

So what had happened?

The Lizards had surrendered.

It was the best-case scenario. The absolute best outcome they could have hoped for. The Lizards, in the person of the individual whose name Wootton had said translated as "the Princess", had conceded everything Katie had asked for without debate or quibbles. The Lizards weren't faking it either. They were acting to make it a fact with an efficiency that was far greater than anything Katie would have dared to demand. It was the opposite of the foot dragging that she'd have expected.

Katie's fleet remained in orbit above Assherraskill to ensure that cooperation. Trust, but verify. It was possible that the corvettes and scout ships fully loaded with marine away parties that they'd dispatched to the neighboring systems with orders to the Lizard fleets to surrender and disarm were walking into a set of traps.

But Katie didn't think so.

It didn't seem to be in the Lizard psychology to do things by halves.

The coming days would tell, but it did look like the Lizards had in truth completely and unconditionally surrendered. Katie and her fleet now dominated them and therefore the local galactic region, too.

That might be a problem. But if so, it was a new problem.

One she could think about after resting from solving her old ones.

\* \* \*

Their hunt had failed.

In the old days, a failure like this would have meant a clan's extinction.

These days, it only meant a change in leadership.

The Princess had requested the Huntmaster's presence in the Grotto of Decision. Under the circumstances, this request was a command, and the Huntmaster prepared himself to be dispatched on his last hunt. A hunt he would pursue alone in the depths of Assherraskill's largest continent. A hunt he would not come back from. His final hunt.

The Huntmaster would meet his fate with discipline and dignity. He found the Princess waiting for him when he entered the Grotto of Decision. They were alone. The usual recording scribe wasn't present. Which was curious. The Huntmaster dipped his snout respectfully to the Princess. "Greetings. Many fat kills in your future hunts, Great Chief-Queen." The unusual title felt strange on his tongue.

"And yours, Huntmaster," the Princess, now formally the new Great Chief-Queen, answered.

The Huntmaster allowed himself a light tooth clatter of amusement. "The final hunt is always successful, my Queen, though the prey may fail to fill the stomach."

"Indeed," the Princess answered, "but I expect it will be many long years before your final hunt. I have need of your wisdom, your experience, and your knowledge."

The Huntmaster blinked in bewilderment. "Perhaps, but our traditions are clear."

"It is clear our traditions have failed us. My father deferred too much to the Broodmother, who was arrogant and ignorant both, as well as power hungry. The mistakes they made, the sending away of our hunters to pursue unfamiliar prey across unfamiliar terrain, were not yours."

The Huntmaster dipped his snout and gave a pleased flick of his tongue. "It pleases me that you believe so."

"The Humans have us prostrate. We lie on the ground, bellies up. Their claws are at our throats. Yet they do not strike. Your thoughts?"

"I believe my Queen caught this scent before me. We were mistaken to see them as prey. Still, although they can obviously be predators and fearsome ones at that, perhaps it is a mistake to see them as only predators." The Huntmaster gave a thoughtful mouth huff. The news that his life might not yet be over had him feeling unbalanced. "I was aware they did not see themselves so. Perhaps it was a mistake on our part to believe that all must be either prey or predator. In any case, it is clear the Humans do not see us as prey to be butchered and feasted upon. It is more like they see us as a defeated clan to be merged with. In that case, we are best advised to co-operate wholeheartedly and act as they expect we should. I sense this is your plan."

The Princess flicked her tongue in approval. "We are at their mercy. We must comply with their wishes. Make ourselves useful to our supposed new clan. We must strive to seem harmless and useful both. We must give every appearance of eager compliance. It will be many generations before we dare do otherwise. I have given orders that it be so. Our ships have disarmed. All that have disagreed have been sent on their last hunt. We can barely defend ourselves against even the meanest of pirate vermin now. But we survive. I need your experience and wisdom to see we continue to do so. I need your help."

The Huntmaster dipped his snout deep. "You have it, of course, my Queen."

\* \* \*

"They're ambush predators," Lieutenant Robert Hood replied.

The reply was in response to a question that was bothering his supposed subordinate, Ensign Tanya Wootton.

They were back in their office after a long day in Commodore Kincaid's command center. They'd stayed there to supply her with any intelligence she might need on a timely basis. Well, Hood had anyway. Wootton probably couldn't have been torn away from the developing events by a pack of wild dogs. She'd been over the moon, documenting them in detail second by second. Like she'd said shortly before, it was a critical juncture in Human history and her part in documenting it would probably establish her reputation among historians for as long as the Human race existed.

Hood had refrained from being a buzzkill and pointing out that if things hadn't worked out, that mightn't have been that long.

They were both very tired, but still too keyed up to immediately hit their bunks and get the sleep they desperately needed.

Hood had a can of beer, and Wootton a container of wine, and they were trying to figure out what the heck had just happened. And, just maybe, what it meant for the future.

Tanya Wootton had watched the Lizard surrender with a growing astonishment. It was a belief well established in her mind that the Lizards were unrelentingly aggressive. That it was a trait inherent to Lizard individuals that was reinforced in every way by the society they'd developed. The submissive compliance they'd shown as they surrendered and dismantled a fleet of space going war craft it'd taken generations to build in less than a day boggled her mind. She found it hard to believe. She'd asked Hood for possible explanations.

"Ambush predators?" she said. "That's prehistory. You can't explain a spacefaring civilization using prehistory. That's like using mammoth hunting to explain the Apollo program."

Hood grinned. He was tired and neither of them was as tightly wrapped as they would have been if they'd had enough sleep. He was getting a rise out of Tanya and rather enjoying it. Better not indulge that urge too much. He put a serious look on his face. "I disagree. Seriously, we were Paleolithic hunters for a far longer time than we've had agriculture, let alone an industrial civilization. Our instincts reflect that. I believe the same is likely true for the Lizards. When the outer layer of social convention fails and is stripped away, we revert to those instincts from an earlier time."

Tanya pouted. Heavens, it was cute. "For the sake of argument, I'll allow that."

"Thank you, ma'am," Hood replied with mock seriousness. "So, their pattern is they sneak up on their prey and rush it as a pack."

"Okay."

"If that fails, they don't try to chase it down like we might, or a pack of dogs might. They accept the loss and look for another unaware, potential victim."

"Still don't trust them."

"Not asking you to. Just saying I don't think they're planning anything sneaky right now, or even in the immediate future. I think they're going to want to regroup and rebuild before trying anything again."

"Okay. Haven't thought much about the future, have we?" Tanya conceded reluctantly.

"Too true," Hood admitted. "We've been too busy just making sure we have a future at all to worry much about what it'll be like."

"Guess we'll have to start thinking about it now," Tanya Wootton said, taking a thoughtful sip of her wine. She paused and inspected the container for who knew what. "Guess we should get some sleep first."

"Yeah, sleeping on it'd be a good idea."

"Then we think about it."

"Definitely."

## 16: What Now?

*"There are more things in Heaven and Earth, Horatio, than are dreamt of in your philosophy."*
From Act I, Section 5, line 169 of "Hamlet" by Shakespeare.

"Why so gloomy?" Bobby asked Amy. They were among the last holdouts in the wardroom. Most of their fellow officers had either gone off to get some well-deserved rest or to celebrate their victory in smaller, more private groups elsewhere.

Amy sighed. She'd felt lost in her identity as Lieutenant Commander Sarkis these last few months. She'd been commander of the *Bonaventure*'s Scout Group for the duration and had buried her personal life and all her personal opinions and feelings in doing that job. Part of that job had been to remain cheerful and so keep up her people's morale despite incredible demands on their time and energy and in the face of fearsome odds. At first it'd come naturally. Towards the end, not so much. "I know I ought to feel elated. It all turned out so well. I know in my head," she tapped that head to emphasize the point, "that we dodged a bullet big time, but now that it's over, I can't help thinking about what it cost."

"So, you're not worried the Lizards are pulling one over on

us?" Bobby, a.k.a. Lieutenant Commander Maddox, Commander Air Group, asked. Bobby was usually pretty cheerful himself. In fact, those that didn't know him well often thought he was unserious to the point of being feckless. Tonight, he'd been rather subdued. Together he and Amy had quietly nursed their drinks while those about them partied in a blow off of contained emotion. That they'd survive, let alone triumph, had been up in the air for weeks now.

Amy puffed up her cheeks and blew out a breath. "People died to make this happen. People who were friends of mine."

"You were at Ganymede. This wasn't the first time that's happened, is it?"

"No, but that doesn't make it easier either," Amy replied. "Besides, I wasn't the one giving the orders that got them killed before. That makes a big difference. I don't think I'm ever going to stop feeling guilty about it."

"Your scouts made this victory possible. We all played our parts, but they did the bulk of the work and paid most of the price. They did what was necessary and so did you. It's only human to feel sad about that, but you should feel proud of them, too."

Amy nodded. "I do. It hurts all the same. Also, I think we've beat the Lizards for the time being, but I don't think this is the end of this. I think we're riding a tiger and there's no getting off of it."

"Yeah, not for us. No false modesty: there aren't a lot of people qualified to do our jobs."

Amy looked into her drink bleakly. "And Katie isn't going to retire anytime soon, and she's going to want to use us in whatever comes next."

"So, you figure she'll keep using us until we're all used up?"

"Yeah, she'll regret that, but she'll do it all the same for the best of reasons."

"Gee, I think that calls for another drink."

"Yeah."

"Still, it was a great victory."

"Yeah."

* * *

Another day, another bar. It was a good thing Shadowguide

wasn't prone to alcoholism. At least, the mood today was better than it had been. Rather raucous, true, but a happy, everybody was treating everyone else like a long-lost friend, kind of raucous.

The crews that'd been stranded at Far Seat, and the dock workers stuck there both were exceedingly relieved the Humans had managed to get the better of the Scaly Ones. Not as relieved as the Humans themselves, though. Shadowguide had the distinct impression that they'd not expected to survive, let alone come out on top. An interesting factoid in a couple of ways.

In any case, all and sundry were busy buying each other drinks. Also, producing all sorts of discordant noise they thought was singing. In truth, Shadowguide didn't expect to overhear any drunken conversations in which useful information was inadvertently shared tonight. Yet he was happy too.

The Humans, for all their oddities, were both less organized and less aggressive than the Scaly Ones had been. More inclined to trade as well. Also, more open; inclined to sharing information carelessly and potentially open to infiltration even by individuals not of their species.

Shadowguide was taking it easy just now and would be keeping a very low profile in the immediate future. Still, he expected his superiors would want him to keep close tabs on what happened with the currently victorious newcomers. He'd be stuck out here past the frontier for the foreseeable future.

This would be framed as a reward for his success in pulling the fangs from the Scaly One threat. It would also be construed as something of a punishment for his exceeding his authority in achieving that success.

Shadowguide didn't mind. He'd just as soon not be rewarded with a promotion and an office somewhere back up-arm. Sitting around, absorbing reports from field agents and meddling from afar in their activities, didn't appeal to him.

Studying a new species that was unusually innovative and had already upset the local balance of power looked to be interesting.

Very interesting.

\* \* \*

It'd been a long time since the Huntmaster had wandered a market. Trading and merchants weren't held in high esteem in the Great People's society. At least, they hadn't been. The Princess seemed determined to change that. At least superficially.

So, the last time the Huntmaster had spent any time in a market was when he was a very junior hunter assigned the task of procuring provisions for his sub-pack. It was a step up from keeping the latrines clean.

It was also preferable to being a slowly mummifying corpse out in the Great Sandy Desert that dominated the interior of Assherraskill's main continent. That's what he'd have been if the Princess had sent him on his final hunt. It was what he'd expected.

It felt strange being alive still. Stranger even than being in a market. Stranger than all the changes the Humans and the Princess, it wasn't always clear which, were imposing on the Great People.

He stopped in front of a stall with a weird variety of odd items. All they had in common was they were all Human in origin. "A fascinating assortment of goods," he said to the skinny, hyperactive merchant manning the stall.

"Absolutely unique and you won't see many items like this again anytime soon," the merchant replied.

"Indeed. How did you acquire them?"

"The Humans have this habit of exchanging little gifts with those they interact with. Our hunters, when they boarded our ships, traded numerous small personal possessions with them."

Technically, hunters didn't have much personal property. The Huntmaster strongly suspected a lot of what had been traded had technically been Pack property. That was unimportant now, though. With all but a handful of hunting packs being disbanded, most of that property was being shared out to their former members to help them in getting a start in their new lives.

The Princess was determined that the centralized reproduction centers the brood mothers had run weren't going to be reestablished. Instead, reproduction was going to be drastically decentralized along the lines favored by the Humans. Small sub-packs, even single couples of a male and a female, were going to be responsible for having and raising broodlings in her vision.

The Huntmaster wasn't sure how this was going to work. It might run counter to not only the Great People's culture but their very biology. Nevertheless, the Princess was determined, and the Huntmaster had no intention of getting in her way.

The merchant waited patiently as the Huntmaster surveyed his wares. Finally, the Huntmaster picked up a compact, but very complicated multi-tool of some sort. "A hand of hands of gold pieces for that," the merchant said.

The Huntmaster flicked his tongue. "Surely you jest."

"I parted with much of my gold to get the original owners to part with their souvenirs. You won't find anything like this again until we start trading with Dirt directly."

It took the Huntmaster a few moments to realize that by "Dirt" the merchant meant "Earth". Something had got lost in translation. He didn't correct the merchant. He didn't wish to betray any particular knowledge or interest in the Humans yet. He wished to appear merely another old hunter looking for a new path in life. He blessed the stars that the leaders of the Great People weren't the well known public figures Human ones seemed to be. "Are many willing to pay your prices?" he asked the merchant.

"You'd be surprised," the merchant answered.

In the end, the Huntmaster bought several items, saying that he knew former pack mates who might like them. He implied that if it was so, he might return to purchase more from the merchant. The Huntmaster hinted he was thinking about getting into trade himself.

Which he certainly would, as the Princess had requested him to. She still had use for him on Assherraskill and the surrounding systems, making sure everyone either accepted the new arrangements or were "neutralized." But she wanted most of all to learn as much about the Humans as possible.

The Huntmaster would pose as a merchant trading with the Humans, maybe even securing passage on one of their ships to

Earth itself, as a cover for that study.

It was important to better understand their new associates.

*  *  *

The main docks and staging area of Goddard Station had been cleared of the normal clutter of small ships and cargo to make way for the ceremonies celebrating the return of Katie's First Anti-Pirate Flotilla to the Solar System.

In fact, the ceremonies just completed had been a victory celebration. The first of many.

Katie had been apprehensive about what she'd find once she returned to Earth and the Solar System. It'd been difficult maintaining communication with home while she was away. It'd become impossible once they'd gone dark for their surprise attack on the Lizard home system.

Katie had been immensely relieved when a small galactic trader, Snout manned of course, had arrived at Far Seat with the news that so far the Solar System was surviving. She'd still only spent a few days at the local galactic trade hub. She'd done the necessary repairs and replenishment of supplies and given those of her people not needed for those tasks a short while to blow off steam. She'd been careful not to notice that on departure from Far Seat many personnel had been either hung over or perhaps still somewhat drunk.

She'd been too busy herself to fully absorb what had happened or to enjoy much relaxation. She'd neglected her multitude of administrative tasks while focused on saving humanity from extinction. She'd not been alone in that; most of her staff and subordinates had been guilty of a similar neglect.

But now that they all had a future - probably - again, suddenly the hoops she was supposed to jump through for the bureaucrats back home mattered once more. They might seem silly, but they did serve a purpose. As much as Katie resented the tedious procedures for managing people and other resources and reporting on various indicators of importance to staffs back on Earth, she didn't want to create unnecessary friction with them. The world was already disorganized enough. Katie didn't need to add to that.

In a way, after all the intense drama, the mundane work

had been pleasantly mind-numbing.

So, she'd been surprised at just how relieved she'd been when the *Bonaventure* had emerged from jump in the Solar System and found it intact and unscathed.

The message of welcome and congratulations from Admiral Tretyak had been a real emotional high. Her eyes had watered, and she'd struggled to maintain her decorum.

Later, in her cabin, during the run into Earth as she read the attachments to his message, her mood subsided. She and most of her people would be spending the next few weeks on Earth and scattered throughout the Solar System, riding in parades, attending ceremonies, and giving interviews. They'd get special leave for this, but it was going to be anything but a vacation.

Apparently, from a political point of view, victory alone wasn't enough. You also had to sell it as such to the folks back home.

"Ma'am, this way please," a diffident voice came. Katie turned around and saw the source. Guess this little moment alone in a glorified closet off of the main reviewing stand was over. Too bad.

The voice belonged to a young lieutenant. Katie would have sworn he was barely out of school. From his bearing and demeanor, that school hadn't been the Academy either. The Space Force had changed. For the better she expected, but it was still disconcerting.

The lieutenant wore insignia indicating he was the aide to someone high ranking. He also wore an expectant expression. "Admiral Tretyak is waiting for you in his private quarters," he said.

Katie smiled at him. "Okay, lead on."

"It's a great honor, ma'am."

"I know," Katie replied.

The lieutenant showed her the way without more unnecessary comment.

Tretyak rose to meet her as she entered his quarters. He dismissed the lieutenant immediately. When that worthy was gone, he sighed. "Katie, it's good to see you again. You're going to hear it again and again, but what you managed was extraordinary and we all owe you an immense debt."

Katie nodded and frowned as they sat down. "It's not like I did it alone and, frankly, we were damned lucky."

"True, maybe," Tretyak said seriously, "but you made good use of that luck. Better use than anyone else could have. You were the pivot it all turned on."

Katie shook her head. "I did my best. Still left a mess out there. I think we left a big vacuum. I've had my people working on it, but I really haven't had time to figure it out. And I guess, there's a lot of politics to sort out here, too. Glad it's more your job than mine. So, tell me, Admiral, what's next?"

"Maybe you'd like a drink first?"

Katie snorted. "That bad?"

"You're right. I'll handle most of the politics, but you're going to have a busy few weeks glad-handing and standing around looking all victorious but modest. There's going to be a victory parade in every major city on Earth. I managed to argue the cabinet down to having you as the guest of honor at only a half dozen of them. London and New York, of course, but Shanghai, Buenos Aires, Cairo, and Johannesburg, as well."

"Always wanted to get to see more of the world. Don't mind good Scotch either," Katie commented. She smiled to indicate it was a joke intended in good fun.

Tretyak chuckled, but it was evident he wasn't fooled. He poured her a small glass of amber fluid. "Sip it carefully. Get used to that. You'll have scores of smaller, more private get-togethers with smaller, but very influential groups of people to attend as well. It'll seem stand-offish if you stick to water or fizzy drinks."

Katie grimaced. "It's all a game, isn't it? A low-key but serious game for high stakes, maybe. But, still, a game."

Tretyak nodded. "True. But, like you figured out while still a kid, an important game. You wanted to make a difference. I don't think you really realized that meant acquiring power and influence and having to figure out how to best use it."

Katie sipped her Scotch by the way of gaining a few moments to think about that. "Neither of us really wanted that, did we?"

Tretyak smiled wryly. "Probably me less than you, though I think I had a better idea of what might happen. But, yes, I was resigned to being a military bureaucrat doing the best he could in a system he couldn't really change." His smile grew wider. "Be careful what you wish for. You might get it."

Katie half huffed, half snorted. She supposed she deserved that. "So, how long do the parades and what-not go on for?"

"A few weeks and then I want you to take a couple more for a real vacation somewhere," Tretyak said before pausing to give her a hard look. "I mean that. You need it. It's going to be hard because there's a lot for both of us to do, setting up Earth's defenses properly and putting the fleet in good order for the long term. We're going to need several flotillas like yours in the end."

"You're planning to raid my people to form cadres, aren't you?"

"Yes. Also, like you said, we have a vacuum that would be better filled by us than someone else and someone is going to need to keep some overwatch on those Lizard people as well."

"How much time are we going to get? And what is the government willing to give us to do the job?"

"Not much, but I still want you to get downtime. Also, we're both going to get kicked upstairs before we're finished."

"Really?"

"Really. And the resources we get will depend to a great extent on how well you play the political game."

"Damn."

Tretyak grinned. "Just so. The reward for a tough job well done is a tougher one."

"Wouldn't have it any other way," Katie claimed.

If you enjoyed this novel, please leave a review.


To be notified of future releases visit my website at
http://www.napoleonsims.com/publishing

## Appendix A:
## First Anti-Pirate Flotilla OB:

**Commanded by:**
> Commodore Katherine Anne "Katie" Kincaid.

**Chief of Staff:** Commander William Cartwright
**Head of Intelligence:** Commander Colleen McGinnis
**Head of Marine Detachment:**
> Lieutenant Colonel Heinrich von Luck

**Flag:** CV 003 Bonaventure
**Flag Captain Bonaventure:** Commander Susan Fritzsen
**Bonaventure CAG:**  LCMD Robert "Bobby" Maddox
**Bonaventure Scout Group Commander:**
> LCMD Amy Sarkis
**Head Galactic Strategic Intelligence Section:**
> LTSG Robert "Rob" Hood

### *Bonaventure* (CV 003) -

"Majestic" class carrier - First of her class. FTL capable. More of a mobile base than an attack platform. She carries a Scout group of FTL capable "Town" class scouts, several "Mountain" class FTL capable utility transports, two squadrons of unmanned fighter drones for defense (no FTL), a squadron of "Wasp" class Torpedo Bombers (no FTL), and a squadron of "County" class ship's boats (no FTL). Also serves as a supply, repair, and command base.

### *Freedom* (CL 001) -

"Values" class cruiser - First of her class. FTL capable. Strong missile defenses, large number of long-range missiles and some torpedoes as well as chaser and rear beam weapons.

Four "Country" class destroyers in two squadrons:

## 1st Destroyer squadron:

"America"            (DD 005)
"Deutschland"        (DD 006)

## 2nd Destroyer squadron:

"Rossiya"            (DD 007)
"Zhongguo"           (DD 008)

Six "Province" class frigates in two squadrons:

## 3rd Frigate squadron:

"New York"           (FF 003)
"Devonshire"         (FF 004)
"Ontario"            (FF 005)

## 4th Frigate squadron:

"Normandy"           (FF 006)
"Queensland"         (FF 007)
"Kerala"             (FF 008)

Nine "Flower" class corvettes in three squadrons:

## 5th Corvette squadron:

"Pansy"              (K 117)
"Daisy"              (K 111)
"Aster"              (K 101)

## 6th Corvette squadron:

"Gladiolus"     (K 120)

"Trillium"     (K 112)
"Begonia"      (K 103)

## 7th Corvette squadron:

"Bluebell"     (K 104)
"Buttercup"    (K 106)
"Daffodil"     (K 109)

Thirty-two "Town" class scouts based on the Bonaventure.

"Lockhaven"
"Honfleur"
"Brandon"
"Deauville"
"Kayersberg"
"Altenkirchen"
"Cuxhaven"
"Herford"
"Shawinigan"
"Allentown"
"Camden"
"Williamsburg"
"Barstow"
"San Rafael"
"Boca Chica"
"Tachov"
"Eger"
"Bran"
"Tokmak"
"Ruza"
"Guna"
"Bina"
"Kothanur"
"Wat Boon"
"Banyao"
"Tanshang"
"Huilong"
"Xikang"

"Tetbury"
"Kilshanny"
"Stephenville"

## Appendix B:
## FTL Propulsion Handwaving:


Faster Than Light, FTL, travel according to our current understanding of science is more fantasy than science fiction. Some physicists have suggested possible workarounds, but the consensus seems to be that although our current physics isn't complete that the speed of light is a hard upper limit on how fast one can travel. And that that is not likely to change.

That said, Space Opera of the sea stories in space variety isn't likely to work without it, so like many other authors I've assumed we somehow beat the odds and discover how to do it. In fact, I've taken a kitchen sink approach and assumed that between ourselves and the various aliens we meet in space that we figure out several different ways of doing it with many variations of them.

I'm also assuming that FTL technology is not something different species readily share without exacting a very high cost.

The main tech I have the more civilized parts of the galaxy (of which Earth and humanity are not a part of and so these do not appear in Katie Kincaid Commodore)using is gates. Basically, the standard SF version of near instantaneous transport between two fixed points anchored on each end by a large donut like structure with its hole large enough to allow a small ocean liner to pass through.

My gates are the proprietary technology of a shadowy species known to most others as the "Spiders". They don't share their technology and they charge a very high price for each gate they agree to install in a system. Their fees for ongoing use are more reasonable, but they insist on operating the gate system themselves and if you cross them you end up cutoff from the rest of the galaxy and your economy will tank.

Their gate stations are located far out (dozens of AU) in each system and are usually way out of the ecliptic plane. They do not allow armed vessels to transit them. They do have instantaneous communication between gates for messages, although it is unknown how this works.

Although transit between pairs of gates is instantaneous or near to it. It's a matter of some debate. Practical interstellar travel and communication are not. The gates to different external systems are often many AU apart and it takes time to transit in regular space between them. Messages, of course, are restricted to light speed between the different gates in a system. If a system has multiple gates; many systems only have one - they are cul-de-sacs.

In this context, it should be noted that although there are a variety of normal space in-system travel methods most civilized species only allow either inertialess drive ships or rather low energy rocket based systems. The use of warp drives, photon drives, or most torch ship drives in inhabited systems is strictly prohibited by most species, even ones not otherwise considered civilized. They're just too dangerous.

Note also that in this context, Humans are considered not just barbarians but particularly primitive and uncouth ones.

On both the frontier and the wilds beyond it, where humanity resides, a variety of other FTL methods are employed.

Warp drives are a primary one. They are the ones species are most likely to manage to invent for themselves. They are also the easiest and cheapest ones to buy from another species. For very liberal definitions of both easy and cheap.

They have the distinct disadvantage of being rather slow. They're often capable of doing no more than a fraction of light speed and at best a low multiple of it. They're expensive to build and inefficient in operation too. Even worse, they're not all that safe. Space is pretty empty but not completely and if you hit anything at all while operating a warp drive ship, a big kaboom can be expected.

For this reason, most warp drives, other than specialized exploration ships, are only operated in lanes carefully surveyed to be free of problematic obstructions.

Less problematic but much harder to obtain the technology for are hyper drive ships.

Hyper drives come in two main types; one, the jump type, and, two, the traverse an alternative space type. In the 24th century, humanity does not understand the actual physics of how either works and, in fact, doesn't even know of a species that does. The actual origin of these technologies is shrouded in mystery.

For practical purposes, jump drives drill a hole in space between two large gravity wells. There are a variety of different restrictions on where and how drilling a hole can be begun and where it comes out. In no case can you just pop out of one place and arrive at some other arbitrary place. (At least as far as most species in humanity's section of the galaxy know.) Given the military implications of it, no species with this technology shares the exact details of how it works.

However, in general, a jump can neither originate near any large mass nor come out near one. Usually jumps are from the edge of a system closest to the target system and require some not insignificant fraction of the speed of light in velocity towards the target system. Very precisely towards the target system. Jumps cannot exceed a few light years and ships that miss their targets are generally never heard of again.

Even rarer than jump drives are hyperspace travel ones. Not much is actually known about these, but apparently they place much loser restrictions on where and how a ship can enter hyperspace and where it can exit. They do so at the cost of a longer apparent elapsed time between departure and arrival. The exact range of these drives is unclear, but it is believed the longer a ship is in hyperspace, the less likely it is it'll succeed in exiting it.

## Appendix C:
## Galactic Units:

### Time:

The basic unit of time is the "Tok".

Earth second =   0.919 Tok
Earth minute =   55.1   Tok
Earth hour  =   3,309  Tok

"A" = one (1)
"Ta" = 10 (10 times)  deca
"Ka" = 100 (100 times)centi
"Ba" = 1000 (1000 times) kilo
"Ma" = 1,000,000 mega
"Ga" = 1,000,000,000 giga
"Da" = 1,000,000,000,000

An Earth day is 1440 earth minutes or 86,400 seconds.
So 86,400 * .919 = 79,401 Tok is about an Earth day.
79,401 * 365 = 28,981,584 Tok =
          Earth year (about 29 MaTok)
79,401 * 30  = 2,382,048 Tok =
          Earth month (about 2 1/3 MaTok)
79,401 * 7  =   555,881 Took =
          Earth week (about 1/2 MaTok)

Work shifts are 10 BaTok usually (180 minutes)
    Most workers do 3 shifts per wake period with a 1 BaTok break in between. For a 33 BaTok working Day. They then get either 33 or 67 BaTok off depending on species and how tight work is.

    33 BaTok = (18 * 33 = 594 minutes or a bit less than 10 Earth hours.)

    So a very common galactic day is 66 BaTok or 1,188 Earth minutes or (1,188  / 60 = 19.8 Earth hours)
    A break of 100 BaToks is not uncommon after one MaTok.

Main working units are "BaTok" of roughly 20 human minutes (bit less: 1000/55.1 = 18 min)

And the "MaTok" slightly less than half a month.

### *Length:*

The length units are all based on how far light travels in a given time.

Distance Traveled in one Tok is 300,000 km * 1.087 = 326,100 km. (approx) and is called a "Byt".

So a "BaByt" is 326,100 km * 1000 = 326,100,000 km, and a little over 2 AU. This is the normal measurement of distance in a system.

A "MaByt" is 326,100,000,000 km. (or about 1/100th a light year) and is not much used.

A "GaByt" which is 326,100,000,000,000 or about 10 light years, is the most used galactic interstellar unit.

A "BiByt" which is 1/1000th of a Byt is about 326 km and mainly used in planetary sub-systems.

More used is the "MiByt" which is 1/1,000,000 of a Byt or 0.326 km or 326 m.

Most used in ordinary life is the "GiByt" which is 1/1,000,000,000 of a Byt or 0.326 m. Roughly a third of a meter or about a foot.

People will often talk about a 10th or a 20th or a half or a quarter of "GiByt" exactly which depends on species and their historical units.

There is no commonly used term of a small unit that's a tenth or thousandth of a "GiByt" outside of technical or scientific circles. So no equivalent to "centimeter" or "inch".

## *Mass:*

Basic unit is about the mass of 1/10th GiByts (0.0326) cubed of gold. This is about 669 grams. (3.26 to the 3rd times 19.3 = 669 grams) and is called a "Git".
A "KiGit" is 1/100th of a Git or 0.669 grams and is commonly used for small amounts of things.

## *Summary:*

The basic units are the "Tok" for time, "Byt" for length, and "Git" for mass.

Other units are derived using multiples of tenths, hundreds and thousands, or fractions of them.
Although it starts from different base units, it's very similar to the metric system in this.

Getting larger, the prefixes are:

| | |
|---|---|
| "Ta" = 10 times | ( metric "deka") |
| "Ka" = 100 times | ( metric "hecto") |
| "Ba" = 1000 times | ( metric "kilo") |
| "Ma" = 1,000,000 times | ( metric "mega") |
| "Ga" = 1,000,000,000 times | ( metric "giga") |
| "Da" = 1,000,000,000,000 times | ( metric "tera") |

Getting smaller, the prefixes are:

| | |
|---|---|
| "Ti" = 1/10th | ( metric "deci") |
| "Ki" = 1/100th | ( metric "centi") |
| "Bi" = 1/1000th | ( metric "milli") |
| "Mi" = 1/1,000,000 | ( metric "micro") |

"Gi" = 1/1,000,000,000      ( metric "nano")
"Di" = 1/1,000,000,000,000      ( metric "pico")

## GREAT PEOPLE UNITS:

### Counting:

"Hands" for counting positively.
"Hands of hands" for tens, Double hands of hands for hundreds, etc.
"Sub-talons" counting fractions is 1 tenth. "Double sub-talon" for hundredths, etc.

### Time:

"Sleeps" for days. (Their planetary one is somewhat shorter than an Earth day.)
"Lunge" for seconds equivalent
"Final sprint" "sprints" for short for minutes equivalent.
"Sub-Talon of a day" or "Day division" for hour equivalent.
"Full turn of seasons" "Full Turn" or "Season Turns" for year equivalent. Slightly longer than Earth year as home further out around brighter primary.

### Length:

"Stride" is basic meter equivalent, but shorter. And count modifiers used for longer and shorter lengths.

Astronomical is "Light Season Turns", "Light day divisions" "Light sprints"

### Mass:

"Mawfulls" about 2 lbs, or a little less than a kilo, the basic mass unit and count modifiers for smaller and larger mass units.

## Appendix D:
## A Rant on Phones and Other Anachronisms:

The future is not what it used to be. It's never what it used to be.

There is a valid opinion out there that it's better for authors not to take too much notice of reviews and criticisms in particular.

However, some reviewers have commented on the characters in the Katie Kincaid series apparently lacking communications devices that are as good as a modern smart phone.

I think this is a natural, reasonable, and mistaken criticism.

It bears some explanation in its own right and it opens up the whole question of predicting what technology, especially the everyday technology people use routinely, will be like in a few centuries or beyond.

It's a can of worms on two major counts.

One is that barring some semi-miraculous *Deus ex machina* that drops the technologies for us to be an interstellar civilization in from heaven (or advanced aliens according to your taste) the time we'll need to develop them will be enough for plenty of other developments to occur at least some of which will be totally unanticipated surprises. No, we didn't predict the fall of the Soviet Union, and neither did we predict super-computers the size of large chocolate bars that even relatively poor people can afford.

Don't tell me different because these things happened within living memory. Within less than 50 years. Centuries bring greater surprises.

I say that despite not believing history is a record of continuous progress, and suspecting that technological progress in particular in our time, is not moving on an exponential curve towards an inevitable singularity. I'm rather inclined to think we're near the inflection point of a logistics ("S") curve. Some, like Peter Thiel, seem inclined to believe we're well past the inflection point.

Change is not a constant, but it does occur, and over a

period of centuries, you can expect quite a bit of it. The world will be a different place, and it will be different in ways that make honest stories that fully portray this less relatable. (Accurate medieval attitudes about sex, status, and freedom if they were given prominence in modern fantasy probably wouldn't help sales.)

So, there's a strong tendency for a lot of science fiction to gloss over this. In at least three ways. By concentrating on character or action and having the tech just be standard accepted conventions that are taken for granted, by using technobabble that sounds scientific to describe what is effectively magic, or by linear extrapolation making future technology just bigger and better versions of what already exists. No reason you can't do all three with say having blasters being used in a gunfight in a big space station that is a cross between a modern mall and an airport, where the space ships are kind of like big planes that go farther faster.

There's a fourth less dodgy dodge that forms the second reason this is a can of worms.

Not only does technology not always get better at the same rate, sometimes we regress. To historians that aren't narrowly specialized, this is no surprise. They can be quite derisive about the outdated "Whig theory of history". The history of civilizations, states, and peoples is that sooner or later and really not that much later, they end, fall, or cease to exist.

There have been at least two Dark Ages where extreme civilizational regression occurred and technologies were not only lost for centuries but in some cases, their very existence forgotten.

It happens, and not only does everyday life become simpler, but common comforts like running water, baths, and central heating disappear for a millennium or more. Jack McDevitt's novels show such a future and I do believe he's been unfairly criticized for showing a society that's too much like modern America.

In Dune and other novels, AI is dealt with by having a future history in which some close calls have led to its banning. Given modern beliefs about how practical general AI is, this might be considered a bit of a dodge. For the record, I don't consider advanced general AI (as opposed to very good expert systems and specialized algorithms) to be either practical or desirable. I believe this makes me one of a distinct minority.

For a modern American technophile nerd (which many of us SF readers are) this is not a very agreeable, or even plausible, point of view. A belief in progress enabled by the power of technology is pretty central to most science fiction readers' belief system I suspect. It's an optimistic point of view, but not one I even really disagree with. I just think we should recognize that that future is not going to happen on its own. We're going to have to make it. We should do so with a view to the pitfalls that potentially await us. Sometimes we'll fail to avoid those pitfalls.

Which brings us to cell, or mobile, phones as they're variously called.

I'm not fond of phones. And, they're fairly new.

The jury is out on them in my mind. I suspect a future in which everyone carries around something that serves as a small computing and communications device is probable. Probably serve as a payment means, too. Personally, I doubt if they'll have the same importance as current phones do.

Right now, we're enjoying the benefits of this new technology without being fully aware of the drawbacks, or at least without a clear idea of how to deal with them.

People have started living on their phones to the exclusion of their physical surroundings and, in particular, the other people around them. I don't think this is healthy or sustainable. And what can't go on won't. I expect some sort of reversal of this trend. Maybe a sudden revulsion, or maybe, like with cars currently, just a fading of interest.

In addition, phones aren't currently secure, and they probably can't be. It's unlikely that there will ever exist a complicated computing device that can't be hacked. And there's possible abuse well short of actual hacking. This is a problem for individuals, especially for parents with children, who are discovering that when everyone on a planet with billions of people is your neighbor, you end up having some pretty sketchy neighbors. Some are predators of some sort who pose a direct physical threat and some are thieves who will steal what they can. Some are well intentioned, but in aggregate waste more time than anyone has with cold calls for arguably useful products or good causes. But in any case, it's a problem that will only grow worse until it's fixed.

In a military context, the security issue becomes one of life and death. If I can geolocate just one sailor out of thousands on a carrier, I can drop a missile on that ship. This is currently something that's being discovered in Ukraine. Lots of guys taking selfies and videos in the war zone, but on the other hand the authorities are taking away phones when they can because just one phone can result in a visit from a drone or some shells.

You can also go on the Internet right now and listen to intercepted calls from soldiers phoning home. Usually complaining while trying not to worry mom too much.

This is not good Op Sec.

So, I don't believe future militaries are going to let their members have their own individual communications devices to use any way they please. In particular, in the ways a modern civilian is used to using them.

No crystal ball, of course, but that's my take on it.

*AvA, September 2022.*